THE DREAMING FOREST

SECRETS OF THE SORROWOOD

BOOK ONE

L.B. BLACK

The Dreaming Forest

Secrets of the Sorrowood: Book One

Wakening from the dreaming forest there, the
hazel-sprig sang under my tongue, its drifting
fragrance
climbed up through my conscious mind
as if suddenly the roots I had left behind
cried out to me, the land I had lost with my
childhood
and I stopped, wounded by the wandering scent.

- Pablo Neruda

PART ONE
TWO ASTORIAS

A Library and a Lighthouse

"Be careful with that book," said Lydia's raven. "It contains a spell that will turn all of your thoughts upside down."

"Tell me more," Lydia said, waving Isst off the desk. The library ravens had been around since she was a toddler and knew its winding corridors better than anyone. If Lydia ever wanted a piece of information, no matter how obscure, Isst would disappear and return a few moments later with a dusty book in his talons.

Clicking his beak, he hopped across the polished tabletop to the brass perch Lydia had dragged behind her through the bookshelves before continuing.

"Exactly as it sounds. You might be taking a stroll through the forest and come across a creek, however, rather than leaping over it, you attempt to drown yourself instead."

"Well, that seems unreliable."

She punched a few notes into her laptop about the book's condition, then re-shelved it. This was only the second time she'd been granted access to the library's collection of esoterica, though her promotion had been approved over a month ago. The head librarian insisted Lydia undergo a round of tests to ensure her presence would not aggravate the more sentient books.

Like the other changelings who'd returned from the fey realm, Lydia had only ever shown an aptitude for a single magical trait, but one could never be too careful.

Isst preened his feathers as another of the library ravens paused to inspect Lydia's work. He did not relax until that bird disappeared into the aisles. "I imagine it was something of an experiment. Human magicians have one obsession: knowing more than the other magicians around them."

Lydia, who spent most of her free time in the library, could not find a proper argument for that. She pulled the next book from the shelf. It was written in a script she recognized as Thamudic Arabic; a language last spoken over five-hundred years ago. The title revealed itself to her instantly.

"What about this one?" she asked, inspecting the condition of its spine. Although Isst was talkative—a trait that had nearly disqualified him from a library position—it was rare he divulged anything about magic. Lydia didn't know if it was because of the spell keeping him bound in bird form, or merely reticence. All the 'animals' in servitude at the compound seemed to show disdain for the Guild and the changelings, but Isst had happily accompanied Lydia since she was old enough to hold a book.

"I don't know everything, Lydia. Those letters look like runes to me."

"It's called *Lost in the Garden of Sorrow* by Omar Najeeb al-Azam," she said, typing a few notes into the system. Until now, the book had been known as *Unidentified Manuscript #9862, Author Unknown; southwest Arabian Penin-*

sula, seventh century CE. Updating the entry gave her the thrill she always felt when translating words that'd been a mystery for centuries.

Isst ruffled his feathers again. "Necromancy. Or spirit-speaking. Get through that one as quickly as you can."

"How do you know?"

"Only a magician would be so needlessly poetic about death. Now, hurry. Lunch started five minutes ago. We're going to miss it again."

Rain tapped against the murky library windows, as it had for the past three days. Shadows slipped down mahogany bookshelves and the green-shaded lamps loomed over her desk. Constant low cloud-cover obscured a view of the lighthouse from her living quarters. She never slept well when her last sight of the day was the sun setting behind that cursed island.

"Fine. Lunch," she said, returning *Lost in the Garden of Sorrow* to its home. "But we're staying here late tonight. There's something I want to look into after hours."

It was not unusual for her to spend time in the library long after she'd clocked out. Under the Guild's orders, external internet access was not allowed at the compound, so when she had a whim, books were the only way to indulge it.

She didn't mention tonight's research session would not be like her usual ones, which were wild and free-wheeling. Lydia might begin reading a book about the geology of the Cascade Mountains, only to have it lead to another about foraging native plants, followed by one on outdated medical practices, and finally ending with the biography of a field nurse in the First World War.

Tonight, she had an agenda. One that involved the books of esoterica she was so painstakingly cataloging. Her raven might be the only one on the compound to understand the true scope of Lydia's gift with languages, but she had no idea how he would react if she admitted…

Admitted what? she thought, trying not to give an audible sigh as she packed her bag and locked the door behind them. That she was hearing voices? That there was nothing she could do to drown out the ocean's whispers at night?

When the changelings returned from the fey realm, many in the Guild theorized they would eventually go mad. Their powers were fairy gifts, which were both generous and cruel, and never offered without expecting something in return. She wasn't about to give one of the mages an excuse to make her translate scroll after scroll of medieval French, high fey, or ancient vampiric.

"Want to try a riddle?" Isst said as Lydia took the stairs heading to the dining room two at a time. The compound was built on the Onners's old estate, expanding around the Victorian mansion in a way that seemed almost parasitic. William and Marianne Onners had died in a sailing accident six years ago, but their portraits were still scattered throughout the compound, like ghosts following the changelings from room to room. Much of the original furniture remained, featuring ornate carvings of ships and dolphins. The heavy drapes were thick and navy-blue, blocking out most of the light and giving the effect of living deep underwater.

"Sure."

"You can find me at the beginning of the end, and at the end of time and space."

"That's an easy one. The letter 'e.'"

"Fine. How about this: Feed me and I live, but quench my thirst and I die. What am I?"

"A fire. Really, Isst, I think you're losing your touch."

Natalie and October were already eating when Lydia

arrived, her raven gliding behind her. They were changelings too, and as such, all three of them had the same stark white hair. Natalie, however, colored hers with dye her boyfriend picked up whenever he went into town. Today, it was a soft shade of orange, reminding Lydia of the popsicles their caretaker once bought them from a kiosk on the Oregon coast.

Lydia had also dyed her hair during her brief stint in the outside world, but all that remained were a few brassy ends.

Neither of her friends spoke as she sat and took a long sip of coffee from a paper cup. Natalie was usually happy to fill the silence with stories about the marine research laboratory where she studied. Lydia had once gone down to the water's edge to see the collections of kelp and jelly-fish bobbing in well-lit tanks, but even before the ocean had begun speaking to her, she'd been afraid of it.

"What's going on?" she asked when she noticed October ignoring her pile of spaghetti. October worked with the Guild's forestry department and always had a huge appetite by lunch.

Thirteen girls had been taken, but only twelve returned, one for each full moon of the year. October still called herself by the hasty identification note scrawled across the Guild's paperwork when she'd appeared at the lighthouse after being missing for twelve months.

"Something happened at the lighthouse. Half the Guild is there, Francesco included. Boats have been going back and forth all day. I swear, I saw *trees* on the island this morning. What do those mages get up to?" Natalie said, popping another turkey meatball into her mouth. The rosy blush on her cheeks made her look younger than twenty-two.

Lydia's stomach churned as the coffee burned its way

down. If there was something new on the island, she would be the last to notice. "Have you talked to Alex?" she asked.

Alex was Natalie's boyfriend—a mage recruited into the Guild after a groundbreaking essay on anomalous physics. When the Onners family was still at the helm, a relationship between a changeling and a mage would never have been tolerated. Their new leader, Francesco, didn't care what the changelings got up to as long as they did nothing to inconvenience him.

"No, but October saw him heading to the island on a dinghy this morning. It must be serious. He usually tells me all the Guild's secrets," Natalie said. Lydia watched Natalie sway as October kneed her under the table.

With the mages occupied, the cafeteria was mostly empty. At Francesco's decree, the changelings raised at the compound had been given a new identity and a bank account at eighteen. Of the twelve, nine had left and of the nine, seven had returned, Lydia included. Francesco had taken one look at her—hungover, pale, and heart-broken—and assigned her a job shelving books in the library.

"Lydia," Isst began. He rarely spoke in the presence of others. She was the only one who understood him, and he found all the squawking and croaking undignified. "I hate to be the bearer of bad news, but I believe those mages over there are looking for *you*."

She swiveled in her chair to catch sight of two men and a woman in their mid-thirties, all wearing yellow rain jackets with the image of a lighthouse topped by an open eye over the right pocket: the crest of the Guild of Light-keepers. The woman gestured at Lydia's table.

"What the hell?" October muttered. Her fork was still clenched in her right hand. Life at the compound had improved immeasurably since the Guild came into

Francesco's care, but there was not a changeling who didn't remember the experiments they'd once been subjected to.

"Lydia Reyes? September? You're to get dressed and come with us. Francesco has asked for you," said one of the men. His eyes remained fixed on the clipboard he was holding as he spoke.

"Wh-what?" Lydia sputtered.

Francesco seemed to have little interest in the ten changelings who still roamed the compound, indulging their hobbies and academic pursuits. With the Onners gone, the Guild had shifted their focus to the lighthouse, and the changelings became little more than curiosities. It wasn't as if they remembered the Green Country, anyway. All had been less than three years old when they were snatched from their beds and replaced with fairy poppets made of bog-wood and alder sprigs.

Those poppets were missing now. Lydia hoped they were stashed away somewhere, and hadn't grown into strange facsimiles of the girls they'd once replaced.

"I am dressed," Lydia said dumbly. Even though there was no required uniform at the library, she still felt a compulsion to dab on mascara every day and make sure her shoes matched her jacket. A good outfit was like armor, she told herself. People took you more seriously when your heels were sharp enough to punch a hole through their foot.

The man didn't respond. He brought a pen to his clipboard and checked something off before looking up.

"Where are you taking her?" October asked. "Francesco has never *summoned* any of us before. We're researchers here, the same as you."

"You'll need a raincoat and galoshes. We're headed to the lighthouse. You're to be on the boat when we go," the man said as if October hadn't spoken at all.

"I have to get back to work at the library…"

"It's been taken care of. Come on. We need to be on the water before the tide comes in."

October put her fork down with more force than was strictly necessary. "If Francesco needs a changeling, I'll go. I'm fine on a boat."

Heat spread across Lydia's cheeks. The last time Francesco had taken the changelings for an outing had been to the aquarium in Newport. She hadn't been able to hide how her knees buckled when she heard waves crashing against a rickety pier.

"Sorry, it's Lydia he's asked for." He turned to address her. "Go with Ms. Gracie. I'll get your food wrapped up. Francesco wanted me to let you know this is library business. I'm sure you don't want to shirk the duties that came with your promotion. Zoya is already on the island waiting for you."

Isst gave a sharp click with his beak.

"Library business?" he said to Lydia. "I've heard nothing about this."

"Will my raven be able to accompany me?" Lydia asked, forcing her body to remain still. A wild thought came to her. She knew all the paths out of the compound; she could run now and return in a few hours, claiming some illness. But she'd worked so damn *hard* for this promotion. A short boat ride wouldn't take that away from her, no matter how much the prospect made her chest tighten.

The three Guild members looked at one another, and the woman shrugged. She had a deep voice with a European accent Lydia could not place. "They didn't mention the raven either way—"

"I need him with me. He's my assistant."

"Assistant?" Isst tutted.

Natalie reached for Lydia's hand under the table and gave it a squeeze. "You'll be fine," she whispered. "It only takes a few minutes to reach the lighthouse. If you feel seasick, look at the horizon. It helps."

"Are you sure you want to do this?" October asked. "They can't *make* you. Francesco promised us our freedom after the Onners died."

"It's fine," Lydia told her, with a tight smile. She wondered if she should try to eat a few more bites before standing, but the thought of being aboard a rocking boat with a full stomach seemed worse than with an empty one.

"I asked for this job. If they need me, I'll go," she added, more for her benefit than anyone else's.

"I'll grab you a raincoat," Ms. Gracie said.

"One of the large ones," Lydia told her. She always had to be creative about altering the late Mrs. Onners's wardrobe to accommodate her curves. "Don't forget the galoshes. These shoes aren't supposed to get wet."

She swallowed the rest of her coffee too quickly, hoping the fire in her throat would bring her body back under control. The heat flooded her chest, aggravating an already uncomfortable pressure.

It's just water, Lydia told herself. It's just a lighthouse.

And yet, she couldn't help but think of those strange whispers she heard from the ocean late in the night, when Isst was asleep on his perch.

Whispers in the only language she did not understand.

"Lydia Reyes. Twenty-two years old. White hair, brown eyes. Can you state your height and weight for the record?"

"No," Lydia said. "What's the purpose of this? I've lived here my entire life."

She wanted to glare at the mage who was asking questions. Instead, she tucked her head into her knees and didn't think she could risk looking up without another wave of queasiness washing over her. The rain had slowed to a light patter, and the coast was an uninterrupted gradient of light gray sky melting into the dark gray of the ocean.

"This is standard procedure before someone steps onto the island for the first time, but all right, we can skip that question. Any history of drugs or alcohol?" the man went on.

"It *won't* be my first time on the island. I'm sure Francesco has this all on file," she told him through gritted teeth. The boat lurched sideways, but with her head down, Lydia did not see the wave that hit it.

There was silence from the Guild members who had ushered Lydia from the cafeteria. Maybe it was a mistake to be snippy with them. Even though the rain may have slowed, the ocean was still so choppy they could convincingly argue she'd fallen overboard.

"I'm sure they have files," came Ms. Gracie's voice. "This isn't about that. Things can get... strange at the lighthouse. We compare our answers every time to check for any psychological changes. Please, Lydia. Do you have any history of drugs or alcohol?"

Lydia swallowed the taste of bile. Isst was gliding overhead, but she didn't trust herself to look. "Not since I returned to the compound two years ago."

"Any sexual partners?"

"Same answer," Lydia said. Over the last few weeks, she'd been unusually successful in not thinking about Dominic. Her promotion meant there was less time to remember the morning she had rolled over in their bed to find his pillow empty, aside from the peace sign button she'd bought him from a quarter machine on their first date.

"And you're of Cuban descent?"

"Your guess is as good as mine."

Lydia had no memories of her brief life before she was taken by the fey. The few clues were the things that remained in her pockets when she returned one year later; a couple of candy wrappers, and a ticket to the maritime museum in Astoria with what might have been her name written on it.

The Onners had done extensive genetic testing on all the girls, but apart from the fact that each had been stolen from their beds on the Oregon coast before they were four years old, there seemed to be no pattern connecting them. Natalie was half-Irish, half-Clatsop. October, Vietnamese, and all the others were equally genetically diverse.

"We'll be there in a moment. One last question. Have you experienced any unusual mental or emotional changes in the last six months? Depression, anxiety? Any intrusive thoughts or voices in your head?"

Lydia took a breath of briny air, hoping the interviewer would assume she was seasick. Even now, she heard the ocean whispering—syllables flowing into one another in time with the sloshing waves. She lay awake at night trying to make sense of it, in the same way that she could make sense of a coyote's yipping, Isst's sleepy clicks, and the hundreds of dead languages preserved in books throughout the library.

"No," she finally said.

The ding of a buoy bell set off the island's seagulls. Lydia saw none of it, but her mind interpreted their shrieks to mean HUMANS! RAVEN! FOOD! She didn't open her eyes until the boat knocked against something firm, and one of the Guild members unraveled a damp rope that snaked across Lydia's feet.

When she eventually unfurled, the first thing she saw was the lighthouse. It rose above the island's dramatic basalt formations, a stark white against the gray sky. The light had been decommissioned years before, but the Guild made efforts to maintain the grounds. Wind-battered grass lined the gravel path from the dock, and the red paint on the house was touched up each June after winter storms did their best to rip it off.

Lydia had not set foot on this island for nineteen years and had hoped she never would again.

Isst landed on the dock as the Guild mages tossed their bags onto dry land.

"I've never seen a human look so green before," he said. "Are you sure you want to do this? Francesco would never actually fire you. You're his favorite."

Lydia wasn't sure if that was true, but Francesco seemed to go out of his way to purchase records of old Cuban music; scratchy tracks that sang of palm trees and longing, and the lightning strike of falling in love. He told the cooks to make flan and rice pudding with milk on her birthday. Sounds and flavors of a place that seemed as distant as the fey realm.

The wind was strong enough to shield her voice from the Guild mages. "I'm fine. I can do this. It's just a lighthouse."

"It's not *just* a lighthouse. Even I don't like it here. The last time I was on this island, one of those accursed mages bound me to this form," Isst said. The wind ruffled his feathers, revealing a hint of puckered gray skin.

"You *like* being a raven," she reminded him. "Stay close to me. I have to prove I can do this job."

Ms. Gracie lent Lydia a hand for the shaky exit from

the boat, and as they walked up the steep path to the light-house, she realized Natalie had been correct. There *were* a number of trees that hadn't been here before. More inter-estingly, they were large, well-established, and most certainly created by magic. It was normally something Lydia would have found intriguing, were she not so afraid.

Isst gave a sharp breath and muttered, "Just what have these fools been up to?"

There were more mages on the island than she had ever seen in one place. Most wore yellow or black raincoats emblazoned with the Guild's crest, but she spotted Francesco in one of his customary gray suits. She tried to focus on walking toward him. It was better than remem-bering she was trapped on all sides by the whispering ocean.

Francesco was in conversation with Zoya Yatsenko, the head librarian. Lydia noticed how many eyes turned to watch her approach; a hush fell across the various groups as if she'd just arrived at a party where every conversation had revolved around her. A cool drop of water slipped from her hair beneath her collar, chasing the shiver already moving down her spine.

"Ms. Reyes! At last. Come with me, we're needed inside," Zoya said. She was an extraordinarily tall woman who always dressed like she was on her way to a funeral. Her dark gray hair was gathered into a tight bun that glis-tened with sea spray.

"What's going on?" Lydia asked.

"We have need for your particular talent, Lydia," Francesco said. He looked to be in his late forties, although mages were difficult to age. She rarely saw him in anything other than a modest gray suit, but when he pushed his sleeves up, she'd glimpsed a network of black tattoos depicting pentagrams, runes, and stranger symbols Lydia had never seen until granted access to the most interesting books in the library.

Francesco was different from the Onners. He denied the changelings nothing; money, knowledge, even influence in the Guild. Still, Lydia noticed the way his eyes darted to the side whenever the window was brought up, as if he wanted to both study the Green Country and forget its existence.

The question of *where* exactly the Green Country was had been a popular source of debate among the Guild of Lightkeepers. It obviously overlapped with their world, the window being proof, but Francesco liked to point out that human perception was limited and even if they knew of the existence of the fairy lands, they might never understand it.

"Thank you for coming," he said in a low voice, leading her into the keeper's house. "I know it wasn't easy for you. Did the Guild members tell you what to expect inside?"

"No," she murmured. The wind blew a strand of hair, tasting like sea salt, into her mouth. For a moment, it felt like she was back on the boat and the world was tipping beneath her.

"All the same. It's not as if anyone can adequately prepare. Just keep your head, as I taught you. We need you to translate a text, then someone will take you back to the mainland. Can I trust you'll keep everything you see and read here a secret?"

This was not an unusual thing to be asked of her, even before her promotion at the library. Many mages spent time among the books at the Onners's compound, and she usually had a decent idea of what they were researching by the volumes they requested. She still felt too ill to speak, but thankfully, Francesco accepted silence as her answer.

"I *am* sorry," he said again. "I don't particularly like coming here myself, to be honest. Isst will have to wait outside."

"But——" Lydia began.

"Even though he is bound, Isst is still a spirit from the Green Country. There may be magic inside the house that lessens the Guild's control over him."

She gave the raven an apologetic shrug. None of the seagulls had returned to the island since he arrived, for captured spirits gave off an aura that normal animals could sense. At times, she caught an oddly familiar whiff of oakmoss and clover whenever Isst darted past her.

"I don't understand. Why did I have to come here? There's too much wind and humidity on this island. The library would be a safer place to examine a book," Lydia said, as Francesco brought her to the keeper's bright red door. She did her best not to lean into him, despite her legs feeling like they were on backward.

"Anomalous physics. This close to the fairy realms, not all of our natural laws are as consistent as they should be. We have to thoroughly examine any object from the Green Country before bringing it to the mainland, lest it have some properties we're not aware of."

Lydia did not have time to ask a follow-up question. The door swung open, and she was hit with the smell of beeswax and wood polish. Old furniture lay scattered across the small living room, each piece a different color and style from the next. It looked as though the house had been decorated with whatever detritus was left when the ocean pulled back at low tide.

Only Zoya Yatsenko and a Guild mage were inside. The latter was a barefoot young man, wearing sweatpants and with a heavy blanket over his shoulders. A chipped mug trembled in his hands.

Lydia tried not to look at the poorly bandaged gash over his right eye, but that meant the only other place to turn her attention was the window.

The window she had not seen since childhood. It didn't even seem that… wrong, if she was being honest with herself. The verdant forest beyond the glass was similar to her usual view at the compound until one realized this window faced west and beyond it should have been the ocean.

Lydia had been on the other side of that window for a full year, even if she couldn't remember it.

Francesco held her arm as her legs gave out.

"It gives me a shock every time," he said with a laugh she knew was for her benefit. "This is Jason Mullan, the leader of our expeditionary team."

Expeditionary team? she repeated in her head. It was common knowledge that the Guild studied the window, but this was the first time she'd heard they went *through* it. As far as Lydia understood, the changelings were the only known humans who'd gone into the Green Country and returned in recent history.

Mullan did not react to Francesco's words and simply stared at his empty mug. It looked as though his bandage needed changing, but he didn't seem to notice the trickle of blood running down his cheek.

Neither Francesco nor Zoya moved to help. They both had their attention on the dining room table, where a small rectangular object lay beneath one of Zoya's silk scarves.

"They're all *dead*—" Jason muttered.

Francesco cut him off. "That's Guild business. Lydia is here about the book."

As he let go of Lydia's arm, she wondered if his trust that she could keep herself upright was misplaced. She rarely touched wine these days, but this might be the evening she shoved Natalie and October out of bed and played Patsy Cline records in the media room until a sleepy mage chewed them out.

On the table, there was also a note written on old parchment, but that couldn't be what Lydia had been summoned to translate since it was written in English.

It read:

> *F,*
>
> *Are you brave enough to come through yet? I have a gift waiting.*
>
> *G*

Zoya took a deep breath. Her hands shook as she lifted the silk scarf from the table, the fabric fluttering in the draft.

Gods, what was going on here?

"We'll need a brief translation, for now. The title and first chapter. Our goal is to determine whether or not this book is safe to bring to the mainland," Zoya said.

The book looked unlike most of those in the library, which liked to show how important they were. Lydia couldn't count the number of times she'd pricked her finger on an elaborate bronze clasp or cleaned dust from a finely etched leather cover. This was more like a traveler's journal. It was thin, probably less than a hundred pages, and the binding was not of the finest quality.

Lydia steadied herself as Zoya passed over a wipe to clean her hands with. The act calmed Lydia's mind. This was normal. This was good. She might detest the ocean and the lighthouse in equal measure, but books were her constant companion. She understood them, and not merely because they had no way of hiding their meanings from her.

"This looks like an old Moleskine notebook. Maybe from the late eighties, judging by the style," she said, meeting Zoya's gaze. "Are you sure you needed *me* here for this?"

Francesco nodded. "Yes, Lydia. Your gift is essential for this."

A sudden motion from beyond the window caught her eye. It was as windy in the forest as it was in their world. Massive sword ferns rattled like they were trying to break free from the dirt. She tried to ignore the low, pained moan Jason gave when branches from the Green Country scraped against the glass.

"Open it," Zoya said.

Lydia gasped at the book's first page. A wild, looping script unlike any she'd seen before filled each available space. It was certainly not a human language, but she didn't think it was one of the fey variants, nor the writing of any other literate species of their world.

"The Notations of a Mapmaker on his Travels," she read out loud. "I'm sorry. There might have been a name, but it's been covered. I can't make it out."

Francesco and Zoya exchanged a glance Lydia couldn't interpret, and he motioned for her to continue. Jason Mullen hobbled to the window and pressed his forehead against it. Blood from his face smeared across the glass.

"Okay," she breathed, "I pray that I'm wrong and this book will never be used for its intended purpose..."

"No!" Jason shouted, beating his fist against his thigh. The room's other occupants jumped. "I've been trying to tell you, it's not safe here. They're all *dead*, don't you understand? My entire team is dead. Open this window and toss that book back in. Those monsters are prepared to kill for whatever is inside it."

Zoya wrung her silk scarf as she looked from Jason to Francesco. "Perhaps he's right. There are warded rooms at the compound. I don't see the harm of bringing the journal back there for examination."

Francesco clicked his tongue like this was an argument he thought they'd already resolved. "You, of all people, should understand why that's unwise. Remember what William Onners learned about their world? You've seen the trees too. They shouldn't be *here*."

Lydia swallowed, unsure of whether she should try to contribute to this conversation. The first few paragraphs were as straightforward as translating any other language, but on the last lines were symbols reminding her of the information she associated with animal calls. It filled her mind with images—a yew tree with a massive trunk, and beyond it, what looked like the wreckage of a boat on dry land.

The thrill of the discovery was so intense she forgot the fear that had accompanied her to the island. Lydia scanned the next few pages. The author had left some notations, but most of the book was written in symbols that filled her mind with forested paths.

This was… a map.

"Zoya—" she began. Her voice cut off as she turned a page because there was her name, glaring at her, in the middle of one of the Mapmaker's paragraphs.

LYDIA REYES WILL KILL THE FEY KING.

She slammed the book shut just as the window shattered.

An arrow whizzed past her head, striking the cabinet. Her hands flew for the book on instinct, and Lydia clutched it against her chest as she ducked under the table.

She caught sight of Jason sprawled across the floor with an arrow jutting out of his shoulder. Francesco's leather shoes skidded across the room, but Zoya was frozen in place.

"Battle mages! We need battle mages," Francesco yelled, as Zoya give a choked sob.

Brilliant red light filled the room. Francesco was an excellent mage in his own right, and the spell created so much heat that Lydia's nostrils burned. She squinted, taking another wild glance around; the front door was a few feet away but Mullen's blood spread across the hardwood floors. If there was already an archer at the window, the time it took her to cross that distance would give them a chance to put an arrow in her back.

Lydia wanted to sob. She wanted to scream. She had always believed the ocean would kill her, but it hadn't been like this. The book pressed against her chest felt like flimsy armor, and despite Francesco's pleas, none of the other mages had rushed into the house to help.

Wards? she wondered. The thought was interrupted by another arrow hitting the table above her. Lydia knew she had to move. A new array of voices had joined the chaos. Fey language was usually lyrical and expressive, but these barked orders sent a spear through her heart.

"Get the book before they challenge the wards on the house! Kill whoever stands in your way!"

There was another thud, and she prayed it wasn't a body hitting the ground. Lydia knew she had no choice but to run. A pair of leather boots crunched against broken glass, and a long shadow fell over the room, cast by the dappled light of a forest in another world.

If she died now, she didn't want to be sitting beneath a table as her pantsuit soaked up blood. Gods, she wished she had more time. She wished she had told Natalie and October that she loved them. She wished she'd left the compound once more; even if it was to get ice cream or ramen or to listen to sad country music at a dive bar where no one knew what'd caused her hair to turn white.

Lydia's hand slipped on blood as she attempted to dart from beneath the table. The attempt failed.

A rough hand grabbed her by the ponytail, yanking her upright.

Her eyes met the pointed features of a fey man with a scar across his cheek resembling a lightning bolt. In Lydia's peripheral vision, Francesco slumped against the room's empty bookshelf. She hoped he was only unconscious. Zoya was missing. Perhaps she'd escaped?

The fey man snatched the book from Lydia's grip. He wore studded leather armor and didn't react as she struggled. The quiver strapped to his back was full of arrows topped by striped hawk feathers, but it was his silvery eyes that made Lydia's breath hitch.

"Got it," he called. The only sign there was another person in the room was a shift in light as they passed in front of the window. "What do we do with this thing?"

They don't know I can understand them, Lydia realized. She was bleeding profusely from a gash across her left forearm. In the rush of adrenaline, she hadn't noticed an arrow had grazed her before she ducked beneath the table.

"The humans had her reading the book. I saw it from the window. Maybe we should bring her back with us. Let Belimar decide what to do," said the unseen man.

She tried to lash out, to rake her fingernails across the fey's face, or kick him in the shins, but the man holding Lydia's hair only grunted.

"You know, they say human women are hideous, but this one's not too bad. Thicker than the girls at home. Might keep the boys at camp entertained for a day or two."

"Cithral! You're a soldier of the king. Act like one. Can *you* read the book?"

The fey called Cithral used his free hand to flick the journal open. "Looks like nonsense to me. Still have no idea why Belimar risked the Sorrowood for this thing."

"That's the king's business," the other man said, stepping into her peripheral vision. His hair was dark red, and his ears ended in sharp points. Every shadow on his face was deep green. Like Cithral, he wore studded leather armor with a bow strapped across his back.

"If she can read it, he'll want to see her. Let's go before the mages break our wards."

"They'll follow us," Cithral said.

"The king's scholars will reinforce the spells properly. Even if the humans manage it, they'll need to get through the forest. They'll think twice after what happened to the last band of thieves they sent into our land. Take the girl, let's go."

"No!" Lydia shouted, but it was the last sound she heard before a fist came down against the back of her head.

The darkness of her unconsciousness was tinted green.

EVERYTHING IS HUNGRY

QUINN WAS ABOUT TO DEFECT FROM THE HIGH KING'S army when a voice called his name from across the camp.

He'd meant to escape into the Sorrowood while the soldiers were distracted with the raid. The forest was dangerous even with a company of trained warriors, but he'd spent most of his life in a village where the trees had long since transformed into the gnarled creatures surrounding him now. If he could get a few hours' head start, he might beat whoever pursued him to one of the towns on the river. There was enough gold sewn into the lining of his jacket to hire a ship.

"Oy! Sawbones! You're needed," a soldier called.

"Dammit," Quinn muttered. The punishment for defection was death, but perhaps Belimar would not bother chasing after a rural medic he'd conscripted less than a year ago. Of course, that meant the king might send his Gyfoal instead.

Quinn looked at the forest again. They'd cleared a few square meters for their camp, and trees loomed over the tents like they were building a cage for a company that'd

willingly wandered into their trap. Someone snatched his
arm before he could take a step in either direction, and
Quinn wasn't surprised to find Rai beside him.

"What are you doing? I've been searching for you.
Someone needs your attention," Rai said.

Rai was dressed in the studded leather armor he'd
worn when preparing to approach the tower a few hours
ago. His red hair was tied back with a leather cord, and
despite the long march of the last few days, his skin was as
pale and lightly freckled as always. It was a sharp contrast
with Quinn's jet-black locks and sun-bronzed skin. No one
would ever guess they were cousins.

"I was checking the supply levels," Quinn lied.

Rai seemed distracted. He took a glance around them,
then leaned in as if to help with the task. "We retrieved the
book, along with a human girl we think can translate it.
This could *be it*, Quinn. If we can get the book to the—"

"Stop," Quinn snapped, his voice low. He opened a
crate and pretended to count the rations inside. "There are
too many ears here, and besides, I've already told you I
want no part of it. My only concern is the Sorrowood."

Rai waved a hand. "There are plenty of scholars in
Astoria. They'll find a way to push the wood back."

"An interesting assumption, considering they haven't
managed it yet," Quinn said.

"You're ornery today. I know you don't like this place. I
know you don't like the army and neither do I, but Belimar
is a more immediate threat, and he thinks whatever is in
that book will cement his power. Word is that he has his
eye on the mountains of the Ettin people. They're
powerful but loosely organized. After them, what kingdom
falls next? The Court of the Salt Lake? The Folk of the
Canyon? You can worry about your Sorrowood once Belimar's head is on a pike outside of the Cloud Pala—"

Rai cut himself off. "I'm sorry. I didn't mean to phrase it like that."

"It's fine," Quinn said. "It doesn't matter. Nor do politics if the Sorrowood swallows the whole of the Green Country. Oh, don't look at me like that, you've made your point. Tell me about the window."

"Less exciting than I imagined. I don't know why the scholars make such a fuss about how they can't travel into the human world any longer. It was horribly bleak. The colors were all wrong, and the air was much too cold, but... I heard the ocean. The *ocean*, Quinn."

Quinn could understand the hitch in Rai's voice. In dreams, he sometimes caught the smell of seaweed drying beneath the sun or the sound of gulls and a distant foghorn. Rai was a few years older and would have learned to sail in the bays that once kept Astorians fed with mussels and bulky red crabs.

"You actually saw the book? The one Belimar dragged us through this forest for?" Quinn asked.

"Yes. It's with the king now. The human needs a medic. Her wound won't close. Are you coming?"

Quinn couldn't help but notice Rai's sneer as he said the word 'king.' Although it was a habit Rai suppressed in the company of other soldiers, Quinn still worried a slip would one day end with his cousin's neck over a chopping block.

A sigh escaped him. He could still run. Rai certainly wouldn't rat him out to the officers, but Quinn was a medic and had taken a vow to help others when it was in his power to do so. It was the one vow he had ever kept; the only that truly meant anything to him.

"Have her brought to my tent, and stop acting like you want to be charged with treason," he said, and didn't fail to catch the tight smile that disappeared from Rai's face as soon as they turned to face the camp.

QUINN HAD NEVER ACTUALLY SEEN A HUMAN BEFORE.

On a surface level, they were anatomically similar to the fey. The young woman had all the proper limbs and facial features, even if her ears were misshapen. She seemed barely conscious when Quinn pushed through the flap to his tent, but bolted upright as she noticed him. Someone had shackled her wrists, and the movement snapped her shoulder in a way that must have been painful.

"Let me out of here," she snarled, tugging on the restraints. The wound on her opposite arm bled through hastily applied bandages.

She speaks our language, he realized. *That's odd.*

"I'm afraid that's not something I have any control over," he said, keeping his voice calm. "But you're hurt, and I can help. I only want to tend to the cut on your arm."

What the hell had Rai been thinking when he brought her here? Until now, Quinn's cousin never had a problem disobeying the king's orders when there was little chance of getting caught. Humans did not belong in the Green Country, not anymore. Even Belimar did not steal changelings or raid the other world in search of captives, as the old fey kings had done.

Not that he could have if he wanted to.

The woman continued to struggle, but he sensed she must have been near exhaustion. Dried blood clung to her white hair and her odd clothes were so tattered, they would offer little protection against the cold of the Sorrowood once night fell.

He sat in a wooden chair by the bedside and spoke as he arranged his tools. A bottle of antiseptic. Bandages and ties. His stitching kit, if the wound looked deep enough once he had the chance to examine it.

"I know you must be frightened, but that cut looks serious. I'm a medic. You'll need to be still so I can clean the wound and re-bandage. If you can't do that, I'll have to sedate you."

The woman glanced at her arm, and he watched her jaw clenching through her closed mouth. Her upper lip was slightly fuller than the lower one—dark eyes shone beneath thick, well-groomed brows. Quinn had always been told humans were a hideous species, but the woman was attractive, even if that wasn't the sort of thing he usually assessed when dealing with a patient.

"What's your name?" he asked. He could tell she was doing her best to keep her breathing even.

"None of your business. I need water. I'm dehydrated. And that brute dragged me through the mud while my wound was uncovered. It needs to be flushed and cleaned," she said. Though she spoke the language of the fey, she had an accent that didn't belong to any region of the Green Country he knew of.

Quinn fetched her a scoop of water in a dented tin mug. "That is my plan if you'll allow me to look at your arm. Are you a healer?"

"No. Listen, I don't know why I've been brought here, but there'll be people after me. Mages. Powerful ones. If you let me go, I can convince them to take me back and leave this camp alone," she said.

He gave an internal flinch. The strange window in the

Sorrowood had made its way into every campfire story of the tiny villages at the forest's edge. Even Belimar's company had lost six men on their journey toward it, despite Quinn using every bit of magic and medicine he had to keep them alive.

The forest would annihilate a group of humans.

He decided it was best not to address her statement directly. If Belimar wanted her here, there was no chance of escape, and she had finally stilled enough to let him examine the gash on her arm. "Do many humans enter the Green Country?"

She snorted but did not wince as Quinn flushed dirt from the cut and applied antiseptic. "Shouldn't you know?"

"If you're talking about changelings and captives, then no. Our worlds have long been closed off from each other. You're the first human I've met."

The woman fell silent, pulling back her arm as he prepared to re-bandage it.

"Are they going to kill me?" she asked in a low voice.

The truthful answer was *probably*. Belimar did not take prisoners, and they were already short on supplies. It would not be strategic to drag a human back to Astoria with them unless she proved to be valuable.

"If they were going to kill you, they would have done so already," he said. "I'm only the sawbones, but I doubt I'd be fixing you up if they intended to do something untoward. Let's get this re-bandaged."

Her arm was limp when he reached for it, as if the fire she'd shown a few moments ago was snuffed out.

Higher body temperature than a fey, he noted. *Pulse elevated, but likely faster than ours at a resting rate as well.*

Quinn was halfway through bandaging her arm when he noticed a subtle golden light flaring just beneath her skin where his fingertips touched her bare arm. The woman spotted it a second after he did and pulled her arm away before the bandage was secure.

"What the hell are you doing? Don't touch me again," she said, tearing the thin linen wrap herself, and tucking it in place.

"What was *I* doing? You… you're a witch."

As the human opened her mouth as if she was going to argue, the tent flap moved and light flooded the space. Quinn's eyes had to adjust before he could make out Rai, who'd swapped armor for traveling clothes.

"Belimar wants to see her," Rai said. There must have been other soldiers lingering around the medical tent. Rai never barked orders at Quinn, except for the sake of appearances.

Quinn glanced at the woman's bandaged cut, then at her frightened eyes. A line from an old song came to him, but he shoved it out of his mind. Even as a boy, he'd avoided thinking about those lyrics, and he was not about to get into the habit now.

Oh, curse me, he thought.

"No," he told Rai. "She's in shock. I'm afraid she's in no state to meet with the king. Not for a few days, at least."

She shifted in the cot at Quinn's words, but thankfully, did not speak.

Rai entered the tent, letting the flap close behind him. His voice was lower when he spoke next. "She's got to go. Belimar will drag her out if you don't bring her, and that won't look good for you."

He doesn't know she can understand us, Quinn realized. Rai didn't heed Quinn's warning glare.

"She can read the book. If we can get her and it back to Astoria, we can contact the rebels and…"

"Enough. If Belimar is going to meet her now, I need to come. She's still bleeding," Quinn snapped. He could feel the woman's eyes boring into him, though he was turned away. This day was getting worse by the hour.

"You usually do everything you can to avoid seeing him. Are you sure, Quinn? Your tender little heart aside, the less Belimar notices you, the better," Rai said.

In truth, it wasn't Belimar who scared Quinn. It was the Sorrowood.

The rulers of the Green Country had politicked, waged war, and executed each other for millennia. All kings eventually lost their favor, and Belimar's skull would one day be tossed into the crypt containing the bones of every dead leader who had hoped to rule the Northwestern court forever.

The Sorrowood was different.

It was impossible to wage war on a forest. Now that it seemed to have hastened its efforts to take over the Green Country, it would only be a matter of time before the blight plowed through their court's city and beyond.

It wasn't only her welfare he was concerned with.

"Yes. I'm sure," he said, turning back to the woman.

The fire in her eyes was back, but it was not the inferno it had been a few minutes ago. This was a slow burn, a dangerous burn; the kind that hid beneath the ground until a stray wind kicked it up and it engulfed an entire forest.

Quinn glanced at the girl's pale hair and bloody bandages. She didn't seem like a mage, and though he wasn't qualified to age humans, she couldn't be much older than twenty. Most of his stronger antipyretic herbs had been used to fight infections after the elk's attack. She'd have to hope the gash didn't lead to a fever too strong to be treated with willow bark.

Rai shrugged when Quinn didn't immediately stand. "I thought the fact that Belimar believes this book has to do with the Sorrowood would be enough to interest you."

"What interests me is getting you out of this forest alive," Quinn said, shooting another warning look that went unnoticed.

"Liar. I've seen how you've been studying this place. Word has it you even tried for an audience with the scholars of the Radiant Eye."

"Belimar is temporary," Quinn huffed. "Once the forest takes our kingdom over, there'll be nothing left to do but run. Come on. Let's get this over with."

A POLE WAS STUCK INTO THE GROUND BY BELIMAR'S TENT, atop which was the freshly cleaned skull of a titanic elk the king had killed on their first night in the woods. The beast had towered over the trees and fatally gored two soldiers before Belimar managed to put it down. Its skull was a trophy now. A way of showing the forest that Belimar was still king of this realm, no matter how much the Sorrowood tried to contest it.

Quinn's eyes flitted to the trees. This was not the first time he'd been in the forest, but it was by far the deepest he'd traveled. The wood had expanded plenty when he was a child, although not at the rates it did now—swallowing farmlands and towns as it marched its way toward the royal city.

He'd lost track of how many refugee carriages had raced out of villages as trees swept across their pastures or grew through cabins even older than the Northwestern court. Plenty of learned men from the country had gone to the college to plead with the scholars for help, but the city at the heart of their kingdom had been in turmoil for decades.

Few had tried to stop Belimar as he and his militia had

dragged the royal family from the Cloud Palace. After all, Belimar—the previous king's huntsman—claimed to know the Sorrowood better than anyone. Claimed to be able to push it back.

But Belimar hadn't, and life in Astoria had gone on, anyway. After all, the wood was a distant threat; the concern of farmers and countryfolk who still lived among the hills as their ancestors had. The monsters that crawled out of the wood may have feasted on fey children, but they weren't Astorian children. At least, not yet.

Except now, the Sorrowood was speeding up.

"Listen to me carefully. Even though Belimar needs you, he has a short temper. Answer his questions quickly and try not to show fear. He'll have a translator who speaks your tongue. Whatever happens, don't let on that you understand us," Quinn whispered to the woman as they crossed the last few yards to the king's massive tent. Rai was a few yards behind, but the bluster of the camp was enough to swallow Quinn's words.

The woman shot him a strange look. She'd struggled as Rai pulled her from the tent, but was now too exhausted to do anything other than jiggle her restraints. "Why are you helping me?"

Quinn was currently asking himself that same question. A snippet of that old song ran through his head.

Here comes the Sorrowood
Gnarled and dark
Bane of the pauper
And the monarch

"You're my patient. It's my job. Don't speak anymore," he told her.

The Gyfoal was not in its stable. Quinn heard it huffing

and pawing at the dirt behind the king's tent, but thankfully, the creature was out of sight.

"Sorry, Rai," one of the king's guards said as they reached the tent flap. "Belimar says the girl and the sawbones only."

"But I'm his command—" Rai cut himself off, likely knowing that even a successful mission into the human world was not enough to spare him the king's anger. He shot Quinn a stern glance.

Quinn knew what it meant. Don't give the king any reason to take an interest in you.

Inside the tent, Belimar stood dressed in hunting clothes—ankle-high boots and a hooded wool tunic in a shade of gray-green. While there was a traveling throne in this tent, he rarely used it, preferring to hover over the maps on his center table. Not that maps were much good out here when the Sorrowood shifted on a whim.

The king looked up as Quinn and the woman entered. Belimar's reputation as a hunter was well-earned. His skin was rugged, with fine lines around his eyes and mouth, and he never used glamours to hide the gray streaks in his hair. If anything, he seemed to embrace the signs of age most fey shunned, even after centuries of life. The ram horns coiling from his skull were tipped with gold caps, his only sign of wealth.

Quinn had to resist the urge to pull out the medical shears he kept on his belt loop and stab the king in the gut.

Another fey stood by the throne, a young man Quinn recognized as a folklorist from the college in Astoria. He looked too nervous to touch anything, including the ground beneath his feet. The folklorist wore a quiver on his back, stuffed with scrolls instead of arrows.

Belimar gestured for the woman to sit, and it appeared she had taken Quinn's advice to heart. She obeyed, though her restraints jangled enough to betray her nerves.

"What's your name, dear?" Belimar asked. The folklorist repeated the question in a language Quinn couldn't understand.

"Lydia," she said quietly.

Belimar retrieved a key from his belt. "I'd like to let you out of those. Can I trust you not to run? These woods are very dangerous, even for ones such as us."

She waited for the translator to repeat the sentences, then nodded. The shackles clattered to the ground. Quinn watched Lydia carefully, but she made no move to try to escape.

At least she had some sense.

The king picked a book from his table. It was a thin volume with a leather cover, appearing no more important than the notebooks the scouts took with them when they went ahead to seek a trail. So that's it, Quinn thought. The thing so many men have already died for.

Belimar tossed the book onto Lydia's lap.

"Read," the king said, and the translator echoed him.

"The Notations of a Mapmaker on his Travels," she began. "The author's name is scratched out, but… there's a bit more. 'I pray this book will never be used for its intended purpose. However, if the need arises, then I must issue a warning: there is nothing to be found by following the paths I've laid out other than suffering and death.'"

"Keep going," Belimar said after the folklorist finished translating Lydia's words.

"I can't," she told him.

Quinn tensed. He watched her brush a strand of white hair from her face with a hand that shook less than it had a few moments ago.

"What do you mean you can't? Do you not speak this language?" Belimar said.

"Not fluently. I need time to translate it. It will take a while."

She's lying, Quinn realized, hoping Belimar would not come to the same conclusion. After all, the king didn't know she spoke their language with the ease of someone born and raised in Astoria.

Belimar crossed his arms and stared at the folklorist. The young man took a few wavering steps toward Lydia, glanced at the book, then shook his head.

"How much time?" Belimar asked.

"Each page will take me several days. I could only read what I'd already translated while in my world. I'll need three months at least," Lydia said.

Belimar chuckled. It was a relaxed sound that somehow made Quinn feel like he'd swallowed a needle.

"Three months. That's a long time for a human or an impatient fey king. The next holiday in our calendar is the Lamb Moon. Have the book translated by then, or you will be slaughtered like one. I'd also suggest you work faster than our scholars, lest you become useless before then. Sawbones, take our Lydia back to your tent. Make sure she is prepared for the journey to the city."

QUINN WAITED UNTIL HE AND LYDIA WERE WELL AWAY FROM the king's tent before muttering, "You *can* read that book. I told you to answer his questions."

"And face execution as soon as I gave him the one thing that makes me valuable? I'm not sure why you're helping me, but I have the feeling you and that red-haired soldier aren't exactly loyal. I just want to go home. If you really care, help me escape tonight. The stars should be the same here as in my home. I can navigate by them," Lydia said. Her voice was weak, like it was too much effort to both walk and speak.

He'd have to fetch her a bowl of elk bone broth from the cook, but there was something she needed to understand first.

"Come here," he said, catching her by the sleeve.

She yanked her arm away. "I told you not to touch me. I gave you permission to bandage my wounds, not use magic."

The old song went through Quinn's head. He clamped down on the thought before it could go on.

"That was *you*—" he began, then shook his head. If Lydia really was a witch, maybe she could slip out in the night, and none of this would be his problem anymore. The other option was too worrying for him to consider.

"I want to show you something before we go back to the medical tent. It's near here."

The Gyfoal was eating chunks of game meat out of a makeshift trough, but it looked up as Quinn and Lydia approached, red eyes blazing like two embers of burning coal. She gasped and stumbled back before catching herself.

It was the reaction most people had when seeing the Gyfoal for the first time. Although it was mostly horse-shaped, there was no mistaking it for a natural animal. It was far too huge, the lines of its head too sharp. Quinn had never seen it open its mouth fully, but the tales said a Gyfoal could unhinge its jaws and swallow a grown fey whole.

"What... what is it?" Lydia whispered.

The stable master spared her a passing glance from

across the pasture. It wasn't wise to be distracted during feeding time.

"The king's mount," Quinn said. "If you try to flee, it won't just be soldiers chasing after you. It'll be *that*. The Gyfoal can outrun a river. It never tires. And deer meat isn't the only thing it hungers for. They say the Gyfoal has coals in its stomach, which it tries to smother with food. You can smell it, can't you? The embers burning it from the inside out."

Lydia nodded.

He turned, urging her to follow him back to the medical tent. They had been seen together enough already.

It was not entirely a surprise to find Rai waiting for them inside. Quinn had hoped his cousin would put off meeting again until nightfall, but at least he'd brought a large bowl of the elk stew and a wooden spoon. It smelled of bone marrow and spices, but Quinn had a hard time choking down the animal that'd killed so many of their company.

Rai handed Lydia the spoon with an apologetic frown. "I know you can't understand me, but orders were to leave your shackles on."

"Doesn't matter. I'm not eating fairy food," she said, sagging onto the bed.

Rai's eyebrows raised as he glanced at Quinn.

"She speaks our language, so watch that big mouth," Quinn said. He turned to Lydia. "It's a myth humans can't eat fey food. You're weak. You need nutrition to help your body recover. Eat."

She shook her head. The spoon thumped to the floor. "It might be poisoned. You might have spiked it with sedatives, or…"

"The king wants you alive, and our medical supplies

are low. We lost most of our crates during an ill-timed river crossing. Even if I had the sedatives to spare, we wouldn't waste them on a bound human who couldn't make it more than a mile on her own. So, eat," Quinn said, wiping the spoon on his tunic before handing it back to her.

Lydia hesitated before taking a small sip of the oily broth.

"If you can understand me, even better. I'm here to offer you a deal, human," Rai said.

"This is not the time—" Quinn began.

"Our company moves out tomorrow. It might be the last chance we get to speak in private. I have contacts in Astoria that can smuggle you through the woods and to your window."

She set the bowl down on her lap and stared up at Rai.

"My friends want that book as much as Belimar does. If you agree to sneak a second translation to Quinn or me, I promise we will get you back home. You won't be able to do it alone, not between the woods and the Gyfoal," Rai said.

"I never said I wanted to be involved," Quinn snarled. He could hear the thud of leather boots on the other side of the tent flap, but casting a silencing ward would draw too much attention.

There'd been a time when he might have been persuaded to join Rai's rebellion, but Quinn had seen too much since then. He knew what Belimar was capable of, and it was more than a handful of idealistic fey would be able to counter. Quinn's main concern now was making sure his cousin didn't get himself killed.

Both Rai and Lydia ignored him.

"This book. What's so important about it?" Lydia asked.

Rai crossed his arms. "Only Belimar knows. After his

scholars uncovered its location, he gathered his best soldiers and charged into this cursed place. I'll admit, I wasn't convinced until I learned humans reached it before us and took it to their realm. Belimar is cruel, but he's also smart. He wouldn't have risked the lives of this company unless he thought it was something important."

Lydia made a face as she chewed a bit of gristle.

"You don't have to answer him," Quinn said.

"I'll do it," she said, staring at the last oily swirl of broth in her bowl. "If it's truly the only way to get back home, I'll do it. But I want to stay here, in the medical tent. The other soldiers—"

"Cithral is a bastard, but he knows Belimar would kill him if he laid a finger on you. Still, I think you should keep pretending to be sick, just in case," Rai said.

Quinn opened his mouth to argue that *he* should get a say in this plan, but before he could get a word out, a sharp trumpet call sounded from outside. Rai slipped through the tent flap.

Dammit, Quinn thought, biting the inside of his cheek.

A few hours ago, he had been prepared to face the woods on his own to escape Belimar's clutches. Now, he'd been dragged into a plot to help steal something Belimar thought was worth risking his and everyone else's life for.

He looked at Lydia, who lay on the bed facing away from him. Her ribs shuddered as if she was holding back sobs. Despite it being his habit to console a patient, he doubted she would be comforted by one of her captors.

He also had no desire to think about the glow beneath her skin as he had changed her bandages, or why it brought to mind some of the couplets the children of his small village used to sing.

Here comes the Sorrowood

And it won't go away
Because our king and his mate
Have a debt to repay...

He'd always known his Aés-Caill blood made him different, but there was already too much on his mind to make room for the stranger implications of the light between them.

His thoughts drifted back to Belimar. Eventually, deciding it might not be the worst thing to steal something precious from the man who had slaughtered most of Quinn's family twenty-five years ago.

THE TALLEST TOWER
IN THE CITY

LYDIA REYES WILL KILL THE FEY KING.

The words snapped her out of a blood-soaked dream, and it took her a few panicked breaths to remember where she was. The Green Country. An army camp. The fey king.

The fey king that a mysterious book proclaimed she was going to kill.

She sat up, wincing at the soreness that oozed through every muscle. It was night. The smell of campfire smoke drifted in as a breeze shifted the tent flaps, but there was no light aside from the scattered points of distant lanterns. The doctor was nowhere to be seen, though there was a steaming mug of tea on his desk.

Lydia considered her options. Lying to the fey king had saved her life. If he had known the book's strange language unfurled for her as easily as a wildflower blooming in the sun, she may well have been dead by morning. She had the feeling Rai would not be so easily deceived.

It had been easier to agree and let him believe she thought he was the key to her salvation.

The truth was, Lydia did not intend to go to this version of Astoria any more than she intended to translate the book. It was the fey that'd snatched her from her bed as a toddler. Their kind had left her with white hair and a gift she did not fully understand, taking away any chance she had for a life outside the compound.

She'd read plenty of books about navigation, and October had given crash courses in hiking whenever Lydia ventured out of the library, which left the matter of the woods to deal with. And of course, the Gyfoal.

A sharp caw interrupted her thoughts. It was so unexpected she briefly wondered if this was a dream and she hadn't woken up after all.

She snuck to the tent flap. Someone had removed the soaking pair of heels she'd fallen asleep in, but the shackles were still in place. They jangled as she moved the canvass to get a look outside.

It was a kind of darkness she wasn't used to. Even in the dead of night, there were lights at the compound and the occasional gleam of a car leaving the driveway. Aside from lanterns marking the location of other tents, the world here was as endlessly black as a raven's wings.

"There are you!" came a familiar voice. "I was afraid that you... Well, you're not and that's good. It's been ages since I've been in this wood. It certainly doesn't like company. Brave of the fey to venture in."

She raised a finger to her lips, hoping he would get the message. Even if she was the only one who could understand him, a raven cawing up a storm near midnight was certain to attract attention. Feathers rustled, and black eyes gleamed at her from atop a nearby tree stump.

"Do you know the way back to the window?" she whispered.

"Certainly. I used to live here," said Isst. She could tell

he was trying to keep his voice low, but ravens had different standards for what they considered quiet. "Which is how I know it's very dangerous and besides, your hands are bound. Francesco and the others are making a plan to come after you. However, there's been a problem—"

"What problem?"

"The fey left wards and traps in their way. It will take weeks for the Guild to dismantle them. Even if they break the spells, there's still the matter of the Sorrowood. The Guild's mages won't be prepared for what they find here."

"How were you able to get through?"

"I told you, I used to live here. I'm as forbidden from speaking more on that as I am my true name, but trust me when I say this is a bad place."

A sound from a nearby tent stopped Isst from saying more. She thought of the doctor's tea, still warm atop the desk. "Listen, Isst, I need to get out of here tonight. Do you think you can guide me?"

"Lydia—"

"Yes or no."

"*Yes*, but I told you, it's not safe. Perhaps if I was in my original form…"

"Wait for me in those trees."

It wasn't safe in the camp either, and the raven had already given her the answer she needed. In the woods, there was a chance; here, there was certain execution at the hands of the fey. She slipped back into the tent, leaving Isst alone in the darkness.

She needed a head start, but the medic could return any moment. An apothecary cabinet sat near the bed. Lydia scanned the handwritten names of herbs, trying to recall what she'd learned during the months she'd helped Natalie and October revive the herb garden at the compound. Lydia had taken an interest in poisonous plants after learning a side effect of her time in the Green Country was the ability to process drugs with surprising efficiency. The first time she'd gotten properly drunk in the outside world, it had taken three shots of naval rum, a mojito, and a cheap beer that tasted like coolant.

Achillea millefolium. Bryonia dioica. Mandragora officinarum. There.

Blessing the doctor for having powdered it already, she didn't bother to measure and instead poured a quarter of the jar's contents into Quinn's tea, and watched it dissolve. Thankfully, it was odorless.

A wave of guilt passed through her. She knew the fey weren't as fragile as humans, but mandrake was wildly toxic in large doses. Quinn had been kind to her, or at least, he had tried to be. Lydia hoped it would merely make him sleep.

She snatched a few pillar candles from the table and crept back into the bed, closing her eyes just as he came back through the tent flap. His clothes smelled of campfire smoke, but if he noticed she'd been rifling through his supply drawers, he said nothing. She heard him drag his chair out from beneath the table and sigh.

Drink, she urged in her mind. Her only chance was to slip away from Quinn's care before dawn. It might buy her a few hours before the soldiers or the Gyfoal started looking for her.

The teacup hit the table with a dull thud.

Mandragora officinarum, commonly known as mandrake root. It would take about thirty minutes to work on a human. She assumed a fey's metabolism was slower. If Quinn wasn't unconscious within the hour, her chances of escaping before the sun rose were null.

Lydia had to wait. And hope.

Pretending to sleep allowed her mind to wander. The

forest—the one she'd heard called the Sorrowood—spoke much as the one back home did. She was well-practiced in ignoring the world's background chatter, but she could have sworn she heard her name as Quinn disturbed the tent flaps.

Paranoia and sleep deprivation, she told herself.

Still, it made her think back to the Onners and the endless tests they'd run on the changelings. Lydia's gift was considered a passive one; it took no special effort to understand languages, and speaking them was little different. It wasn't until Francesco arrived at the compound that interest in Lydia's abilities was revived.

"It's not merely humanoid languages," he'd explained to William Onners. "I heard her talking to one of the library ravens."

Francesco would wrap her in his oversized scarf and let her stroll through the compound's nature trails with a Styrofoam cup full of hot chocolate in her hands.

"I think you're more special than you let on," he'd once said, crouching down to meet her eyes. "Tell me what the forest says."

Lydia shrugged. "It's confusing, with everything talking at once. The animals are usually hungry. The trees… the trees speak slowly. About the weather. And the dirt. And the wind."

Francesco reached into the soil and uprooted a sprig, hardly longer than one of her chubby fingers. Yellow petals were already fighting their way out into the world from the bud on the end.

"It used to be said that language was a kind of magic. Some were born knowing it, and others could learn, with practice. Certain cultures forbid the use of certain words, for fear of the power inherent in them to summon spirits or bad luck. Many religious traditions speak of a divine language—one used by the gods and angels."

She wasn't sure what to say to that. Francesco had always spoken to her as if she were another Guild member, not a child with hot chocolate on her chin. Her silence didn't seem to matter. He continued without waiting for a response.

"Can you understand what this little bud is saying?" he asked.

"It wants to bloom," she murmured.

"There is a hormone in the leaves that senses the length of days. When the sun shines for long enough, the bud opens up. We're still a few days away, so tell it to bloom early."

She was uncertain why a tremor of fear passed through her. The scarf suddenly felt too tight around her throat, the chocolate too hot in her mouth. She understood what Francesco was asking of her. He wanted Lydia to do magic.

"I can't," she said.

"Just try. Nothing will happen if it doesn't work."

That wasn't what she was afraid of. If it didn't work, she knew Francesco would march her back to the compound and she could sneak back to the library to finish the book she'd started this morning.

But if it did...

Even though the Guild of Lightkeepers might not fear magic, she did. Lydia couldn't remember the Green Country, but she still had murky dreams about waking up in the lighthouse keeper's home, one year after she'd been taken. Everything had shimmered like she was underwater. Witches, fairies, and magic were fun in her books, but in the real world, magic was terrifying.

Lydia stared at the bud, saying nothing, not even in her

mind. She squinted her eyes, hoping Francesco would believe she was concentrating.

"Nothing's happening," she told him.

"It's okay. It's getting cold out here, don't you think? Let's head inside. The other girls are getting ready to watch a movie." Francesco smiled as he adjusted her scarf. The smell of his expensive hand cream mixed with that of the melted marshmallows in her drink.

After attempting similar experiments a few more times, he'd eventually given up. Lydia tried not to think about those incidents too deeply. At least, not until she was ten years old when she'd just finished reading *The Last Unicorn* for what was likely the hundredth time; a story filled with magic lush and wild, like a forest.

For all of Lydia's insatiable curiosity, magic should have enthralled her the most. But like the ocean—just as vast and mysterious—thinking of it made her feel like gravity had somehow been switched off.

She wasn't sure exactly what compelled her to do it. Perhaps her mind still hadn't left the dreamy world of the unicorn in her lilac wood. Lydia looked at the sad little cactus on her nightstand. A gift from October, who even then preferred plants to most people.

There were no flower buds to ask to bloom, and Lydia's black thumb meant the poor specimen was already a week away from becoming compost. It had spoken nothing she could understand for days.

"Die," Lydia muttered to it.

Instantly, the cactus shriveled into a gray husk, and she burst into tears.

She had been right. Magic was just as awful and dangerous as she'd assumed.

Lydia vowed never to try it again. She quietly tossed

the cactus away with the evening trash and never spoke of it to anyone. Not even Isst.

She risked opening her eyes to find Quinn asleep in his chair, his head lolling back. This was the first time she'd had a good chance to study his features. His dark hair was gathered back into a short ponytail, with the sides of his head closely shorn. It was a similar haircut to what Rai sported—likely army regulations.

Aside from the pointed ears, he might have passed for human, were it not for the unnatural smoothness of his skin or eyes that were slightly too large for his face. The fey were said to be beautiful, but she had always taken fairy tales with a dose of skepticism. After her time in the library, she knew that any culture writing too fondly about itself was twisting the truth at least a bit.

Still, Quinn *was* undeniably attractive, at least by human standards, and just because Lydia spent most of her time among books didn't mean she couldn't notice something like that. Her first few months away from the compound had been a blur; neon lights through a haze of vodka and kissing beautiful strangers in bathrooms smelling of cigarette smoke and multi-purpose cleaner.

As she rolled off the bed, the gash on her arm pulsed beneath its bandage, and a flash of red pain swam behind her eyes. Quinn had cleaned the wound once, but she'd refused to comply when he asked to change the bandages.

Fairy medicine seemed similar enough to human's, if a little outdated, but fairy magic was another thing altogether.

The young medic didn't stir as Lydia snuck into the darkness beyond the tent. The shackles around her wrists weighed her down, but searching for the key meant making noise. Aside from the distant lanterns of two guards doing rounds at the clearing's edge, the area was motionless.

Quinn had said the company had been decimated by their journey in the woods. Could there really be so few men left?

"Isst," she whispered, stumbling in the direction of the trees. They were only silhouettes, a touch darker than the already impossible blackness. The moon was a mere day into its wane, offering little to go by. It was as if even light refused to go near this place.

"Here. To your left," she heard.

Isst flew to a low branch as Lydia took the last few steps away from the clearing. The trees curled around her so that even the short distance back to the camp seemed treacherous.

"I told you, this is madness, even if your hands were free," the raven said. "There are plenty of beasts in the woods that would be excited for the chance to hunt a bleeding human woman."

She ignored the wetness of her bandages. She could get proper medical attention once she returned to the compound.

"I can't wait. They're going to kill me—"

Before Lydia could take another step, a hand snatched her wrist, yanking her back. Isst's wings brushed her head as the raven dove for her captor, but his instincts were too quick.

He released her wrist, dodged, then grabbed her arm before Lydia could process what'd happened. This time, his grip wasn't as careful. Strong fingers dug into the tender skin beneath her bandages, and another hand covered her mouth before she could gasp. The shackles clattered.

"Don't struggle. Don't make a sound. I told you; it's not only soldiers you have to worry about," Quinn whispered. His breath tickled her neck.

She heard Isst's wings rustling, but there was no other movement. Perhaps he'd hit a tree and was stunned.

"The mandrake was clever, but I told you, our supplies are low. I've been diluting it with magnesium powder," Quinn said.

As Lydia's eyes adjusted, the tree trunks appeared to be expanding, as if drawing in a breath. The pain in her arm was maddening. There was no longer any plan save to wrench herself out of Quinn's grip and run blindly into the woods, but it was difficult to draw her attention away from the forest.

She could have sworn it was whispering her name again.

He seemed to notice the movement, too. The branches, already tangled above them in a makeshift cage, knotted more tightly together, hiding the moon.

"Come on. The Sorrowood has noticed us. It's only a matter of time before something else gets curious." With another sigh, Quinn added, "Although Rai can be impulsive, he is a fey of his word. Coming to Astoria is your only hope. Truly."

"He might be right," Isst said from the dark. This was the first time she'd ever noticed a waver in his voice. There had been nothing to be afraid of in the library. It was why she had been so desperate to return there after her foray into the outside world.

Quinn gave no indication he'd heard Isst. The woods were already full with the song of nighttime birds, and an insect with an unearthly shrill she was certain didn't exist on her side of the window. He hadn't even seemed phased when the raven attacked him, as if Quinn expected violence from the forest's creatures.

"If you nod, I'll take my hand off your mouth."

And I'll bite your damn fingers off, she thought, but Quinn was several inches taller than her and from the way he'd dodged Isst, much faster too. He shifted his hand off her bandages, still keeping a bruising grip as if he expected her to run again.

"*Please*," he said.

Lydia nodded, feeling a defeat as deep and heavy as the surrounding darkness. Quinn's hand left her mouth, and though she could finally take a proper breath, it was not the trees making her claustrophobic.

"I took you to relieve yourself," he said. "You lost your way and wandered a few feet into the woods. Let's go."

She cast a desperate glance at Isst before allowing herself to be pulled back to the camp, but the raven had again disappeared into the forest. Her last tie to home. To the world she'd come from. Gone again.

"Why were you at the window?" Quinn asked.

Neither of them had spoken for well over an hour, and Lydia had begun to wonder if he was asleep. Hell, she wasn't sure whether or not *she* was asleep. Her exhaustion was so profound, everything around her seemed like a dream.

"Why are you asking?" she countered, not in the mood to entertain a curious fey.

"We were told humans were invading our lands and that they had stolen a book precious to our kind."

"And? You think I'm a thief."

"That's why I'm asking. You have suspicions about me

and my cousin. Suspicions that could get both of us killed if they are voiced to the king. I want to know who I'm putting my trust in."

"I didn't steal the book. I was brought in to read it. I'm... a linguist," she said, opening her eyes. Quinn sat hunched over his desk, his face in profile, lit by one of the pillar candles. An aquiline nose above a full mouth. Thick lashes and a sharp jawline.

He shot her an odd look. "The language I just spoke to you—it's one myself and friends from my village made up as children for when we wanted to have a conversation the adults weren't privy to. There's no way you could have understood it. You *are* a witch."

Damn trickster fairies, Lydia thought. She tried to shift, but the motion made her arm hurt. "I'm not a witch. I'm a changeling. I was stolen to the fairy lands when I was a child and returned a year later. When I came back, I was able to understand every language. Read every language. *That's* why I was at the window. Are you going to let me sleep now?"

His eyes narrowed. "A changeling? Perhaps that explains why— Never mind. We can theorize later. You're bleeding through your bandages. You should let me fix them."

"Maybe in the morning. I'm going to sleep."

"Even if you aren't a thief, you certainly are a liar."

Lydia looked up, accidentally making eye contact before turning her head away. She'd read enough medical textbooks to name several unfortunate outcomes if her arm was left untreated.

"Fine. Only if you cover your hands. No more magic," she eventually said.

Quinn opened a box above his apothecary cabinet and returned with a pair of lambskin gloves. They weren't exactly medical grade, but perhaps the fey couldn't transfer diseases between each other as humans could.

He gently cleaned her arm and applied another few drops of an herbal-smelling antiseptic. "I'll see about getting the shackles off. Be careful with your arm for the next few days. If the wound opens up again, I'll have to stitch it. Though, it might not be a bad idea to pretend as though you're in pain. It'll give me an excuse to stay near you."

"Why are you helping me?" she asked for the second time. "It would have been safer for you to leave me in Belimar's clutches."

"For Rai," Quinn said, and did not elaborate. The word shouldn't have stung. Quinn was a fey, a fairy, just like the cruel beings that had stolen her and the other changelings out of their beds in the night. Of course, he only cared for his own.

"The Sorrowood," Lydia said, needing to change the subject before her eyes filled with tears. The word sounded thick in her mouth like she was attempting to speak through a mouth full of syrup. "It's not... this isn't a regular forest, is it?"

Quinn shook his head. "No, it certainly isn't. One day, trees began to grow in places they had never been before. And they crept closer and closer, growing straight out of the ocean as if by magic. The curse corrupted the animals and birds, turning them into monsters. Wards that had once kept the Green Country protected from ancient spirits fell as the wood swept across them. Many of those spirits are loose now, wandering the forest, perhaps plotting revenge against all who imprisoned them."

Lydia breathed out forcefully, remembering the trees on the island in her world. Trees that certainly shouldn't have been there.

"Is it still spreading?"

"Faster than ever," he replied with a shrug.

"Can't you take me back home?" she asked, picking at a loose thread from her bandages. "I thought fairies could travel into our realm. It's just us humans that need a window."

"The Sorrowood has disrupted that magic as well. Since it appeared, not even our mages have been able to go to the human realm or the other courts. The exact reason is a matter of dispute, but the result is the same either way. All in the Kingdom of Astoria are trapped here with the Sorrowood."

"And Belimar thinks the book holds the key to stopping it. That is, if I can translate it for him."

"You didn't seem so curious before," Quinn pointed out, eyebrows raised.

"Of course I was, but I was also extremely terrified. I mean, I'm still terrified, but it's better to be terrified of something you understand than something you don't."

Quinn looked as though he was searching for an argument before continuing. "Belimar was the previous king's huntsman. He spent a lot of time in this forest. Some say it was the Sorrowood that drove him mad. Anyway, it's best not spoken of here and you need to rest."

Gods, how she wished for Isst. She wished for the soft footsteps of Guild members on carpeted hallways. She even wished for the distant sound of the ocean swirling around a lighthouse.

If Quinn really was her best hope of survival, she'd use him, just as he and his cousin were using her. If the trees on the lighthouse's island were related to the Sorrowood, then she had to get back to warn Francesco.

"Fine," she said. "Now, be quiet. I want to sleep."

HER DREAMS WERE OF THE FOREST.

She heard the distant huff of some large animal, but it was the trees that truly frightened her. Their twisted, tortured bodies. The shapes in their trunks that resembled eyes.

There was something so familiar about them. Something that called to her.

When she tried to look beyond them into the darkness, it felt like the darkness was looking back.

THE CAMP WOKE BEFORE LYDIA DID. QUINN WAS ABSENT from the tent but returned while she was blinking crust from her eyelashes. He carried a bundle of wool clothes similar to his own, and a key.

"Orders are the shackles can come off long enough for you to change," he said, with an apologetic smile.

Despite the tunic being cut for a man, it was still better than her sweat-stained blouse. Quinn turned away as she dressed, then replaced the shackles before helping her hobble to a privy. She scanned the trees for Isst but only crows perched, waiting for their chance to pick at the company's leavings.

Most of the camp was already cleared. Fey soldiers packed what supplies remained onto carriages helmed by nervous horses and a variety of other mounts. Enormous dogs. A roan-colored stag. Even a huge goat with a saddle on its back.

Most of the fey soldiers looked similar to humans, were it not for their blade-sharp ears and large eyes, but others were small and winged or had mottled fur like that of a calico cat covering their bodies. One small figure was hidden beneath a heavy robe, with only glowing red eyes visible beneath its hood. Two of the carriages were abandoned, toppled over at the clearing's edge.

"Not enough mounts or soldiers left," Quinn told her. Before he could offer further explanation, a familiar fey man came jogging toward them. "Be careful. That's Belimar's prize general. They call him the King's Cleaver, and for good reason."

Cithral. The stove-warmed water Lydia was splashing on her face seemed to lose all of its heat. A scar ran from behind the fey's left ear and across his jaw. He wore a short sword at his side, the hilt emblazoned with an oak leaf.

"Hope you've had your fun with the prisoner, sawbones. She's riding with the king," Cithral said.

Lydia forced herself not to react, though it felt like she'd been punched in the stomach. She swore Cithral smiled at the way her fingers twitched.

"Impossible. She's in no condition to go on horseback. She'll be in one of the supply carriages with me," Quinn replied.

Cithral laughed. It was unexpectedly high-pitched, like a coyote's yip. "There you go again, thinking the opinion of a yokel medic matters in this army. Your orders are to tend to Trystan. The bite on his leg is oozing again."

"Fine. If the king insists," Quinn said, then turned to Lydia and leaned in to inspect the bandages on her arm. He spoke slowly, miming along to his words as if Lydia couldn't understand them. "Make sure these don't get wet, or you'll risk an infection."

There was a shift in his voice, and she realized he had switched to the secret language he'd spoken last night. "Whatever you do, don't let on that you understand us. Remember, the king needs you *alive*."

No, Lydia thought. *Please no.*

It wasn't as if she trusted Quinn, but at least it didn't seem like he wanted to feed her to his horse for fun.

"What was that?" Cithral asked.

"Just cursing this damned wood and this damned army. Here. Take the girl. The king charged me with seeing she gets to Astoria alive. If anyone so much as bumps into her, they can visit another medic the next time they have a sore on their prick that needs draining," Quinn said.

"Human scum," Cithral muttered, steering her through what was left of the camp. His heavy steps punched holes in the early morning mist.

Lydia's instincts urged her to run again, but she doubted Cithral would be as forgiving as Quinn. She instead focused on words Zoya Yatsenko had spoken when Lydia began her work in the library. 'Some questions can seem big enough to be unanswerable. Start with one fact. One page in one book, then another, then another. Soon, you'll have a mosaic of knowledge that's as powerful as magic. Remember, a single book can do the work of an army.'

Fact number one: her potential allies in the Green Country were nowhere to be seen.

Fact number two: the king of the fey was mounted atop the Gyfoal, which snorted billows of red steam from its nostrils.

Fact number three: this was the very king who wanted her to translate the book that prophesied she would kill him.

The king's translator was also on horseback, though his skittish brown mare was several feet shorter than the Gyfoal. Cithral stopped a few yards away and shoved Lydia forward.

"Be careful, you brute, this girl is a guest in our realm.

Help her up," Belimar said. He was dressed in riding clothes; on his cloak, a brilliant gold brooch in the shape of a stag's head. The caps at the ends of his horns looked sharp enough to pierce armor.

It seemed Cithral was less afraid of the Gyfoal than he was of Belimar. He caught Lydia's arm and dragged her the last few feet to where the beast stomped its hooves against the ground. Hooves large enough to crush her head.

"Tell her I'm trying to hoist her up," Cithral barked at the translator.

It was strange to hear English spoken from the mouth of a fey with a quiver full of scrolls strapped to his back. "Go on, let him help you."

A moment later, Lydia found herself atop a leather saddle. She searched for something to grip, but her palms were so damp, she couldn't get a proper hold of anything. Every time the Gyfoal breathed, she almost toppled off. The animal's skin was burning hot, as if there was a roaring hearth where its guts should be.

So hungry, the Gyfoal hissed. It did not speak again after that.

"Take hold of the king's waist," said the folklorist, exasperated. "You don't want to fall off that creature. It's a long way to the ground."

Belimar chuckled as she wrapped her arms around his torso. She couldn't bring herself to do more than let her skin graze his clothes. It was like forcing herself to hug a corpse. One of his hands left the reins and pulled her closer until her chest was pressed against his back.

"It'll take the rest of my army days to leave these woods and reach Astoria, but on the Gyfoal, we'll be there by late afternoon. You need to hold on tight," Belimar said.

She was dimly aware of the translator repeating those

words. His brown horse was covered with brands in the shape of runes. Lydia read them in an effort to calm herself—speed, guile, speed, strong bones, speed, speed, speed. The saddlebags on both his mount and the Gyfoal were sealed with enormous bronze padlocks. Did they contain the book that had started all this trouble?

Belimar gave no warning. He clicked his tongue against his teeth, and the Gyfoal moved. There was no trot. No cautious steps to test the forest floor. She imagined this was what it was like to be shot out of a cannon.

Lydia tried to glance back at the army camp, but it was already disappearing. Even the heavy smell of campfire smoke was swept away as the Gyfoal ran, the translator's horse a few yards behind them.

Twigs snagged her skin and hair. After a few minutes, the trees seemed to crowd in, as they had when she'd tried to escape. They were traveling deeper into the Green Country, Lydia remembered. Further away from the window. Further away from home. Further away from vanilla lattes, buttery popcorn, and late-night Patsy Cline dance parties with Natalie and October.

She did not allow herself to sob, but her heavy swallow must have been noticeable to Belimar, whose back she was firmly pressed against.

"Horrible, isn't it? This wood, I mean. Once, this was an ocean. My people built enormous ships and conquered distant lands, both in the Green Country and in the human realm, until the forest put a foul curse on our country. The old kings were weak. They couldn't stand against the Sorrowood. Not in the way I will," Belimar said, his voice coming out in breathy puffs.

Fear struck through her. Did he know she understood him?

"Do you know what's in the book? The scholars of the

Radiant Eye are divided," the translator asked, spurring his horse on.

Although he did not seem excited about the chance to address the king directly, Lydia realized why he'd spoken. The woods had grown still. All birdsong ceased as the Gyfoal shook its huge head, sending plumes of red smoke through the trees. It was unsettling.

"The Sorrowood's secrets. How to command it," Belimar said simply.

She was glad to be at the king's back. It hid her flinch.

"But—" the translator sputtered, "How can that be?"

Belimar clicked his tongue, and this time, it was the translator who winced. "This wood is magic. Like any magic, it can be controlled. One simply needs to know how."

There were times she caught glowing eyes watching from the shadows, but the Gyfoal moved so quickly, they were always gone by the time Lydia blinked. Their party didn't slow until they reached another clearing, dotted by what appeared to be fey-made structures. She caught sight of wooden planks, bent into a ribcage, like the body of a rotting ship. Next to it lay an ancient figurehead, covered in moss—a bear carved from oak, slowly losing its features with a large tooth embedded in its neck that looked as ancient as the wreckage.

"The ocean is just... gone?" Lydia whispered to herself, falling back into English on instinct. She was surprised when the translator answered.

"I pray to the yews and the alders that it's not, but no one has been able to reach it yet," he said, before seeming to catch himself. "Don't speak, girl. If you are in this wood, then you are being hunted."

Belimar held up his arm.

Now that they were still, the whispers of the Sorrowood returned.

Lydia Reyes.

No. No, that was impossible. She was hungry, dehydrated, and frightened. Stress could cause both visual and auditory hallucinations. Lydia scanned the forest. Through the gnarled trees, she caught sight of a raven on a high branch. Isst! He had come back for her.

"Wards, now!" Belimar barked. His right hand flew from the reins and traced a sigil that shimmered in the air.

Lydia eyed the large hunting knife in a scabbard at his hip, knowing there was little chance she'd be able to snatch it away without him noticing, but if they were attacked... perhaps in the chaos...

"I'm sorry for disappearing. I went to search for an old friend who might be able to help you," Isst crowed from the branch. "You're being followed. You need to hide."

Hide? Lydia thought. *How am I supposed to hide?*

Her question was answered a second later. The Gyfoal reared as she slackened her grip on Belimar's waist. The fall happened so quickly she was only aware she was slipping a moment before landing on the forest floor. She rolled to avoid the Gyfoal's hooves, but as she stood to run, her path was blocked by an enormous black cat with huge tufts jutting from each ear.

Resembling a lynx, though markedly larger, it was so devoid of color that the dull reflection in its eyes seemed to glow against its fur. There was a shining red ribbon looped around its neck.

"Whatever you do, protect the girl," Belimar shouted. She heard the song of a weapon leaving its sheath.

The cat crouched and took another step toward her. A deep rumble came from its throat, but she could not tell if its eyes were fixed on her or the Gyfoal. Her breath had been knocked out by the fall, and there was a sharp pain in her ribs when she tried to inhale.

One fact at a time, Zoya's voice reminded her.

With the lynx in front of Lydia and the Gyfoal behind, there were only two remaining directions. She dove for the shipwreck as the lynx leaped, but the escape was so narrow, she smelled its breath as it passed, like mulch and freshly tilled dirt.

Lydia turned in time to see the lynx recoil as the Gyfoal kicked in its direction.

"Lydia," Isst called. "It's a cat-síth. It will steal your breath. Cover your nose and mouth!"

Across the clearing, the translator pulled a scarf over the lower half of his face. The cat-síth hissed and the forest air seemed to go stale. What had been a fresh breeze with a hint of sea salt now smelled of a swamp on a windless day. Lydia's chest pinched as if something was being dragged out of her.

Belimar's mouth was uncovered. The hunting dagger gleamed as he reset his grip on the hilt and threw it straight at the cat-síth in one fluid motion. The cat dodged so quickly it moved like a black ink stain against the backdrop of trees.

Then its attention turned to her. Even with her mouth covered by the tunic, it felt as if someone was yanking on a rope coiled in her belly. Gods, this was what she always imagined drowning to be like.

"Oh, aren't you full of precious breath," the cat-síth purred.

Think, Lydia told herself, *think.* Several wooden planks lay half-buried in the surrounding dirt. She tugged one free from the ground. It was not the most aerodynamic object in the world, but she hurled it with enough force that the cat-síth had to dodge again.

This time, the Gyfoal was ready.

A massive hoof came down on the cat's back, forcing it to the ground with an echoing crunch. Birds scattered from branches as the cat yowled. Its back should have been broken, but it continued to thrash wildly against the dirt.

Red plumes of smoke billowed from the Gyfoal's nostrils. Its mouth opened, and any illusion it might have been a horse was shattered. Rows of sharp teeth gleamed as its jaws spread impossibly wide, and the Gyfoal bent to retrieve its prize.

Belimar traced another sigil in the air and a ward swelled around them, glowing faintly green. The Gyfoal ate like a snake, tipping its head back to swallow the cat-síth in a few easy gulps. The creature's wails were still audible until the tip of its tail disappeared into the Gyfoal's mouth. The king watched, gently stroking his mount's neck, as he muttered, "There you go, girl. You've needed a proper meal."

Lydia turned and vomited into the dirt. She was still retching when Belimar hauled her upright.

"Come," he said, "If a cat-síth was foolish enough to attack us now, it means the woods are upset. Best we move on."

The translator repeated the words, but Lydia could hardly feign attention. She was too focused on forcing her body to move toward the Gyfoal. It sneezed and gave a satisfied huff.

She was made braver knowing the raven watching from the trees was not merely there to see what carrion it could pick from the wreckage. And Lydia had learned something else useful as well. The Gyfoal was vulnerable when it was eating. And more, Belimar seemed to love it as he would a child.

The realm of the fey was not at all what Lydia
expected, though the Green Country was an accurate
name. Wherever she looked, there was only one color
stretching in every direction.

The woods thinned as she was getting so saddle sore
that she contemplated throwing herself off the Gyfoal
again for the chance to stretch. The pain in her ribs made
it easier to follow Quinn's advice and she groaned whenever they hit a rough bit of trail. Finally, Belimar dug a
wineskin out of his saddlebag and forced it into Lydia's
hands.

She had thought this would be a land of immeasurable
beauty, but the woods had proven her wrong. Even as the
gnarled trees straightened into normal-looking trunks of
birch and oak, something was still unsettling about the
occasional overturned boat or the cathedral-like ribcage of
what might once have been a whale.

"This was once an ocean," Belimar had said.

She again thought of the trees that had suddenly
appeared on the island back home. Had Francesco been
right to distrust everything that came through the window,
or were they merely Guild magic?

The woods soon vanished, giving way to farmland, and
then to small towns. Their architecture was at once
familiar and not. They comprised a loosely organized gathering of rectangular buildings made of long cedar planks,
all elaborately painted with swirling vines and runes, but as
far as Lydia could tell, every village was empty.

Or maybe the fey hid when the king and his Gyfoal
were about?

When at last the city came into view, Lydia's fear lifted
long enough to allow a glimmer of wonder. A myriad of

towers rose into the clouds, birds circling the tallest steeples. As far as she could tell, none of the structures were made of glass or steel. From a distance, the towers might have been enormous trees, constructed from hardwoods and crisscrossed by suspension bridges.

Astoria.

There was one in her world too, though she had the feeling it was not in the same place since they were traveling east, away from the ocean in the human realm. She also doubted the fey city was named after a fur trader. Her gift informed her that Astoria was actually Ast-o-riea, meaning the storm river.

Isst, who had been trailing far enough behind to avoid Belimar's attention, caught up and gave a low croak. "Astoria. A city half on earth, half in the clouds. Just as impressive as I've been told."

Lydia wished she could ask why Isst had never been here, even when he lived in the Green Country. *Soon*, she vowed. *Once I get out of here.*

The Gyfoal slowed as they approached the city walls, and from above, someone shouted,

"The king is back!"

A great set of doors opened to allow them entry. The city was on a riverbank, but instead of sprawling across both sides, it seemed confined to the southern shore. Lydia glimpsed a tall bridge before entering through the gates.

The villages may have been empty, but here the squares were full of fey, some carrying large woven baskets full of fruit, or leading strange animals resembling goats and dogs as much as the Gyfoal resembled a horse. Like the king, a few of the fey were horned; others had hoofed feet, or tunics cut to accommodate shimmering dragonfly wings. A hush fell over them as the king and his companions passed. Most bowed, but Lydia noticed some ducked behind walls and pillars to avoid being seen.

LYDIA REYES WILL KILL THE FEY KING.

She'd hardly had time to think about the book, or that her name was in it. Let alone what else was scrawled on those pages.

They rode past a collection of enormous treehouses to the front steps of what may well have been one of the tallest towers in the city. The fey in this area wore robes of a green so dark they appeared black until sunlight touched the fabric. Like Quinn's eyes, she thought, unsure why his face had come to mind.

Someone greeted the translator as Belimar steered their group into a large stable, where troughs were already filled with piles of raw meat.

"Tasgall! The woods didn't kill you," a young fey woman shouted. Small antlers poked through her creamy blond hair. Like Belimar, she wore a brooch pinned to her tunic, but hers was fashioned into a lantern with an eye at its center instead of a flame. It reminded Lydia of the Guild's crest, even without the lighthouse.

"It nearly did. Wait 'till you see what I've brought the scholars. I'll get my brooch for sure," Tasgall laughed, urging on his mare, who did not seem interested in sharing a stable with the Gyfoal. She snorted and danced in place, before at last relenting.

"Enough, or you won't have a head with which to enjoy your promotion," Belimar called. His voice rumbled against Lydia's chest, irritating her already-pained ribs. The king dismounted, then hauled her off the Gyfoal as easily as if she were a sack of grain.

"Bring our saddlebags up to the tower. I'm going to show our linguist to her new quarters."

"I'M AFRAID EVEN MY MAGIC DOESN'T FUNCTION WELL around the college. The scholars have been here for longer than there was a city. There are too many books that should never have been read. Too many doors that should never have been opened. The rules governing the rest of the Green Country are here easily bent and sometimes discarded altogether. So, we must climb," Belimar told her when they reached the base of the tower.

Tasgall repeated the words in English, less enthusiastic than he'd been with his colleagues a moment ago. The spiral staircase before them wound upward until the distance made her eyesight blurry. Her legs already felt like they might crumple should she shift her weight carelessly.

"Go," Belimar said. This Tasgall didn't bother to translate. The meaning was clear enough.

Her knees buckled after the first five minutes. If Belimar hadn't been there to catch her, Lydia knew she would have tumbled down the stairs. He hauled her up and forced his wineskin into her hands.

This time, she drank. The last rational part of her brain reminded her this was fairy wine. Its strong liquor would seep into her blood, binding her to this world forever, but the screaming in her brain was drowned out by the screaming in her body, and the wine eventually calmed both voices.

Her head swam, but when Belimar put his hand on her lower back and pressed her onwards, she obeyed.

They climbed until Lydia could no longer look down without feeling off-balance and the air coming through the planks smelled of clouds and ozone. When she tried to rest against the walls, Belimar forced more wine into her mouth, and they continued onwards.

She didn't notice they'd lost Tasgall until they reached a heavy oak door that Belimar unlocked with a key from his belt. It opened to a sparsely furnished circular room with a small cot covered by a heavy wool blanket, and a lantern and ink well atop a writing desk. Lydia caught sight of a chamber pot under the bed, and a fierce heat spread across her face.

"You have thirty days," Belimar reminded her, once Tasgall's thudding footsteps were again audible. The translator, red-faced and sweating, gasped out Belimar's words in the language of the world Lydia had left behind.

"The book will be with you during the day. Once the moon rises, it will return to my scholars. I recommend you work quickly. If they manage to translate it before you, we'll have no more use for you here. The Lamb Moon requires a sacrifice. Our ancestors would be pleased with a human offering."

Lydia tried not to flinch until Tasgall finished repeating the words. "And if I finish the translation before then?"

"Then you will be given a mount and I'll point you in the direction of your window. If you're clever, you may find a way to return home. If not, everything in the Sorrowood is hungry."

"I need medical attention," Lydia said, lifting her arm. Quinn's work had been thorough. She was no longer bleeding and the dull throb of potential infection was gone, but her ribs were certainly bruised, if not broken.

Belimar nodded. "One will be sent to you when possible."

Her mind reeled. How could the man who had a moment ago threatened her life sound almost regretful about her injuries?

"Our people differ in many ways," Belimar said, as if

he understood the frown that passed across her face. Lydia almost didn't hear Tasgall's weary repetition of the king's words.

"Humans believe the Good Neighbors cannot lie, but this is untrue. The sky is pink. Your hair is black. The fairy wine I've given you is poisoned. Now do you understand? The difference between humans and fey is that we see no point in deceit. If you do not translate the book, you will burn along with our sacrificial animals. Before then, you will be held captive, but you will be treated with the dignity of any prisoner in our kingdom."

Before Lydia could answer, the great oak door swung shut.

ON LYDIA'S FIRST DAY IN THE TOWER, SHE MET A FAIRY resembling a small hare with a pair of opalescent wings poking through its threadbare shirt. It did not speak as it set down the book, along with a bowl of warm oats topped with a dollop of honeyed cream, and a mug of rosehip tea.

The small creature also brought her clothes. A fine gown blue gown woven with silver stars that Lydia would once have been thrilled to wear. Now, it made her feel like her skin had been replaced with sandpaper.

"Wait. Please, can you tell me..." she began, then trailed off as she understood two things. One, she had no idea what she had been about to ask. And two, the fairy either wouldn't speak to her or couldn't.

She did not work on her translation that day, even though the fairy also brought up a new ream of paper. Instead, she read the book in its entirety, and when she was done, she paced from one side of the room to the other until her ribs hurt too much for her to stand.

The fairy returned to take the book away in the evening and did not comment on the untouched paper.

On Lydia's second day in the tower, she spent all morning looking out the window for Isst. The local crows screamed gossip to each other from tower to tower, but the larger silhouette of her raven was always absent.

Twenty-nine days. I only have twenty-nine days to live.

She translated the first few lines of the book, but soon realized she could not accurately describe the strange runes filling her mind with images instead of words. So, instead, she attempted to draw them—fields full of standing stones, creeks, and trees so heavy with ancient wasp nests it looked like a small city had grown around the trunk.

It is a map, she confirmed, with a thrill in her heart she hadn't felt since her first few days in the library.

A map that led to... a tower?

Lydia did her best to recreate the images in her mind, page by page, until she reached the passage with her name in it.

"My research has granted me many gifts, if one is foolish enough to call them that. Humans see time as a river, flowing inexorably in one direction; the Aés-Caill viewed time as an ocean. Time may have tides. It may slosh and rise and fall, but it would be a mistake to argue that one drop of water comes before or after any other. Once I reworked my mind to look at time as they do, I understood a few vital truths: You, Lydia Ryes, will kill the fey king. Only the blood of the Aés-Caill can end what I have begun."

The Aés-Caill. The People of the Yew, it meant, though she hadn't heard the term before now. Some books in her library back home spoke of the beings that had preceded the fey of the Green Country; monsters of the rivers and forests, even older than a spirit like Isst.

She did not read further, nor did she sleep that night. Lydia tried to imagine the Mapmaker who knew her name but couldn't bring a face to mind.

On her third day in the tower, the king returned.

He was dressed as a hunter, with the only signs of his status, the deer brooch and a golden diadem resembling oak branches fitting snugly over his horns. The translator trailed behind Belimar, wearing scholar's robes and looking paler than he had in the Sorrowood.

"Lydia," Belimar said, patting her shoulder as though he were greeting a friend he hadn't seen in years. The force of it was enough to make her want to buckle beneath him, but she braced herself against the desk.

"Don't look so frightened, girl. It's been but a few days. I suspect most of your time is still occupied with planning your escape," he went on, Tasgall dutifully repeating the words. "I want to show you something. You see that window, there? Look through it."

It felt as though there was a boulder in her stomach, but she feared what Belimar would do if she didn't obey. In this small space, there was nowhere to avoid him.

The window was barely wide enough for her face, the tower's thick wooden frame filling her peripheral vision. She had already spent hours looking out this window, studying the small square below. It seemed to belong to a college; most of those who came and went wore robes and caps adorned by a long blue feather. Sometimes, small wooden tables and chairs spilled into the street, but the scholars' chatter was always muffled.

Today, the square was mostly empty. She spotted a few groups of fey huddled beneath an awning, but the silence seemed deliberate. After a moment, the stable master walked into view, the Gyfoal trailing behind him.

"The view is wonderful from up here," Belimar said,

leaning into the window next to her. "Don't look at me. Keep watching."

She heard the Gyfoal's frustrated huffs from the tower room. Then another sound joined it as two guards dragged a fey woman into the square. She was blindfolded, but not gagged. Her screams seemed to excite the beast, whose hooves beat against the cobblestones.

"That young scholar was caught distributing pamphlets suggesting I may not have the ability to stand against the Sorrowood, as I claimed. My Gyfoal hasn't had a good meal since we left the wood," Belimar continued.

"No." The word left Lydia's mouth involuntarily, but Tasgall had already finished most of his translation.

The scholar was forced to her knees, enveloped in the stream of red smoke from the Gyfoal's nostrils. Lydia tried to back away when she understood what was about the happen, but Belimar clamped a hand on her back, locking her in place.

"Watch, changeling. I want you to know how serious I am about my kingdom. About that book. Keep looking. If you close your eyes, I'll drag someone else out of the prison."

It happened fast. The Gyfoal's jaws unhinged, as they had when they'd encountered the cat-síth. The birds that normally flitted from tower to tower quieted, and the only sound left was the fey woman's screams. Lydia's tears were a mercy, for they blurred the square beneath her as the Gyfoal wrapped its mouth around the woman's shoulders, then tossed its head back, swallowing her in gulping bites like a snake would devour a rat.

The woman screamed until only her legs were visible, but by the time her pointed boots reached the Gyfoal's teeth, there was nothing except for the beast's happy rumbles.

Belimar released Lydia and she reeled back as if pushed. She whirled on the king, unsure of what she was about to say or do, but the sight of his stern eyes caused her to freeze.

"Work fast," he told her. "The quicker you translate, the less time the scholars have to gossip. My Gyfoal will be the only one who doesn't thank you."

He turned, cloak flaring out around him. Tasgall nearly made eye contact with Lydia, but looked away before she could meet his gaze. The translator had a hand pressed against his stomach as if he was also trying to prevent himself from retching on the floor. Lydia wondered if he'd known the young woman in the square below.

"You helped this happen," Lydia muttered, loudly enough for Tasgall to hear. She was going to be sick herself, but waited until the door closed before she vomited into the small wastebasket next to the writing desk.

The fairy servant arrived to clean it a moment later, bringing along a tray stacked with plums the size of volley-balls and elaborate pastries that made Lydia nauseous just to look at them.

On Lydia's fourth day in the tower, Isst arrived at the window.

"There you are!" she gasped, nearly spilling her ink pot.

There was a thin pink gash on Isst's chest, visible through his feathers, but he puffed up as he laid eyes on her. "I'm sorry. I tried to reach you earlier, but there are so many wards against my kind around the college, it took me ages to figure out how to get through them. Are you okay?"

No, she wanted to cry. *I'm alone with a book that knows my name, and I'm pretty sure the fey king is going to kill me as soon as his translators catch up. I think I have a broken rib, and all fey food tastes like honey. I hate the chamber pot. I hate the scratchy wool blanket. I want to go home.*

"I'm fine," she told him. "I need to get out of there."

"I know," he said. "I found my friend, but he can't come into the city. You'll have to find a way to get to the woods. Can you think of something?"

Lydia glanced at the ink pot and the ream of paper.

"Yes," she said. "I need you to take a message to someone. Give me a moment."

She rushed to the desk and wrote out a few words in the fey language.

The king is keeping me in the tower next to the college. I have the book when the sun is out, but his translators work on it at night. I don't know how far they've gotten. He will kill me and lock the book away before or on the next full moon. NEED HELP IMMEDIATELY in exchange for my translation. Give your answer to the raven.

Lydia paused before addressing it. There were only two fey she might trust in the Green Country, Quinn, and Rai. After a moment, she wrote Rai's name at the top of the paper.

"There is an officer in the king's army with dark red hair and freckled skin. Make sure you give this to him and no one else. Don't let anybody see you."

"I will. Be careful, Lydia. I'll come back as soon as I can," Isst said, before taking the message in his beak and disappearing.

On Lydia's eighth day in the tower, she started crying and could not stop. She wondered if this might be the start of a new fairy tale. A human girl, locked away, who cried so many tears she filled her room with water and drowned.

She had a wild, stupid thought. At least she wouldn't have the inconvenience of having her period in captivity. Perhaps it was their quickened metabolism or a side effect of their magic, but the changelings only bled twice a year —in spring and fall.

On Lydia's tenth day in the tower, she finished writing her translation and stashed the pages beneath her mattress. It was not a faithful transcript. It left out her name and any details she thought might get her killed, but she had no confidence the king would make good on his promise to let her go. She had to buy herself time.

As far as she could tell, the book contained two prophecies.

The first was about her. It read: You, Lydia Reyes, will kill the fey king. Only the blood of the Aés-Caill can end what I have begun.

The second prophecy, she might have thought unimportant, if she hadn't seen the trees herself—the horribly twisted trunks that appeared overnight on the island in her world. This one read: Oh gods, what have I done? Their forest won't stop with the Green Country. The force of their anger and pain was too much. No world is safe if the window isn't closed.

That proclamation was decidedly more confusing than the first, but the Mapmaker didn't elaborate. Lydia turned the phrase 'their forest' in her head, over and over again. Quinn hadn't been able to say who created the Sorrowood. Perhaps the Mapmaker had someone in mind?

She pictured Francesco's face as she'd stepped onto the island. He'd been polite and jovial as usual, yet there was something frantic about the way his eyes skittered across the lighthouse keeper's home. Had he known those trees were the vanguard of an invading army?

On Lydia's eleventh day in the tower, the door opened, and it was not the fairy servant she saw, but the dark-haired sawbones from the army.

"Quinn," she said. Her voice cracked as if the word itself burned her mouth.

"I'm sorry," he breathed. "I tried to come sooner, but there was an accident on our journey back through the woods. I had to tend to the soldiers before the king would allow me to…"

"You let him *take me*," she cried. "You handed me over."

"I had no choice. You were safer with him than the army," Quinn said. It looked like he wanted to go on. Instead, his eyes darted around the room.

"I don't care—"

"How's your arm? The fairy servants should have been changing your bandages. Any sign of infection?"

Lydia sagged onto her mattress. Her anger had been a steady simmer during her first few days in the tower; now it felt like something cold and rotten, something poisonous. When the door opened, she'd hoped to see Rai, or one of his agents, or even Belimar—it was beginning to feel like dying would not be as terrible as waiting to die.

"I've been told your ribs were hurt as well. Did *he* do this to you?" Quinn went on, a deep-seated anger in his words. His voice changed slightly, and she knew he had switched to the invented language of his childhood.

She shook her head, unsure of how to answer.

"We need to be careful when we speak. Magic doesn't work properly around the college, but someone could still be listening. The translator will be up those stairs in a moment. We can thank the gods I'm in better shape than he is. I have a message from Rai. He got your letter. The king's scholars have made little progress. His spies don't expect their translator will be done by the full moon. Stay the course. There is a plan in place."

She nearly laughed with relief, but the translator's panting breaths came from the staircase.

"Stop," she muttered, noticing that Quinn had taken hold of her bandaged arm, and there was a faint glow beneath his fingertips.

His eyebrows furrowed as he pulled his hands away and rummaged through his satchel for the lambskin gloves. The red-faced translator burst into the room a moment later and slumped against the wall.

"Wolf's piss, those stairs. You'll be treating me next, medic. Has she said anything?" Tasgall said.

"No," Quinn told him, returning his attention to Lydia's wound. The skin beneath her bandages was pink and textured from the press of the linen wrap against her arm, but the gash was fully closed. Even the scabs had fallen off.

"Tell her to signal when it hurts," Quinn said. He set to work on her ribs next, gently pressing against her torso.

Tasgall repeated the sentence, and Lydia decided she was tired of this back and forth. "How do you speak English, anyway?"

The translator looked taken aback to be addressed directly. He'd only said a handful of words to her that hadn't come from Belimar, and it was as if he'd forgotten they shared a common language.

Tasgall pulled a handkerchief from his pocket and wiped his brow. "My parents lived in your world. I was born there as well. I returned to the Green Country when I wanted to further my studies in Astoria. This Astoria, I mean. That was before Sorrowood's curse spread, and we lost the ability to travel between our realm and yours."

The poisonous anger inside Lydia filled her mouth with bitterness. Quinn attempted to catch her eyes, but she ignored him. "So you willingly aided in a raid on the world you once called home? People were killed. I was nearly killed. I probably will be before I can leave this place."

"Don't upset my patient. I'm trying to examine her. I can't feel for injuries if she's shouting," Quinn snapped at Tasgall.

Lydia took a shuddering breath as Quinn found a sore spot just below her right breast. Perhaps it was meant as a warning.

"Of course, I did. They were orders from the king," Tasgall said, addressing Lydia as if Quinn hadn't spoken. "Anyway, I'm not supposed to talk to you any more than is necessary. Just let the sawbones work, and you can be rid of us."

I need Quinn alone, she realized. The plan came to her as his gloved hands pressed on her upper back as she took a long breath. "Tell the medic I've got a strange bruise on my side. I got it when I fell off the Gyfoal and it won't heal. It may be internal bleeding."

Tasgall pinched the bridge of his nose and gave this information to Quinn in what sounded like a long sigh that happened to include words.

"All right," Quinn said. "Lift your dress."

"Not with you in the room," she told Tasgall, once he finished his translation.

"I'm to stay the entire time. I'll turn around if you're so worried," Tasgall said.

Quinn seemed to understand what Lydia was getting at and spoke in the fey-tongue. "Just step outside and close the door. Do you think she's going to jump out the window?"

Tasgall's mouth opened slightly, revealing nervous bite marks on his lower lip, but apparently deciding this argument wasn't worth the effort, he turned and slipped from the room.

Lydia darted to her writing desk and scrawled a note on a scrap of paper. *Need to speed the plan up. Something in the book will get me killed if the translators reach it before the full moon.*

Quinn narrowed his eyes and muttered, "Yes, there's a bad contusion here. Probably sustained from falling off the king's mount. Might a soft tissue injury."

He took the pen and answered, *I'll do what I can. The king is planning something. Increased guards. New wards on the palace.*

Lydia wanted to shout, "So? You seem to hate him, anyway."

Tasgall stretched against the door.

Quinn wrote another sentence before she could snatch the quill away. *Keep up the ruse that you're ill. I'll try to come back when I can.*

Why should I trust you? she wrote back.

"I'll have the servants bring her willow bark for the pain," Quinn said to himself and wrote: *I cannot give an answer that would satisfy you, but I'd be beheaded should anyone find these notes. So you keep them.*

He held onto the quill for a moment, turning it in his hands, then wrote another sentence: *Do not act until the rebels do.*

Quinn crumpled the paper as soon as she had the time to read it and shoved it under the mattress. Then he ripped a page from his notebook and wrote out instructions for an herbal blend before calling Tasgall back in.

"She needs to take this, or she'll be in too much pain to sit and write," Quinn told him. "The human has other injuries I'll need to check up on—"

"The king will call if you're needed," Tasgall said with a sort of finality that made her wonder how a folklorist had won so much favor with Belimar. He switched to English to address Lydia. "I've also been told to inquire about your progress with the translation, and collect any pages you've already completed."

It felt like the blood rushed out of her brain, leaving her light-headed. Quinn made a sudden show of digging through his satchel for a jar of ointment, but Lydia remembered the old cryptography books in the library back home.

"I'm afraid that's not possible. The books are written in a sort of code that's laborious to translate. If I give any of my pages up, I'll be missing a part of my key," she said.

"Then make a copy. I'll wait," Tasgall said.

"My notes won't make sense until I—"

She wasn't able to finish the sentence. A rock came crashing through the tower window. All three of them jumped, and Quinn took a step between her and the shattered glass. There was a commotion from the street below, though they were at too much height for her to make out what the fey were shouting at one another.

"Hells, what now?" Tasgall murmured. "Those idiots are going to blow up this whole college if they're not careful. I'll be back in a few minutes, girl. Have the copies ready."

Lydia met Quinn's eyes, but he was expressionless as he followed Tasgall down the winding stairs. She was only consoled by the sight of a raven's black wings cutting through the air when she looked out of the shattered widow. Isst always had good aim.

He landed heavily on one of the balconies across the way and shouted, "I'm doing what I can. Just say alive, Lydia. Stay alive. Stay alive." He was gone before she could beg him to come to her, disappearing into the low clouds that always swirled around the college.

Lydia let herself cry for a full three minutes, then she picked up the quill, knowing Tasgall would return at any moment for her progress. Yet it was the fairy servant that arrived first, carrying the tray of fruits and pastries Lydia had been forced to eat for every meal until it felt like her teeth were gritty with sugar.

A wild thought came to her. One that ignored Quinn's final message. *Do not act until the rebels do.* Even if she could produce a fake translation, Lydia might have no other choice.

It didn't hurt to be prepared.

"I'm human," she snapped at the little thing, who blinked with enormous golden eyes. "Can you understand me? Humans eat meat. Raw meat. Bring me a slab of venison and let no one cook it first."

SEVERAL CHOICES

"You were supposed to meet me an hour ago. I've been forced to drink all this wine alone," Rai said, though his speech was as clear as usual. Rai had the sort of tolerance for alcohol just short of being a marketable skill.

"We're alone?" Quinn asked. When Rai nodded, he went on. "I checked in on our translator. They have her locked up in one of the college towers. She's convinced Belimar is going to kill her sooner rather than later."

"How is the translation going?" Rai asked, rotating his empty glass on the table. He lived in a small house near the soldiers' barracks, tucked away behind so many winding alleys that few were likely to notice if Quinn came and went more than their professional relationship demanded.

"Gods, is that your first question? Her life is in danger," Quinn said, helping himself to a swig directly from the bottle. It was sweeter than his normal preference and tasted of black plums and early fall, the time when any fruit left on the vine rotted.

"And we'll save her if we can, but that book might hold

the key to getting Belimar... Hells, Quinn, I thought you would want him dead more than anyone."

Rai's home was sparsely decorated, and Quinn had the feeling his cousin spent most of his time at the training courses near the barracks. A few drawings were tacked to the wall; birch trees with spears of sunlight between them, a scene of the Astorian fish market, and a loose portrait of a curly-haired fey woman Quinn didn't recognize. Rai was talented with a stick of charcoal.

"She's entrusted to my care," Quinn said, which was a partial truth. He had to admit there was more than simply Lydia's skills with language he found intriguing, but it would be impossible to bring up the odd glow when their bare skin touched without arousing suspicion about his parentage or bringing up that cursed song. That he some-times caught himself thinking about her pale hair or the writing callus on her middle finger, was something he'd also have to keep ignoring.

"You're a sawbones, Quinn, not a saint. This is bigger than some code. You of all people should know that—"

"I'm not doing this for her. I'm doing it for the Green Country," Quinn said. His jaw ached from tension.

"Whatever you say, cousin. She's not so bad looking for a human, and the gods know you need to loosen up," Rai said with a shrug.

Something inside of Quinn bristled, and it was not the part of him that was a medic, a soldier, or even a fey. It was his Aés-Caill blood. The blood of a beast, petty and jealous and fierce, rearing its head at the least opportune moment. He had always struggled to feel at home with the other fey. Sure, they were decadent and hedonistic, drinking fairy wine and spinning tales until dawn, but Quinn had the feeling even they would be frightened by the hungry, ancient thing living inside of him.

Why was it that any mention of Lydia was enough to make the monster stir?

"Speak of her again, and I'll remind you how often I used to clobber you during sparring practice," Quinn said.

Rai lifted an eyebrow.

"My, my, cousin, I don't think I've ever heard you defend a lady's honor before. I'm not sure whether to be nervous or impressed."

Quinn snatched the wine bottle out of Rai's hand and repeated, "I'm doing this for the Green Country. If the book really tells of a way to control the Sorrowood, and she's the only one who can read it, then she needs protection."

The last two verses of that damn song ran through his mind, unbidden.

It's the mother's blood
Her tears and her pain
That made the wood grow
And it won't stop again...

Till the king drives his sword
Through his queen's beating heart
And the wood and its mother
Are no longer apart.

They went silent as voices rose on the street outside. Even though Quinn hadn't seen what caused the commotion outside the tower today, he doubted it was a raven snatching the wig off a scholar as the witnesses suggested.

"We need to move the timeline up. Get her and the book out of that tower," Quinn said.

Rai sneered. "Oh, and what's your plan? Stroll a band of rebels into the most heavily fortified part of the city?

My contacts at the college all say the same thing. Belimar's scholars have made little progress in their translation. It's up to the human. The king will keep her alive until the full moon. There's no doubt of that. Besides, you've been insisting for weeks that you're not getting involved. What's changed?"

Quinn took another long swig to delay his answer. In truth, he had thought about that question a lot in the past few days, and no conclusion could explain the tension inside of him, as if something was wringing out his organs. He hadn't been lying to Rai on the day Quinn nearly fled the army camp in favor of the forest. Belimar's power was too entrenched, and with their ocean gone and the wood spreading, there were plenty of fey in Astoria fearful enough to surrender their freedom to the Hunter King.

Even if he had risen to power in a tide of blood.

The book was important enough for Belimar to willingly sacrifice his best soldiers, put his own life at risk, and lock a changeling girl in a tower. Quinn remembered the last words his mother had said to him, her hair fanning out on the river's surface as her head slowly sunk beneath the water. "A curse is nothing but grief and pain too profound to be expressed through language. These fools will never be rid of the Sorrowood, because they haven't bothered to look for its heart."

"Oh, stop thinking and just answer. It's annoying when you do that. Where's the fun if you never let what you're actually feeling slip?" Rai said.

"I was thinking you're an arrogant prick. You're impulsive, and you never stop to wonder about whether or not the odds are in your favor before you start stabbing. I could have run when I was conscripted, but you're the only cousin I have left, and so I stayed to keep you from bleeding out every time you did something spectacularly idiotic. But maybe this time, you're right. Maybe Belimar has a kink in his armor."

Quinn traced a bit of woodgrain with his index finger.

"This whole plan hinges on *you*, Quinn," Rai said after a period of silence. It was the beginning of a conversation they'd had many times, but now, Quinn didn't argue.

Instead, he said, "I think it hinges on the human girl locked up in Belimar's tower. You weren't lying to her, were you? When you said your people would escort her home?"

The words Quinn couldn't say lingered in his throat like they were trying to choke him. He loved his cousin, but too often, Rai looked at those around him as mere tools.

The sun was setting, and though Quinn could not see the sky behind Rai's curtains, a cool violet light filled the room. Rai finished the wine, but instead of getting up to fetch another bottle, he reappeared with a stack of maps showing Astoria and its great river sketched in detailed lines.

"I'm afraid you'll be waiting to see your sweetheart again until the full moon. We have a plan, and it involves most of the city being at the Lamb Moon market. Please tell me you've kept up with your training."

"She's not my sweetheart, she's my patient, and you never answered my question—"

A heavy knocking sounded at the door, and Rai shoved the maps into the nearest drawer. He and Quinn exchanged a glance. There was nothing more incriminating between them than an empty bottle of wine, but they'd always made it a point to keep their distance in public. He and Rai were only related on his father's side, and Quinn took after his mother. It would be difficult to tell they were cousins at a glance. Still, there wasn't any reason to raise questions.

"Rai," came a voice a second later. "Open up. *Now.*"

Rai seemed to recognize the visitor, a slight woman with swirling white tattoos on her face, wearing a dark robe emblazoned with the lantern of the Order of the Radiant Eye. She looked younger than most of the scholars from the college, but then again, the fey did not age as humans did. Quinn suspected many found streaks of gray hair to contribute to their academic credentials.

She gave Quinn a sideways glance, as Rai bolted the door. "It's okay. He knows everything. What's going on?"

Quinn had never spoken to any of Rai's rebels. Slipping medical supplies to them now and again was one thing. Being caught in their ranks was quite another.

The woman tried to steady her breath. Droplets of rain stuck to her hair like her hood had fallen back as she ran. "Something is happening at the palace. The scholars aren't getting the book tonight as planned. Rumor is that the human has finished her translation."

"That's not possible," Quinn muttered. "I was treating her today. She told Belimar's little weasel she wasn't done yet."

"I don't know the details, but she and the book are currently in transit to the palace. A carriage pulled by the Gyfoal and flanked by soldiers was spotted a few minutes ago. If they make it, Rai…"

Quinn didn't need to know the whole of their plans to understand what the woman was implying. The palace was heavily warded by magic and guarded not just by soldiers, but also by several creatures with no name. Belimar had *earned* his title of the Hunter King. The Gyfoal was not the only wicked beast he had dragged out of the woods and enchanted to serve him.

Once Lydia was inside, there would be no getting her out until Quinn was called to pick up the body.

Rai turned to the closed window, a finger against his

chin. Quinn's heart gave a double tap as he anticipated the words Rai was about to speak, but it hurt to hear them all the same. "We need to move now. Quinn and I will slow the carriage down. Dzune, gather whoever you can. Have our forces ready themselves at the Cloud Bridge. Tell no one to make a spark until you see our signal."

Dzune nodded, pulled her hood up, and disappeared into the night.

"And how do you plan on slowing the royal carriage down?" Quinn snapped once the door shut behind her.

"You're the smart one. I was hoping you would figure it out," Rai said.

"I never agreed to—" Quinn began, but Rai was already fastening the straps on his leather armor.

"No, but you're still going to. Your weapon is in the cabinet at the end of the hall. Go fetch it."

Again, Quinn didn't argue. Rai already knew he had lied to the king about Lydia and instructed her to lie as well. That he'd risked execution for a human girl with a nasty scrape on her arm, even before Quinn knew what was in the book.

He looked at the bardiche. It was an unusual weapon for the Green Country—a cleaver atop a four-foot pole, good for keeping an enemy from getting too close. His was superficially plain, but in the right light, an etching was visible on the axe head; a stylized, flowing kelpie. If the water-horses still existed anywhere in the Green Country, they were rare, but it was a common motif in Astoria.

Quinn sighed, blood pounding in his ears, and ignored Rai when he called out, "Really hope you weren't lying about keeping up with your training."

ASTORIA MOSTLY SPRAWLED ACROSS THE SOUTH SIDE OF THE
river; there were markets and the college, and farther into
the hills, small residential towers, crisscrossed by ladders,
ropes, and whatever trees were resourceful enough to take
root on the mud smeared across structures for temperature
control. The palace lay on the northern banks, connected
to the city proper by a high bridge that, in the days before
the Sorrowood, had nearly always been obscured by rolling
clouds and ocean mist.

Those clouds were gone, but the name remained.

There are too many people out. This will end badly, Quinn
thought, as he and Rai moved through the shadowed alleys
off the main road in an attempt to catch up to the king's
carriage. Astoria's population had swelled with refugees
from the farmlands who'd fled the encroaching forest. A
city of fey that had once lived under hills and in barrows
now stacked together in towers swaying in the strong
winds.

News that the king's carriage would make its way
through the streets didn't seem to have reached the population. Young fey couples sat on wooden benches drinking
wine, and a street musician played a fiddle while others
danced around him, their laughter spilling into the square.
A group of small, winged fairies with enormous ears had
unfurled a rug ladened with opalescent jewels from the
Sunrial mines, far to the east. Their high voices competed
with the fiddle for attention.

Quinn smelled the Gyfoal before he saw it. Too often,
his medical tent was erected near its stable, and he was
more familiar with the scent of raw meat than he preferred
to be.

"Hope you've come up with a plan to slow this thing
down, cousin," Rai said, as they climbed a wooden ladder
to a balcony affording them a better view of the road.

Across the street, the musician sang a ballad about a swan maiden who'd flown too high and found herself trapped on the moon.

"You didn't exactly give me notice," Quinn said.

"Aren't medics supposed to be good under pressure?" Rai said. Quinn did not like the breathless excitement in Rai's voice; there was very little chance of them escaping this evening alive, let alone recovering both Lydia and the book.

The weight of the bardiche against his back was not unfamiliar, but he'd fallen out of the habit of carrying weapons, aside from the silver medical tools on his belt. The bardiche's cleaver was made of meteorite iron, deadly to humans and fey alike.

"A medic," he repeated, feeling something click together, like a dislocated bone sliding back into place. "How much coin do you have? I've got a request for the bard, but he'll likely charge extra."

A grin spread across Rai's face. His teeth—devoid of sharp points, like all the fey—glinted in the light of lanterns strung across the street.

Rai climbed down from their hiding place, and a moment later, he whispered something into the bard's ear. The bard leaned back with his mouth open, an arm across his chest as if whatever he was asked was deeply offensive, but when Rai unhooked his coin pouch and handed it to the other man in its entirety, the bard shrugged and nodded.

Quinn spotted the banners from the king's procession turning the corner. He hoped the bard was a decent actor.

The musician dropped his lute gently against the cobblestones and took a few shaking steps into the road as the surrounding crowd gasped. He spun, the back of his hand pressed against his forehead, and collapsed with more flair than necessary.

In Astoria, a drunken bard might be amusing for a moment or two, but it would not hold the attention of a crowd. This was the biggest city in the court. They'd already seen a curse, a coup, and whatever the hells crawled out of the sewers below the college every now and again.

"Everyone, clear the road!" Quinn shouted as he ran toward the fallen bard, knowing it would have the exact opposite effect. "He's injured. I'm a healer!"

That captured a few eyes. It was at least more interesting than the vendor attempting to sell dried river fish smelling of low tide.

Quinn did not think himself a particularly talented actor, but he'd delivered plenty of bad news with a straight face. The opposite couldn't be so difficult. He felt for a pulse while the bard opened his left eye and winked at him.

"He's not breathing! Give him space," Quinn shouted, which caused the crowd to jostle closer, hoping for a better look. This bard was a common fixture on the neighborhood's corners. The audience for his final ballad would have something interesting to tell their friends in the morning.

The king's carriage turned and slowed as it met the throng blocking the road. Out of the corner of his eye, several fey disappeared into the alleys once they caught sight of the Gyfoal, but in the commotion, not everyone appeared to realize whose procession was behind them.

If Quinn was being honest, he hadn't entirely believed the king's carriage would slow at all. Belimar had sent his best soldiers into the wood, knowing most would not return. A few civilians meant nothing to him, but at least the fey man driving the carriage was hesitant to plow the Gyfoal over his neighbors.

"Out of the way! King's orders!" someone shouted. The crowd separated, but the bard—who Quinn decided deserved more than whatever Rai had given him—began to speak.

"Oh, the pain in my chest! The Lady Philomena Rorrit refuses to leave her husband for me as she promised she would. Help me, sawbones."

Philomena Rorrit was not only a high-born fey but also married to one of Belimar's top generals. The statement was enough to cause those who were fleeing the scene to pause. Gossip was as good as gold in this city.

The bard gave Quinn another wink and fell back on the street. Coin wouldn't be enough for the kind of performance that might end with his head rolling across the cobblestones. He had to be one of Rai's rebels, or at least sympathetic to the cause.

The Gyfoal snorted and took several steps forward without direction from the carriage driver. A woman screamed as a cloud of red mist from the Gyfoal's nostrils hit her bare shoulder, and the square filled with the smell of fried skin. Even the bard scrambled off the street and into the alleys.

Quinn took the opportunity to dart sideways with the crowd, hoping the chaos would keep him anonymous. He was at last able to get a better look at the procession. There was the head carriage, led by the Gyfoal, which likely housed Belimar and Lydia, and behind this, were another five coaches, no doubt packed with guards and mages.

He searched the balconies for Rai, but as the carriages resumed their trek, Quinn's view was obscured by flapping banners bearing Belimar's crest. A stag's head with an arrow in its eye.

I've done my part, Quinn thought. He'd stalled the procession for as long as he could, and if he ran now, there would be enough of a distraction in the rebels' attack to mean no one would care if a single army medic went missing.

His eyes were stuck like a fox in a hunter's trap, unable to move away from the deer's head crest making its way through streets that had not so long ago run with blood, just so that flag could be hoisted above the palace.

The screams of Quinn's father had once echoed through these alleys. Even now, there were neighborhoods left in tatters by Belimar's coup; buildings scarred by sword marks and fire, abandoned to whatever ghosts now occupied them.

Fuck, Quinn thought, again aware of the bardiche's weight.

He'd go to the bridge. He'd make sure Rai and Lydia got out of this alive.

Then he'd leave this city forever.

QUINN HADN'T GROWN UP IN ASTORIA. HIS FATHER HAD already been married when he met Quinn's mother, and her pregnancy was not exactly conventional, even by fey standards. Their baby had come into the world at the bottom of his mother's lake, his first breath full of cold water rushing into his lungs.

His father had wanted nothing to do with his bastard son, half-fey, half... whatever the Ladies of the Lower World were. So, the lake maiden handed the soaking baby on to a passing farm girl and sang a song that ensured he'd be well-cared for. Even if it was in a village at the edge of the wood, where monsters sometimes snatched fey children out of their cribs, as the fey had once done to human infants.

He didn't know Astoria as well as Rai and his rebels, but Quinn had a talent for finding his way to water. He ran north, winding through narrow alleys clogged with fey, trying to avoid the king's procession. Snippets of conversation drifted past, all with a slightly panicked edge that cut into his eardrums like a scalpel.

The hill climbed steeply upward, and the main road soon disappeared. Only the king and those on his invitation had any reason to venture to the north bank, so access to the bridge was restricted by both guards and wards. He felt the shimmer of magic as he neared the river crossing, but something about it was strange. Magic had a feeling to it, the way a good wine tasted of the land where its grapes had grown. This magic's feeling was one of *wrongness*, like those grapes had been nurtured in soil fertilized with blood.

Quinn hoped it meant Rai's rebels had reached this place with time to spare. That the scholars who opposed Belimar had tinkered with the wards they had built.

He drew the bardiche from the strap on his back. There was little sound near the bridge, aside from the sloshing of water. He understood why Rai would choose this place for a confrontation and yet was nervous for the same reason. Only one way on, only one way off. When the fight began, there was no choice except to carry on until you or your enemy were dead.

The king's caravan reached the bridge and slowed to navigate the narrow passage. Quinn thought he saw a hooded figure on one of the wooden supports, but the bridge was heavily populated by statues of ancient fey monarchs and their heraldic animals and he wondered if it was just another gargoyle, crouched above to scare away water spirits.

Rai had only divulged the bare bones of their plan. Quinn looked to the west, searching for a glimmer of orange light on the river, yet there was nothing but murky violet darkness.

Once he could get a proper look at the bridge and the procession, his chest tightened. The rebels may have had to prepare at a moment's notice, but he was sure Belimar knew this was coming. The bridge's two towers were alight with magic, bright enough to show the silhouettes of archers stationed inside. The caravan was larger than expected, now that ramshackle buildings no longer hid its length.

Quinn tried to swallow, but his mouth was too dry. He looked at the river again. There was still no signal from the rebels. No hint of wood smoke. Only black water rushing toward an ocean that no longer existed—at least, not anywhere near here.

He had to get closer to the bridge. The wards hadn't truly fallen, not yet. Still, he hoped they were weak enough to let him climb the wooden supports on this side of the river without shaking him off.

The bridge rumbled as the Gyfoal reached the edge and reared, attempting to take a few steps back. Monsters from the Sorrowood hated running water. The carriage driver looked too nervous to use his riding crop until a shout came from inside the coach. Teeth snapped as the Gyfoal turned and lashed out at the fey who'd whipped its haunches.

Quinn's attention was pulled in two directions as Belimar emerged from the carriage and dragged the driver from his seat. On the river below, a brilliant flare of red and gold was rushing toward the drawbridge.

He recognized the ship, though the fire had already engulfed its sails. The Kelpie. The most prized warship of the previous king's navy, crafted from the sacred oaks of the Green Country; trees that had given the king their blessing. The frigate resembled a forest. Its masts curved and branched out, and clumps of hanging moss dangled from the crow's nest.

Even Quinn, in his childhood far from Astoria, had grown up hearing tales of the great floating forests that had once carried their people to fog-shrouded lands on the other side of the ocean.

A chorus of shouts began from overhead as guards spotted the flaming ship barreling toward them. Archers dove from the towers into the river, landing with bone-breaking splashes. Quinn realized he might also be too close to the impact, but before he could assess his surroundings, the Kelpie and the Cloud Bridge collided.

He fell. Sprawled against the cobblestones, the heat of the fire swept across him so forcefully it felt like his skin had peeled back. He became aware he had dropped his bardiche and snatched it up while struggling to his feet. In the chaos, it was difficult to tell what direction he was facing. Fey rushed from their homes at the burst of light and noise, but those who had already been in the streets were now running, a slack look of shock on their faces.

He pushed his way toward the sound of a loud crunch. It became easier to tell where he was going once the Cloud Bridge caught fire, for the towers of flame acted like beacons over the river. The remaining wards must have been damaged by the Kelpie's magic.

He ran, ignoring the pain in his shoulder. The king's guard had drawn their weapons, but he could see no sign of Rai or the other rebels. It was not until an arrow whizzed past his head that Quinn realized the attack was already underway.

"Dammit," he hissed, ducking behind a smoldering chunk of the bridge on the riverbank. He scanned the chaos for a sign of the Gyfoal or Belimar, but the guards had broken ranks. The force of the impact had not completely destroyed the Cloud Bridge, but it was engulfed in flames and impossible to pass.

Or so Quinn thought.

He glimpsed an enormous black horse with red eyes. It was no longer hitched to the carriage. Atop the Gyfoal, Belimar had a sword drawn, a ward of blue light surrounding him.

Quinn was most concerned with the blindfolded young woman with white hair, slumped forward in the king's saddle. Belimar held Lydia upright with his left hand, clutching his sword and the reins in his right. Being hampered this way didn't stop him from successfully cutting down the lone rebel who stood between him and the ramp to the bridge.

Quinn searched for Rai's helmet, a unique piece of armor adorned by fins on either side. He knew the rebels had a sizable force in the city, but there hadn't been time enough to gather their full numbers. The Gyfoal and its passengers raced toward the bridge with no one to stop them.

No one but me.

He waited until the Gyfoal was so close he smelled the coal in its stomach, then stuck his bardiche across the only path not blocked by debris. The Gyfoal noticed the obstruction and tried to halt, but it had too much momentum. It stumbled over the weapon, righting itself before it could fall completely. It was enough to make Belimar—still gripping the reins with one hand—tumble from the saddle, taking Lydia with him.

There was a second large crack as another of the supports failed and one of the towers at the river's edge crumpled. Shards of wood fell on both sides, some splashing into the water below, others forming a smoldering barricade at the bridge's entrance.

Quinn glanced wildly from side to side.

Walls of flame at either end of the bridge.

And at its center, no one but himself, Lydia, Belimar, and the Gyfoal.

The fall had broken Belimar's ward, but the magic had likely shielded him from injury. Lydia writhed beside him, unable to push herself upright with shackled hands. Belimar climbed to his feet and caught sight of Quinn's face.

"Sawbones?" he said in a low, smoke-filled chuckle. "I never figured you for a rebel."

The bridge creaked and the Gyfoal gave an angry huff, unhappy to be trapped over running water with no way to escape. The smoke from the flaming ship reached Quinn's nostrils, reminding him of a forest fire. Lichens, mushrooms, and oak, cooking in the heat.

Belimar's eyes narrowed as he spotted Quinn's bardiche, and the water-horse etched into its cleaver. "Wherever did you get *that* weapon?"

Lydia propped herself upright on a piece of debris. The blindfold must have slipped from her eyes in the fall, and her attention was focused on the Gyfoal looming over her. The red mist of its breath nearly obscured her face, but as she locked eyes with Quinn, he saw something sharp and determined in her gaze.

"I found it in the Sorrowood," Quinn lied. He took a step back, but too much of the path was blocked by debris.

He tightened his grip on his weapon. Although Quinn had been honest when he told Rai he'd kept up with his training, the last real fight he'd been in was against bandits in Brittlerun. Certainly not on a collapsing bridge against a powerful king, who had both magic and a horse-like demon at his command.

Belimar's mouth twitched into a wicked smile. He didn't flinch when a piece from the ship dropped onto the bridge, causing the beams to sag beneath them. "You know, I'd always wondered what became of Llewel's bastard son, birthed by his mistress from the Lower World. I assumed he'd had you drowned."

Quinn did not react when he saw Lydia inch away from the Gyfoal. She was struggling to retrieve something from inside her jacket, despite the shackles constricting her movements.

I have to keep him talking for as long as possible, Quinn thought.

"I can't drown. A gift from my mother," he said, hoping it was enough to keep the king intrigued.

Belimar twirled his sword and stepped into a fighting stance, his leading foot angled slightly outwards. "All the more for my scholars to study when they drag your body out of the river."

Still, the king did not attack. He kept his weapon trained on Quinn as he took several steps back and snatched Lydia by the hair. The flames behind him made an impenetrable wall, yet somehow, the king summoned another ward with his sword hand. Unlike the first, this one flickered, especially when Lydia kicked out in an attempt to free herself.

Quinn saw a flash of pink in her hands as she wrenched herself out of the king's grip and threw something over the edge of the bridge. The Gyfoal sniffed, and followed the arc of the object with its eyes, before darting toward it. Its body disappeared into the flames, reappearing a second later as it tumbled over the edge and into the blackness of the water below.

"No!" Belimar roared. He turned his sword on Lydia, and Quinn saw his opening. The bardiche caught the light of the fire as it swung, making it look as if the weapon was aflame. It crashed through the king's ward, losing momentum, but forcing Belimar to release Lydia as he dodged the blow.

She scrambled away, and Quinn lost sight of her as he struck again.

This time, the king parried and swung back, but Quinn's muscles seemed to come alive. *Strike, dodge, strike, parry.* Just like Rai had taught him. He could hear Lydia shouting and the bridge crackling beneath them, muffled by the roar of adrenaline in his ears.

Gods, how long had he spent hating this man from a distance? He'd trained to fight out of necessity. Because even in his rural town, he knew that one day, soldiers from the city might come to drag him out of his home.

They had, just not in the way Quinn expected.

Belimar attempted another spell, but it seemed there was still some magic at work on the bridge. The glowing missile whizzed past Quinn's head, as something other than his bardiche struck the king's armor.

An arrow. Had the rebels made it past the blockade?

Quinn knew he could not risk a glance back, but again, Lydia was shouting something in her native language, the urgency in her words unmistakable. He attempted another jab at the king's torso, but Belimar anticipated the move and turned sideways, causing Quinn to stumble forward.

Another arrow flew past them. Then another. If Quinn didn't get out of the way, he was just as likely to be struck as Belimar. Yet, the king refused to cede his ground. He lunged at Quinn again, not giving him a chance to escape the fight.

"Quinn, get out of there!" he heard.

Rai. He'd made it.

The rebels were not the only ones. There was a clatter of steel as the king's guards also fought their way through the blockade.

"You can't win this fight, sawbones," Belimar panted. With an unexpected bit of footwork, he forced Quinn to the left, so that now it was him with his back to the wall of fire. "Lay down your weapon and I'll feed you to the Gyfoal. It'll be a quicker death than any other I can offer."

Quinn did not waste his breath with an answer. Intense heat scorched the back of his neck. One of his strikes landed against Belimar's hip, but the king's armor was as enchanted as his sword and the bardiche merely bounced off it.

But Belimar did not expect the strike from behind.

Lydia's shackles hit the exposed skin between his helmet and his backplate. A dangerous strike to the cervical vertebrae that caused the king's eyes to briefly lose focus. Quinn did not hesitate. He dashed to the side, took hold of Lydia's arm, and dragged her away.

The rest of the bridge was a blur of fire and fighting, but there were more rebels in black than guards bearing the king's crest. Quinn finally made eye contact with Rai, directing the battle from a perch on the mast of the Kelpie, which was sinking and burning at the same time.

"Come on!" Rai called. "Bring her here!"

Quinn didn't move. He looked back at Belimar, who had steadied himself, and was again approaching with his sword drawn. Then Quinn looked at Rai, who was urging him and Lydia to come.

All of this violence. All of this death. When there was something far worse barreling toward them.

"We have to jump," Quinn muttered.

"What?" Lydia said. Her voice sounded exhausted, despite the chaos.

"Jump! Now!" he shouted, pulling them both toward the edge.

They went together, Quinn still holding onto Lydia's shackled arms as they plummeted toward the river. The soft glow beneath their skins did not extinguish, even as the black water rushed in to surround them.

THE LADY OF
THE LAKE

LYDIA KNEW SHE WAS ON A BOAT BEFORE SHE OPENED HER eyes. She hoped most of the water beneath her had come from the damp gown clinging to her skin; it was the last one the fairy servant had brought her, and surprisingly practical compared to the others. It fell to her mid-thigh, with a pair of leggings stitched to it. A modest dress. A dress to be executed in.

The air had cleared, and it no longer smelled like a city. There'd always been chimney smoke and the scent of roasting food creeping through her tower windows, but now there was only pinesap and fresh water.

Gods, the city. The tower. The fire.

She'd hoped it was all a dream.

When she eventually opened her eyes, the world grew no brighter. The night was lit by a crescent moon, barely visible through a cloud bank. A waxing moon, days away from being full. One that could have been her last.

Her shackles had been tossed aside. The metal was dented as if it'd been struck by a weapon to force them open. Quinn was at the boat's opposite end, his right hand on a lever she knew was called a tiller. Lydia had once tried to abate her fear of the ocean by learning everything she could about tides, wind patterns, and sailing. It had done nothing to make her less afraid, but now, she knew exactly how many ways there were to make a shipwreck.

At least they were heading west. Toward the window.

Quinn didn't seem to notice she had woken up. He stared past Lydia at the river, as if trying to read some message spelled out by dim moonlight on dark water.

The book! Her throat already felt raw from the smoke, but it clenched so tightly at the thought that her next breath came out as a wheeze. The sound snapped Quinn to attention.

"How do you feel? Any pain or dizziness? You fainted as soon as we crawled onto the boat."

Lydia remembered very little after they'd leaped from the bridge. There was only the sensation of falling and it being a surprise, though she knew she had chosen to jump. Her body had never stopped being sore since she'd been brought to the Green Country. She imagined her heart looked like a bruised apple.

"Where's the book?" Lydia asked.

Quinn nodded to an empty seat where it rested. It was bone dry, but since so many of the library books back home were enchanted, this was not surprising. "I can't believe you managed to take it," he said.

"It was in the Gyfoal's saddlebags. The lock shattered when we hit the magic on the bridge."

"A linguist, a thief, and now a pickpocket," he said, in the same tone he'd used to calm her when he'd first attempted to bandage her arm. Lydia found she'd had quite enough of Quinn's bedside manner.

"No, just a librarian. Where are you taking me? Why didn't you hand me over to your rebels?"

"Don't get up. I'll look at your head once I find a safe place to drop anchor. Now, tell me what happened. Why did the king drag you out of the tower early?"

She ignored a wave of dizziness as she tried to get to her feet. The boat trip to the lighthouse had been the first she could remember, and no amount of reading could teach her how to keep balance on rocking water. At least she was able to stand without tumbling overboard.

"Apparently, his translators are not as useless as I'd hoped. I've had *enough* of your cryptic nonsense. I've been dragged through the woods, locked up in a tower, and had to jump off a burning bridge. You claim to want to help me, so answer my questions or I'm diving into this river and I'll find my own way home."

He didn't need to know she couldn't swim. A gust of wind whipped her hair across her face. Around them, tall hills swept by, reminding her of the landscape she'd seen when her ex had driven them through the Columbia River gorge. Just *where* was the Green Country?

A bardiche rose behind Quinn's right shoulder, the sharp curve of its blade lighting with a silver flash each time the clouds separated. He tapped his fingers against his knee twice before nodding.

"I'm sorry. You're right. The answer to your first question is… I'm not entirely sure. My one thought was to get us out of the city, and the wind made this direction the fastest. We're also heading back toward the Sorrowood. That alone will make it harder for anyone to follow us."

"I notice you've said nothing about taking me home," Lydia told him, crossing her arms. The motion was enough to make her lose balance again, but at least she could sink into the spare seat in a way that looked slightly natural.

"Because I don't want to make promises I can't keep. Surviving the woods will be unlikely enough, and we've humiliated both the fey king and the rebel leaders. I only said it would be harder for them to follow us. Not that they wouldn't try."

"So, what about my second question: why not hand me over to the rebels? They're your friends, aren't they?"

Quinn made a show of checking the way ahead for obstructions, and Lydia thought she'd never seen stalling so obvious. He spoke before she could mention it. "They are my friends, but you would have been a prisoner with the rebels, just as much as with the king. Whatever you've read in that book makes you both valuable and dangerous. The rebels wouldn't have set you free any more than the king would have, and… perhaps you really can help to stop the Sorrowood."

Sometimes, hearing the truth out loud was even more painful than the silent realization. The only hope she had of returning home was with this strange fey who smelled of medicinal herbs, could sail a boat, and hold his own in a fight against the king. Even though he didn't appear particularly confident about their chances.

"I heard what Belimar said to you," she told him, her voice barely audible over the flapping sail. "You're not just an army doctor."

"Yes, and no. I grew up in a rural village, where I apprenticed with a healer. I was conscripted into Belimar's army because we lived at the edge of the Sorrowood. We hunted in it. Foraged for herbs. No one ever went more than a few miles from our town, but we knew how to tell when the forest was trying to trick you. To lure you into a trap. He saw it as a useful skill set."

Lydia listened quietly, searching the skies for Isst. She doubted she would see him unless the clouds parted. The pain of his absence was worse than any soreness in her body. Quinn fell silent. The sound of the river against the hull made her jaw tense, but at least it wasn't the ocean.

"I wasn't born in that village. I was hidden there," he went on. "My father, the High King Llewel of Astoria, wanted his bastard son tucked away in a place no one would ever find him. It worked. Even Belimar, who executed the entire royal family on the steps of their palace, had no idea the sawbones tagging along with his company was technically the rightful heir to his throne."

Her eyes widened as Quinn's words sunk in. "He murdered your family. How could you stand to *serve* Belimar? How could you even look at him?"

"Because it kept me alive," he said. "And it kept Rai, my cousin, alive. He's the one who taught me to how to fight. When my aunt saw the political tides in Astoria shifting toward a coup, she left him on the steps of a temple in the guise of an orphan. Her enchantment meant he could not speak of his true family except to another who shared his blood."

"So, that's what this is all about?" she snapped. "One side wants to use me to stay in power, and another wants to use me so they can take it back. And you, you want me to…" Lydia realized that the only person who had never asked her what was in the book was Quinn. "What do you want me for?"

"You won't like the answer."

"I haven't liked any of them so far. I'm used to it."

"The Sorrowood has been spreading. It gets faster every year—it used to move in inches, but now, miles of the Green Country are overtaken in mere days. The trees swallow up villages, and those who can't or won't run die. And the people in Astoria don't seem to care. They'd rather fight over whose banner flies over the palace than pay attention to the fact that soon, the only thing occupying the throne will be monsters and sentient trees."

"Why not run? There must be other fairy courts."

"There are, but those paths have been blocked off as well. Even if they weren't, traveling between them is as complicated as traveling to the human realm. There are rules, protocols, and the fey are notoriously territorial."

Even in this darkness, there was a heaviness in Quinn's expression that was nearly enough to make Lydia feel sorry for him. "I can't help with that," she said quietly. "You can have the book. I only want to go home."

"Have you ever noticed anything strange on your side of the window? Here, it began as a whisper. Something only a few mages were able to hear. Something full of pain and grief. Then, one day, people saw trees in the ocean, as if on distant islands. The fisherman and sailors dismissed it at first, but the trees continued to spread. They overtook the shore. Soon, you could walk from the beach to the reef, as if there'd never been water there at all."

Lydia did not speak. She did not breathe. She recalled the Mapmaker's second prophecy.

Oh gods, what have I done? Their forest won't stop with the Green Country. The force of their anger and pain was too much. No world is safe if the window isn't closed.

"It happened slowly at first. Every year, there was less ocean and more Sorrowood. Until one day, soldiers rode into the forest and realized they couldn't find the sea at all. Now, it's moving so quickly that a village can be there one morning and swallowed up by the time the sun sets. I don't know how the window between our worlds exists, but I suspect what's happening to the Green Country will happen to yours in time."

"I'm not a mage," she said. "And I've read that book

from cover to cover twenty times. I can promise you that—"

Lydia stopped herself. There had been a few things she'd understood as she studied the book for hours upon end in the tower. For one, the Mapmaker may not have been the one to create the window, but he knew who had. And he'd attempted to recreate their magic himself.

It was what had driven him mad, but also what had allowed him to see into the murky river of time and know that one day, a changeling named Lydia Reyes would read his words.

LYDIA REYES WILL KILL THE FEY KING.

If Quinn noticed there was a hitch in her breath, he didn't show it.

"It's fine. You don't have to tell me anything. I won't force you. If you wake up tomorrow and you still want me to take you to the window, regardless of whether or not either of us survives, so be it. All I ask is that first, you let me take you to see my mother. She may have some knowledge of the book."

The river had widened and slowed. She knew from her books it was a decent place to drop anchor and when Quinn stood, Lydia realized he was doing exactly that.

"There's a canvas and a few hides wrapped up here. We can string them up and make a tent," he said.

She looked over the side of the hull to find it was called the Avalon. Another strange similarity between their worlds. It was apparent there were more than even the Guild of Lightkeepers were aware of.

"The Avalon?" Lydia asked. Switching between languages was usually an unconscious choice, but she felt the English word heavy in her mouth.

"It's from an old myth in the Green Country. Avalon is the island where the ancient fey King Artuin learned magic from the Aés-Caill—the creatures that lived here before."

The Aés-Caill. The People of the Yew. An electrical shock ran through her. "The Aés-Caill?"

"A difficult thing to explain. There were many creatures here before the fey emerged from their barrows to form courts. Only a few descendants of the Aés-Caill remain. It is said they were supremely powerful magicians. Even more so than my kind."

Lydia had a thousand more questions but attempted to keep her face neutral. Quinn hadn't pressed about the contents of the book and that alone made her suspicious.

"Funny," she said instead, feeling brave enough to run her fingers along the paint on the boat's hull. Water sprayed across her arm, and the cold shock of it grounded her. "It's similar in my world, except we have tales of King Arthur, a human."

Quinn shrugged. "It doesn't surprise me. I've heard that humans call us the Good Neighbors. The Green Country and the human realm have always been entwined, sharing stories since the beginning of time. Before the Sorrowood, we fey could pass freely into your world and there are plenty of human mages who spent time here in turn."

"And the Sorrowood blocked the paths between our realms?"

He nodded, lifting his shoulders in another half-shrug. "Not even the scholars can say exactly why. The Sorrowood is thought to be a curse. Whoever or whatever created it wanted our worlds separated."

Her mind reeled, but even with all her curiosity, she was too tired to think more deeply about that now. "Where did you get this boat, anyway?"

"On top of being a deserter and enemy of the crown, I

am now also a boat thief. Figured I might as well continue the crime spree while I was able."

Lydia chuckled. The emotion was gone as soon as it had arrived, but this was the first time in weeks that her smile was genuine.

QUINN STRUNG UP THE CANVASS AND LAID THE HIDES beneath it with surprising efficiency, considering there was a large weapon strapped to his back. When Lydia crawled her way into the makeshift tent, he didn't join her.

She breathed a sigh of relief into the fur wrapping her body; it had been cured, yet still smelled of animal musk and oil. Her fingers found a knot of rough skin, perhaps from the place an arrow had pierced the creature's side. Thankfully, the river did not whisper as the ocean had. There was only the gentle susurration of water lapping against the hull, and the muffled sounds of Quinn moving about the boat.

He hadn't protested when she tucked the book into the inner lining of her jacket. It was a cursed thing, the very reason she was here in the Green Country instead of in her library, but she'd still felt a hint of panic whenever the fairy servants snatched it away in the evenings. It was her name on its pages and despite wondering if she should set fire to the damn thing, she couldn't shake the feeling that his book belonged to *her*.

She was certain it was the line with her name in it that'd caused Belimar to drag her out of the tower, but if his translators managed to finish their work, he was sure to be disappointed. It contained no instructions on how to push the Sorrowood back, nothing but the two passages she still refused to think of as prophecies.

Their words had repeated in her head the entire time she'd been trapped in Belimar's prison. The mages in the Guild of Lightkeepers had never spoken highly of prognostication. Even the thick books of prophecy in the library spent most of their time gathering dust until Isst reminded her to clean them.

But how could the Mapmaker have known she would be the one to translate the book?

Her name was mentioned one other time, near the book's end, as was part of another apology. It read: Lydia. I am so sorry. It has to be you. I'm so sorry, I'm so sorry, I'm sorry, I'm sorry...

And so on, until the Mapmaker ran out of space.

Lydia drew the hides more tightly around herself. A dark part of her wondered if Isst's distraction of the rock through her window had been his last gift and that he had returned to the woods and abandoned her.

It wasn't long before she realized sleep would not come. Quinn, at last, seemed to have settled, but the boat continued to creak. In the hills, loons called to each other —declarations of longing and love in the cold spring night.

She hardly noticed her teeth were chattering until the crude tent flap moved and Quinn said, "You're shivering."

"I'm trying to sleep," she muttered. The fey had sharper senses than a human, but it still seemed far-fetched he'd been able to hear the rhythm of her breathing over the river.

"You've been tossing and turning for an hour. How are your ribs? Can't get comfortable?"

"Are you actually trying to examine me *now*?"

"I have a vested interest in keeping you alive. Hypothermia will complicate things, and magic doesn't work properly over running water. Move over, let me lay down next to you."

Lydia opened her eyes and sat up, catching sight of Quinn's silhouette against the dark sky. He no longer wore his bardiche, and at some point, the leather cord tying his black hair back had been lost. It hung loose, just past his ears. She was about to ask if he was serious, but her teeth were chattering so violently, it was difficult to speak.

"I won't touch you," he said when she didn't answer. "I swear. Whatever those brutes in the army said… I promise I'm not like that."

It was difficult to force her body away from the meager pocket of warmth she'd created. She trusted Quinn barely more than she trusted any of the other fairies, but he had rescued her twice now. He could have left her to Belimar or Rai, saving his own life and reputation. Yet here they were, on a boat, with two warring factions after them and a corrupted wood full of monsters ahead.

At least she could be warm for one fucking night.

"No skin on skin," she managed, remembering the soft glow between them the last few times he'd tended to her arm.

"That really wasn't your witchwork?" he asked. Lydia's back was turned, but she felt the hides shift, and his body settled into the small space beside her.

"You're the fey. I don't have magic."

Her teeth still chattered, but the small space warmed within a few moments once he lay beside her. She could feel the press of his lean but well-muscled leg through the hides and resisted the urge to inch closer.

"Your gift with languages would certainly be considered a form of magic," he said, his voice half-muffled by fur.

"I told you, I was a changeling. I spent a year in the Green Country when I was a kid. The mages say it's some sort of fairy gift."

"Hm," he said. "There used to be more travel between our worlds in centuries past. People would wander into fairy rings or find their way into one of our barrows. Slipping from one realm to the next and not noticing until returning the way they came was impossible. Some mages found the paths deliberately, and attempted to steal our... Well, that's just how the old stories tell it. Perhaps you were enchanted in some way."

Lydia turned over. In this light, all she could see of Quinn was a sliver of his profile and a pointed ear sticking out from the hides.

"Can we try to touch again, for a moment? Call it scientific curiosity," he went on.

"Is this really why you came in here? I thought the whole point was to help me sleep."

"No. I came in because I heard your bones rattling from the other side of the ship, but you can't tell me you're not curious."

Lydia sighed. He was right, dammit. There'd been plenty of mysteries to contemplate since being stolen from her world, but why her skin glowed when in contact with the dark-haired army sawbones was perhaps the one she'd been least eager to confront.

Not merely a sawbones. The son of a fey king. The rightful heir to the throne.

LYDIA REYES WILL KILL THE FEY KING.

No. If it was indeed a prophecy, it referred to Belimar. It had to. And either way, it wouldn't matter once she asked Quinn to take her back to the window.

"Fine. Just for a second," Lydia said. As she spoke, she imagined Isst chiding her curiosity. He was right. It *was* likely to get her killed.

She moved her hand from her ribcage and held it toward him. Quinn sat up enough so she could see his face as he seemed to consider her outstretched arm. Then, he too shifted and took her hand in his own.

It didn't begin immediately, and she started to wonder if it'd been an illusion after all. But after a few breaths, Quinn's face was illuminated in a soft golden light dancing between their connected palms.

It reminded her of the bioluminescent jellyfish Natalie kept in tanks at her laboratory. The light brightened until reaching a steady glow, almost like a camping lantern. And it wasn't only light. It was warmth too. Warmth that started in Lydia's hand and raced toward her chest.

Okay, it was… nice; she thought. In the quiet of their makeshift bed, the light was not as frightening as it had been at the army camp.

"What is it?" she asked. His palm felt rough against her own—calluses, small scars, burn marks. The hands of a healer and a fighter.

"I'm not sure. My mother might know more," he said. His voice sounded distant, as if his mind had wandered elsewhere.

There was another thing about the light she hadn't noticed before. Now that they took care to stay in contact, a pattern formed. The glow sectioned itself into curves and lines that almost looked like runes.

But the symbols—if they were symbols at all—were incomplete. Anytime one looked as though it might click together, it shifted, connecting with those around it to make something new. It was the only language, aside from that of the ocean, Lydia wasn't able to read.

"Can you see runes if you look closely?"

"I suppose," Quinn said, after a moment. "Not any I recognize, though. It might be… pareidolia. Seeing patterns where none exist."

"That's a big word for a sawbones from the farmlands," she whispered, hoping he could hear her smile. It must be the light making me loopy, she told herself, without pulling away. Why do I even care what he thinks about me?

"There's a lot about me that might surprise you."

Is he *flirting?* she wondered. It wasn't as if she was particularly happy to be trapped on this boat with Quinn, but at least he wasn't Belimar. Or Cithral. Or Tasgall. Or any of the other fey she'd met so far. Sure, they might all be unnaturally beautiful, but even a lovely flower could be full of poison.

Still, it wasn't completely unpleasant to have those dark-green eyes focused on her. She'd caught some of the Guild mages glancing at her occasionally, but she was the changeling who had returned from the human world drunk, in tears, and with a bad dye job, then promptly retreated to the library. Most assumed she was too much trouble.

"I already know your secret, lost king," she said in a hushed voice, not sure of her intentions.

"I have more," he told her.

"So do I."

Another wave of warmth passed through her, though this time it lingered in her stomach and thighs. Sure, Lydia had read plenty of romance novels in her time at the library, but it wasn't until the outside world when a beautiful woman with black lipstick and skull earrings dragged kisses down Lydia's throat that she had woken from what seemed like a long sleep. Even Dominic had called Lydia insatiable.

"What would you have been, if not a librarian?" Quinn asked, bringing her back to the boat.

"That's an odd question."

"This is very awkward. I'm trying to make conversation."

She sighed. "I guess I'd have a record store."

"That must be a human thing."

"Someone who sells music to others," she told him, struggling to find the appropriate words in the fey language.

"Like a bard?"

"Not exactly. More like a curator. What about you?"

Quinn was silent for a moment. "I've always liked herbs. Perhaps a gardener."

She had to stifle a laugh at the thought of the fey king, wishing he had more time to grow flowers. "Should we stop?" she whispered.

"I suppose," he said.

Neither of them moved. Lydia made eye contact with Quinn, and a heat spread across her face that had nothing to do with the magic between them.

Let me read you, she thought, and for a moment, the runes seemed as if they were about to lock together. A wave of fear washed over her, breaking them apart like a puzzle shattering. She pulled away and brought the hand to her chest, where the warmth lingered for a moment before fading.

The light was frightening enough. That it had felt so good, so pleasurable, was even worse.

Darkness fell over them again, thick and heavy as the hides they were tucked beneath. The twinge in her ribs was hardly noticeable as she turned, pulling the blankets up to her chin. She was uncomfortably aware of Quinn, separated from her by less than an inch of fabric and fur. What would happen if she shoved the hides away and pressed against him, toe to forehead?

The thought sent a strange ache through her, one she

hadn't felt since Dominic and her disastrous year in Portland, but she shoved it aside.

It's just been a long time since anyone touched me properly, she
figured.

Perhaps she'd agree to meet Quinn's mother, but that
would be the end of it. No matter what the fey woman had
to say, Lydia would insist he bring her to the window afterward. She would relay the information to Francesco. He
would know how to stop the woods from spreading into
their world.

She pretended not to hear when Quinn sighed and
rolled over so they were back-to-back. But before Lydia
drifted off, she noticed how their torsos expanded and
contracted in rhythm, as if they were breathing together in
perfect time.

Lydia woke alone, the hides still keeping much of
Quinn's body heat. It took a long time to force herself to
get up. The sun had risen enough to fill the valley with
light, but the hilltops were shrouded in thin mist. They
were again racing westward, though she noticed the river
had narrowed significantly while she'd slept.

For the first time, she allowed herself to find the Green
Country beautiful.

The lush hills were tall enough to be called mountains
in the human realm, cutting into the underbellies of slow-
moving clouds. Occasionally, there were ruins—almost
always statues of women and animals or combinations of
the two. Nothing was whole in the fairy realm. The statues
were always broken off at the neck or hip, the missing
shards of pale rock jutting out of tall grass. Any farms they

passed seemed empty, save for the occasional group of goats or wild horses, feasting near decaying buildings.

Lydia turned to where Quinn stood at the stern, adjusting the tiller to navigate the current.

"After we speak to your mother, remember your promise to take me to the window. If the wood really is spreading, the Guild of—the mages on my side will know what to do."

"I forgot to mention that my mother inconveniently does not live by the river. We're going to have to dock our boat and hike. Although it's not far, I should warn you, it might not be pleasant."

She remembered the cat-síth, and the branches that'd looked as if they were interlocking to build her a cage. She must have paled because he said, "We're at the edge of the woods here. It won't be as bad as where you came in through the window, but things can still get strange."

"And your mother *lives* there?"

"She's... unconventional. We're not far now. I foraged a few berries from the shoreline before we set off this morning. You should try to eat."

The berries reminded her of the ones that'd topped the elaborate cakes and pastries the fairy servant brought her in the tower—impossible shades of violet and pink, so sweet as she bit into them, her tongue stuck to the roof of her mouth. She had given up on rejecting fey food within the first few days of being dragged through the Green Country, figuring she had no chance of escaping if she was too weak to run when the opportunity arose. Still, there was something unsettling about their perfection.

In a way, Lydia preferred the gnarled trees at the edge of the wood. Even though the trees were wicked and happy to inform you of such, the perfection of everything else in Astoria reminded her of a gleaming, ornate coffin hiding a rotting corpse.

Quinn, apparently having decided checking and re-checking the sails was more interesting than answering Lydia's questions, said nothing when she found a place to plop down and turn her face to the sun. After weeks in the tower, the warmth of the day prickled against her skin.

She was the first to see the raven flying at pace with the ship.

"Isst," she called, scrambling to her feet. Quinn's attention snapped to her, but she didn't bother explaining as the raven circled their boat before coming to a shaky landing on the Avalon's pulpit.

"Where have you been?" she said. There was a bubble of anger in her chest close to popping. Isst had been her remaining link to home. The one thing she thought she could trust, and he had abandoned her for days.

"I'm sorry," he croaked. "I told you, I was looking for a friend. Then, the wards around Astoria started making me feel... unstable. I was no good to you if I wasn't myself."

"A friend? Are you going to explain, or do you plan on flying off again?"

Quinn stood watching her shout at a raven, who cawed back at appropriate intervals, as if for once, Lydia might be the strangest thing in the Green Country.

"I am as forbidden from speaking his true name as I am mine, but you won't have a hope of making it through the forest without his help. He will meet us a few miles downriver once we're in the Sorrowood proper. My friend is very shy. You may not see him, but he'll be there."

A thousand questions sprung up in her mind, much like a classroom full of rowdy students all vying for atten-tion. Quinn interrupted before she could get any of them out.

"Excuse me. Is that *your* raven, Lydia?"

She turned to find Quinn had sheathed his bardiche and fastened a slightly damp mantle cloak over his shoulders with a pin similar to a caduceus from Lydia's home world. The Green Country's version was a slender, wingless dragon wrapped around a sprig of alder. His cloak matched the color of his eyes.

Something about it made her feel slightly off-balance. Perhaps the current had shifted beneath them.

"He's my assistant," she said, trying to decide on the simplest answer. Isst bristled at the word. "The library in my world is staffed by ravens. He flew in through the window after me."

"I can feel a glamour on him, but it's not fey magic. He's not a true raven, is he?" Quinn said.

"Well, well, you've managed to befriend the lost King of the Barrow-folk and in less than three weeks, I'm impressed," Isst said. This statement kicked the cacophony in her head into high gear, but she thought this might be a conversation to have with her raven in private.

"No, he's not," she answered, ignoring the raven. "Creatures from the forest sometimes sneak into our world through the window. Our mages bind them to the forms of animals, and they serve the…"

It was difficult to find a word for the compound that Quinn might understand, so she settled on, "They serve our college."

"Dangerous business, trapping those creatures. They may look and sound like animals, but they're not. The resentment of being imprisoned grows within them. If they ever get loose, it can be deadly," Quinn said.

"Pssh. I, for one, enjoy this body. It can fly and be very loud. Tell the Barrow King I've just come from Astoria. Both Belimar and the rebels have already sent scouts after you, and are preparing larger forces to begin the chase. Even if one side wipes out the other, you're going to have trouble. Best to get into the Sorrowood as soon as possible."

She relayed this message to Quinn, whose face remained impassive. "I expected as such. We'll lay our anchor down up ahead, in those reeds. They'll hide the boat. It's a short hike to my mother's place from there."

Lydia waited until Quinn was occupied with preparing the Avalon to anchor, then muttered, "Lost King of the Barrow-folk?"

"My people were in the Green Country long before the fey arrived and burrowed into our hills. It's... one of the least derogatory names we have for them," Isst said.

"How do you know who he is?" she asked in English, hoping Quinn would assume she'd switched back to her native language out of habit.

"I know his mother. Which is why I want to warn you now: whatever she tells you, whatever she asks, do not get close to her lake."

THERE WERE MANY THINGS LYDIA WANTED. COFFEE, A shower, and a change of clothes. A mug of hot chocolate, spiced with cinnamon, chili, and possibly rum. More coffee and most of all, her jaw to stop clenching anytime she accidentally made eye contact with Quinn.

She wasn't close to getting any of those at the moment, but at least she was on dry land again, and Isst hadn't flown away as she'd feared. The forest grew dense the moment they stepped off the ship and started heading uphill, but she spotted the raven overhead any time the canopy thinned.

"We're still at the wood's edge," Quinn explained. "Another mile or two, and things get strange. Gods, it has spread fast lately. None of this was Sorrowood when I came here with Belimar's men a few weeks ago."

They followed a narrow game trail. The soil beneath them was lighter, perhaps churned up by deer hooves. What came as a surprise was the occasional pile of stones or fey trinkets, dangling from string tied to the branches. Most were the equivalent of common human objects; coins, arrowheads, and bits of jewelry. But some were so distracting that Lydia fell far behind on the trail and Quinn had to call out to her.

A swirling cloud of black mist in a jar, balanced atop a trail marker. A pale pink moth in a small birdcage it could not escape, despite being small enough to slip through the bars.

"The fey visit this lake for advice sometimes. It's customary to leave an offering," Quinn said, walking back a few yards to fetch her. "Don't touch anything."

The trail soon plateaued, then continued steeply downward over loose gravel. She concentrated on her tattered shoes, not willing to give Quinn a reason to catch her if she fell. It had been easy not to think of the light between them with the excitement of Isst's return, but now that there was nothing to focus on except her balance, her mind wandered back to how she'd felt, huddled beneath the pile of hides, with his hand against her own.

"The lake is just over these boulders," he said. "I'll give you a boost."

At least he was wearing gloves. He cupped his hands around Lydia's shoe, lifting her with a surprising amount of ease as she pulled herself over the ridge. She gave a sharp inhalation at the sight of the lake and barely noticed when Quinn stood on the rocks beside her.

The lake was smaller than she'd expected and perfectly round. The trees stopped a few yards from the water's edge, giving way to a neat swathe of grass dotted by yellow wildflowers. The water was a clear blue near the shore but darkened to black at the lake's center.

"I expected a cabin," she said, dropping to the other side of the boulders. Something was missing, she realized, and it was not merely the absence of a home. There had been such a heaviness inside of her for the past few weeks —a combination of fear and pain that had taken residence in her like a stubborn ghost. She could still feel it, but Lydia wondered what it would be like to wander the Green Country freely and of her own will.

She imagined it would be a bit like exploring the library that had secrets hidden even in the corridors most familiar.

"I may have failed to explain properly. My mother doesn't live by the lake. She lives *in* it," Quinn said.

Isst swooped down to rest on a low branch. "She is one of what our folk call the Ladies of the Lower World. Even with her son here, she will ask you to join her for a swim. Shameless and violent, those Ladies. Our people greatly admire them."

"The Ladies of the Lower World," Lydia repeated, unsure of why she felt the need to clue Quinn into the half of the conversation he couldn't understand. Damn Francesco, insisting she grow up with manners. "You're only half-fey?"

Quinn nodded. "Half-fey, half Aés-Caill. Or at least, what remains of the Aés-Caill. When there are a number of sentient species in your world that can procreate with each other, you get some interesting results. Let me tell her we're here."

Only the blood of the Aés-Caill can end what I have begun.

Lydia wondered if he noticed how her body froze at the thought.

He found a smooth rock near the lake's edge and sent it flying across the water, where it bounced several times before sinking. The memory of Natalie and October skipping rocks on the small irrigation pond at the compound made Lydia bite the inside of her cheek.

Several minutes passed before there was any movement, aside from the ripples. Lydia could rattle off a hundred folktales about sirens and mermaids, but that still didn't prepare her for the long dark hair that rose to the water's surface, fanning out like strands of kelp.

A face emerged next; feminine, but not mistakable for human or fey. The Lady's eyes were too large, with dark-green irises that left no room for white and her skin too was tinged green, aside from where it transitioned to a deep blue around the gills slashed into her neck.

"Oh. It's you," she said to Quinn, rising out of the lake to her shoulders. Lydia saw the silhouette of fins moving beneath her, but the water was dark and the Lady's hair swirled, obscuring the body underneath. In a strange way, she resembled Quinn. Even their eyes were the same color.

"Hello, mother," he said, coming to the edge and sinking to a crouch.

Isst clicked his beak when Lydia attempted to take a step closer, and quietly said, "Your curiosity is even more likely to get you killed here than in the library."

"You've brought friends," Quinn's mother went on, looking first at Lydia, then Isst. "It's been a while since I've seen you, Isstulmanad. However did you end up trapped in this form?"

"I wandered where I didn't belong," Isst said, with another pointed look at Lydia, as if she had somehow *asked* to be dragged into the Green Country.

"Our time is short," Quinn interrupted. "Mother, I need to ask you about something you told me the last time we met. You said no one had been able to conquer the Sorrowood, because they couldn't reach its heart. What did you mean?"

The Lady looked at Lydia and grinned. The expression made Quinn's mother look even more inhuman as her skin pulled taut around her mouth, revealing the odd bone structure underneath. "Every curse has a heart. A powerful moment of sorrow or pain from which the hex spreads, corrupting everything around it. Perhaps you've heard the trees crying to you, little changeling? Does their hurt remind you of your own?"

Lydia remembered the way the forest had whispered in the army camp, but shook her head. "I don't understand anything about this world. I was stolen by the fey from my bed when I was a child."

The Lady's hair writhed around her like tentacles. Lydia took another step back, fearful one might leap out and grab her by the ankle.

"A rare gift, that of understanding. We hear much in the Lower World. Those above speak and it echoes down upon us. So, I can tell you it was not a fey who snatched you from your world. It was another human."

"That's not possible," Lydia said. She desperately wanted to splash water on her face, but nothing was inviting about the lake now. The Lady's hair had turned it into a seething mass of blackness.

"We hear everything, from everywhere. Your Mapmaker was a human mage, a traveler, just as the Aés-Caill. However, while our people open their windows naturally, the Mapmaker could not. He needed power. The sort of power that runs in the blood of the Aés-Caill and their descendants. Your gifts do come from the Green

Country, but you had them long before you ever set foot here."

Lydia met Isst's eyes, knowing she would not be able to keep the waver from her voice. "That can't be right. The Guild would have known. Is this true? Did you know it?"

"The Guild's enchantments prevent me from saying many things," was all the raven offered.

"Tell me," the Lady said, "During what month were you brought to this realm?"

"September," Lydia managed. Quinn stood and crossed his arms over his chest, his expression unreadable.

"Ah, the Goose Moon. Very auspicious. The moon of journeymen, the harvest, and the hunt. My son was born beneath the Crow Moon of October. That's why he's so hard-headed."

"Mother, *please*. I told you, we're short of time—" Quinn began, but now it was Lydia who interrupted.

"If the Mapmaker knew about the window, and he could already travel between the Green Country and my world, why did he need to steal us?" she said.

The Lady sank back into the water until even her pointed chin was submerged. "The Green Country and your world have always been connected, but there are other realms existing alongside our own. I do not know where the Mapmaker was trying to go, but the Aés-Caill understood the consequences of trying to pry open a tear where none should have existed."

"The wood. I always believed it was a blight, a curse from a rival kingdom—" Quinn began.

"The Sorrowood sprang up around a tower, which once stood alone on an island far from the ocean shore. Before the forest cut off our paths, we Ladies watched him attempt and fail to open a window of his own. We do not know what planted the seeds of the Sorrowood; only that

there were thirteen great ripples of pain, felt even in our
chambers below the Green Country. After that, the forest
began to spread."

"The tower. I have a map. I know how to get there,"
Lydia finished. She touched the end of her stark white
ponytail. What the hell had the Mapmaker done to her?

A thought struck her like a blow to the back of the
head. "You say I have Aés-Caill blood. The other
changelings must have it too. Thirteen ripples of pain.
Thirteen of us used in rituals traumatic enough to strip the
color from our hair. Was it us? Did *we* create the
Sorrowood?"

Whoever or whatever created it wanted our worlds
sealed off, Lydia thought. It was the curse of the children
who never wanted to set foot in the Green Country again.

"Soon enough, you'll be able to ask the Sorrowood
itself," the Lady said. "My cousins and I have not been
able to get near the tower for some years now, but we must
assume the window is still open. The changelings may have
created the spark, the first flames of the curse on this land,
but the window continues to fuel it. Why it has begun to
hasten now, I do not know. We suspect it has to do with the
death of Llewel, for the high kings of the fey are tied to
this land."

"An opportunistic infection," Quinn murmured. "The
Sorrowood sensed weakness. The changelings wanted to
hurt the Green Country, and their curse has found its
moment. Can his window be closed?"

Whether or not he was deliberately choosing not to
address Lydia's revelation was unclear.

"Perhaps," the Lady said, her words causing bubbles
on the lake's surface. "I do not know the secrets of the
ancient Aés-Caill. I have heard only whispers from the
Lower World. Ladies forced to abandon their lakes.

Dryads, their trees. The wood spreads, but worse accompanies it; corruption. Animals turned into monsters. Creatures such as me turned into demons. Demons like my old friend, Isstulmanad, freed from the magic that bound them."

The Lady's head briefly sunk below the surface and reemerged covered in water droplets that shone like emeralds. "The magic of traveling between worlds has been lost to us, but the price of ending the curse will be the same as the cost of starting it. Blood for blood."

"You *have* to know more," Quinn urged.

A tentacle of hair rose from the water and snatched a passing canary. A flurry of yellow feathers scattered across the surface of the lake as the Lady crunched bird bones between her teeth.

Don't be afraid, Lydia told herself. *Everything here is hungry.*

"Mm. You will not find one of my kind willing to sacrifice themselves for the Green Country, nor do I believe it would work if you did. However, you are both tied to this land. Quinn, as the rightful king, and Lydia as one of the Sorrowood's mothers. You must go to the Mapmaker's tower. Learn what witchwork he did there. Perhaps you will find some way to pay his debts."

"And if we don't, it'll spread?" Lydia asked. "You're certain the wood will spread into other worlds? Into my world?"

The Lady's mouth was smeared with blood, running pink as it mixed with lake water. "At times, we hear the whispers of your ocean, as we did before the paths between our worlds were cut off. Lately, it cries in pain."

Isst landed on the boulders behind Lydia. His claws scraped against the rock. She hadn't even noticed he'd gone.

"We need to move," the raven said. "Ships flying Belimar's colors are headed in this direction."

"You can hide in my lake, changeling. Come to the
water's edge. You will be safe in the Lower Worlds," said
Quinn's mother.

"An admirable attempt, Lady," Isst said. "But the east-
wardly winds are in Belimar's favor. We must go."

Lydia repeated the raven's words, which spurred Quinn
into action. He moved toward the rocks, pulling himself
onto the first ledge with a soft grunt. "I'll come back to visit
when I can," he told his mother.

"Mm. Don't forget the offering next time. A young
goat will do nicely. I have one more thing before you go. A
gift for the changeling," the Lady said, lifting a finned arm
from the water and tossing a satchel onto the grass. It was
surprisingly dry and too unwieldy to have been thrown
with such ease.

"What is it?" Lydia asked, surprised by the satchel's
weight. Whatever was inside was heavy. Plenty of books in
the library warned about fairy gifts, but perhaps it wouldn't
count as an acceptance until she opened the wrapper.

"Something to protect you in the Sorrowood."

"She needs nothing from you, mother——" Quinn
began.

The Lady of the Lower World cut him off.

"My son's concern is justified. There is no such thing as
a gift in the Green Country, only favors that must be
repaid. However, I can promise what I demand in
exchange will be fair, and I will not ask until we meet
again. If you die in the woods, you will be free of your
debt."

Isst shifted his weight impatiently. "She'll ask for a
single strand of hair, or a pinch of dirt, or your name, or
your shadow. Perhaps she will ask for a cup of tea in which

the full moon is reflected, or to bring her the ocean, one bucket at a time. She may ask for your happiest memory or your saddest one, or the one in which you betrayed yourself most thoroughly, and whichever she takes will be lost to you forever. But it will be worth it. Just as in the human realm, it is wise to accept a gift from the Lady of the Lower World."

"Armor?" Lydia asked as she opened the satchel with unsteady hands. She was still reeling from the thought that it might have been… her and the other changelings. That the force of their pain had been enough to curse the Green Country.

"It belonged to a great warrior who fell in love with one of my sisters and left the Upper World forever."

"You mean, one of the Ladies seduced and drowned her," Quinn said flatly.

"Perhaps. Take it, Lydia. You'll need it where you're going," said his mother.

Quinn clicked his tongue. "You don't have to do that, mother. You shouldn't do that. Lydia, throw that parcel back into the lake."

"No," Lydia said, straightening from her crouch. "Your mother is right. I need armor. I want armor. I've spent too much time in this country feeling defenseless. I don't want to be at its mercy anymore."

It was the first time she'd admitted it to anyone, including herself. Knowledge is power, the old saying went. Francesco and Zoya had driven that into her mind, again and again. But what if knowledge wasn't everything? What if sometimes you needed strength to back it up?

She thought of the magic that potentially flowed through her. Lydia had always been too afraid to use it, but now… she might have no other choice.

"You don't know what you're asking," Quinn said, but

he was wrong. She knew exactly what she wanted. It was a way out of the Green Country alive. It was a way to stop the spread of the Sorrowood in both her realm and Quinn's, and it was a way to keep her friends safe.

"I accept your gift, Lady," she said, ignoring Quinn's previous sentence. "Thank you."

"Anything?" Quinn asked Isst, as the raven returned to the pulpit that had become his favorite perch.

"They've had to slow in the shallows. Our boat is faster, but they're coming as quickly as they can. We need to go deeper into the woods, where my friend is waiting," Isst said. Lydia barely remembered to repeat the message.

Nausea had settled into her, and it had little to do with the Avalon's constant rocking. If the Lady had been telling the truth, Lydia had Aés-Caill blood. All the Guild's changelings did. Her power with languages did not come from her time in the Green Country, but from her distant ancestors. And the man who had written the book tucked against her chest had been the one to steal her from her family.

"Are you okay?"

She looked up to find Quinn standing over her, the sails billowing out behind him. A strand of black hair had come loose from its tie and whipped across his forehead.

"I don't know," she said.

She thought of the Pacific Ocean, dried up beneath a cursed forest. She saw the city of Portland overrun with monsters. Massive wolves tearing through Powell's bookstore, gnashing through pages with their fangs. The bridges she'd loved to ride a bike over collapsing as people attempted to flee. Would the Sorrowood begin its spread slowly in her world, as it had in the Green Country, or would it sweep across the landscape as if claiming the earth for its own?

The guilt made her feel like she was back in Belimar's tower, trapped on all sides by thick walls, with no path out save through a door whose lock she didn't have the key to. The rational part of her knew she had not been brought to the Green Country of her own free will, not then and not now, and that the Mapmaker was responsible for the effects of his rituals.

But it didn't mean she could look at the wood without knowing in her gut that it was here because of her. That it might swallow both the Green Country and her world because she hadn't been able to control the magic in her blood.

"Don't," Quinn said, his voice hardly louder than the creaking sailboat.

"Don't what?"

"Don't feel guilty. You were a child, stolen from her family to be used as fuel for a mage's delusions of grandeur. You're no more responsible for the Sorrowood than I am."

She had never heard of the fey being gifted with telepathy, but the way Quinn always seemed to know what she was thinking unnerved her. "Oh? Then why are *you* so set on driving it back?"

The question wasn't meant with any cruelty, but something in her squirmed when his eyes flitted to hers.

"You want the truth? Because no one else seems to notice. No one else seems to care."

"There's more to it than that. You have a trade that'd be sought after wherever you went. As far as I can tell, you have no close friends and aside from Rai, your only other family is a mother who you apparently don't visit enough. You could run, Quinn."

"Not forever," he said, biting his lip as if he was debating whether or not to continue. "Even if the other courts were open to us, it's just a matter of time before the forest reaches them, too. But you're right, it's not just that. I'm the one dragging you into the Sorrowood. You deserve the truth. I suppose I feel some sense of... responsibility. My father was the king of this court. It was his duty to fight the Sorrowood and he didn't. We fey are tied to the land of our birth, the royal lines even more so. Belimar wiped out Llewel's entire family, save for Rai and myself, and Rai has chosen his own battle. There's no one left but me."

Lydia fell silent, listening to water slap against the Avalon's hull. A vulnerability shone in Quinn's eyes she'd never noticed before. Their gazes met and held until the sailboat shifted in a current and he returned his attention to the tiller. A flush raced through her body, similar to the warmth she'd felt when their skin touched.

"I meant what I told you before. If you want me to take you to your window, I will, but I'm going to search for the Mapmaker's tower either way."

Lydia hadn't yet explained that searching for the tower would not be necessary, because she already knew the way. She closed her eyes and again thought of Natalie and of October. Of Francesco and Zoya Yatsenko and the library and Patsy Cline records and ice cream sandwiches and romance books and clean socks and coffee with too much sugar in it.

"What if you can't close the window alone?" she said, her voice hardly louder than the river. She didn't speak her other thought. That closing the window might require a sacrifice of Aés-Caill blood. If the Mapmaker was correct, Quinn's blood specifically.

"I'll still try."

She set the book beside her and wiped her hands on her gown. It didn't make them any cleaner. "If the wood is spreading to my world, it won't be long before I don't have a home to go back to. I know how to get to the tower. This isn't just a book, it's a map. It was left for me."

Her foot met the side of Quinn's boot. She hadn't meant to touch him, but he did not move away. Nor did he speak.

"So, I'll come with you," she said. "To find the window and stop the wood. And afterward, you'll take me home."

Quinn smiled. Though half his face was in the shadow of a hand shielding his eyes from the sun, the expression made him look much younger. She wondered if the Green Country would be different were he on Astoria's throne.

Belimar had entered the wood because he thought it would cement his power. Quinn was entering it because he thought it might save a world that had been cruel to him, again and again.

"Do you have any idea how we're going to close the window? It was opened with human magic," Quinn asked.

She sighed, wondering if she should mention she'd only done real magic twice in her life, and had been too afraid to ever try again.

"I recently got access to the esoterica books in my library," Lydia said instead, "But human magic is based on balance. Like for like. Theoretically, the power needed to break a curse would be the same as the power needed to create it."

"Any chance you can convince your changeling cousins to help us?"

"Unlikely, even if there were time to gather them.

We're on our own, Quinn."

"Well, at least you're decent company. Thank you. You're a brave woman, Lydia Reyes," he said, with a smile that made her feel like she'd noticed a new and achingly beautiful lyric in a song she'd heard a thousand times before.

LYDIA REYES WILL KILL THE FEY KING.

No, thought a hissing voice inside her head. The Mapmaker lost his mind trying to open the window. Whatever snippets of the past and future he saw or thought he saw were nonsense. Besides, the fey king was Belimar and Lydia had already decided she wouldn't feel too guilty about sticking a dagger into his gut.

"How far do we take the river?" Quinn asked, settling back into his usual place at the helm.

She had read the book so many times that she didn't have to consult it to answer. "We'll come to what looks like the ruins of an old harbor. Then, we head south."

"I know the ruins. If this wind keeps up, we'll be there before nightfall," Isst cawed from the ship's helm.

Lydia opened the book in her lap, and stared at the pages, wishing she could find some passage she'd missed. She heard Quinn hum a few bars of a song, as painfully pretty as all fairy music, but when she looked up, he stopped, as if she'd caught him trying to steal the last bit of her lunch.

She remembered the warmth that had swept through them as they held hands within their makeshift tent, but that was a thought to be pushed away. Ignored. One day, she'd be home, and this would all seem like a distant dream.

LYDIA REYES WILL KILL THE FEY KING.
LYDIA REYES WILL KILL THE FEY KING.
LYDIA REYES WILL KILL THE FEY KING.

PART TWO
THE SORROWOOD

Miles to Go Before I Sleep

Even as a child, when the Sorrowood spread only a little faster than a normal forest, Quinn wondered if it was endless.

The village of Brittlerun was the residence of not more than two hundred fey. Quinn didn't have parents in the sense the other children did. He was simply passed from home to home, briefly living with whoever had a spare cot and the most meat in their salt cellars. Though no one in Brittlerun ever guessed he was the offspring of an ancient elemental being and the High King of Astoria, it was plain there was something *wrong* with him, even as an infant.

He could lie beneath bathwater for half an hour before surfacing for air. The chickens and goats went silent as he walked past, dropping into reverent bows. Many were surprised when he apprenticed under the barber-surgeon —a surly man named Gwenallt Teague, who'd fled to the countryside after mending the broken hands of an Astorian thief. Most in Brittlerun assumed Quinn would leave for the city as soon as he was able. He was quick-witted, handsome, even by fey standards and skilled as a fisherman and sailor.

But Quinn had studied and Quinn had stayed. Until Belimar's army arrived in Brittlerun and demanded a medic who knew the dangers of the wood and how to traverse it.

Gods, Quinn had been so afraid of the Sorrowood then. He and his friends may have spent plenty of time trapping rabbits a mile or two into the forest, but even there, he had felt the wickedness of the trees. It was as if they were waiting for someone to trip, to stumble over a root, so they could reach out and drag them into the heart of the woods.

Years later, there was still dread in his stomach.

Lydia spoke quietly with Isst near the pulpit, both oblivious to the fact they had entered the forest proper. The world was darker here, though it was closer to noon than twilight. The Avalon, theirs simply because it was the first boat that was easy to steal, had been quick as they fled the city. Now, Quinn found himself wishing the winds would turn against them.

That old song. The one he couldn't keep out of his head.

It'd been long accepted as a prophecy by Astorian scholars, considering it had predicted the Sorrowood before there had been such a thing. But Quinn had never had much of a reason to consider it deeply until now.

He stole another glance at Lydia, feeling an uncomfortable mixture of emotions knotted within him. Quinn had sworn to himself he would protect her, ever since she'd been dragged into his medical tent with a gash on her arm.

She was his patient. That was his duty. Sure, he hadn't failed to notice she was beautiful—stark white hair stunning against tanned skin and dark eyes. Even her calluses had intrigued him. They spoke of books, of quills, and of curiosity. He'd made it a point not to keep *looking*, not in that way, no matter how enticing her curves had been beneath the damp tunic.

It had been ages since he'd been with anyone in that way. He'd had to turn his back to her last night to hide the sudden, unwanted erection as the glow flared between their joined hands. Quinn wished they'd had the chance to ask his mother about that. At least he hadn't been forced to admit that anytime he wasn't worried he was about to die, he was thinking about Lydia.

And to be honest, he thought about Lydia the times he was worried he was about to die too.

Lyrics ran through his mind.

It's the mother's blood
Her tears and her pain
That made the wood grow
And it won't stop again

Till the king drives his sword
Through his queen's beating heart
And the wood and its mother
Are no longer apart.

Lydia. The mother of the Sorrowood. Or at least, one of them. Lydia's revelation—that it had been her and the other changelings who'd cursed the Green Country—had been a stab to the gut.

Put it out of your mind, Quinn told himself. He was the one who had dragged Lydia into this. She was under his protection. If anyone had to die, it would be him.

"Isst wants to ask you a riddle. He says it's a way to

reveal your character," Lydia said, pulling Quinn from his thoughts.

He gave a throaty chuckle. "Well, I'm terrible at them. The fey are supposed to be good with wordplay, but I've always found it easier to speak plainly."

"Isst is stubborn. He won't let it go."

"Fine, then."

The raven croaked and shrieked, and a few moments later, Lydia said, "There are two of me. I have eyes, but cannot see."

She bit her lip, pondering the question as if it had been meant for her. After a few moments of listening to the Avalon's groans, she was the one to answer.

"A storm, and...?"

"A needle," Quinn finished. "I only guessed because there was a stitching kit on the boat, and it was already on my mind. Please don't make me do another. Look. There are the ruins up ahead."

Lydia and Isst looked up, but it was Lydia's face that made him feel like he'd run their boat into rocks. The rings beneath her eyes were dark and although her figure was still full, there was a gauntness beneath her cheeks that hadn't existed before she'd been trapped in Belimar's tower. She needed proper nutrition and a night of uninterrupted sleep.

That's better. She's your patient. Nothing more.

The raven took off, and Lydia came to join him at the stern. It turned out his mother's gift for her had been a change of clothes—hunting trousers, a linen shirt, and a piece of torso armor that looked like it was made from kelpie leather. Strong, waterproof, and nigh unheard of in the Green Country for centuries.

Battles had been fought over armor so fine. A sigil was emblazoned over the heart, but it was not the coiled kelpie that signified his father's royal line, nor did it belong to any of the ancient fey families Quinn was aware of. Three running hares, arranged in a triangle so that they each shared an ear.

The armor came equipped with two accessories—the first, a strap beneath the breastplate, the perfect size and shape to fit the Mapmaker's book. There was also a scabbard to wear against her hip, though Lydia had no weapon to fill it. She'd already searched the Avalon for a fishing knife, but whoever owned the boat had taken everything except for a few survival supplies.

Lydia had accepted the offer of Quinn's cloak, and pulled the book from beneath it. The pages all looked like nonsense to him; blocks of strange runes that were not any variation of the fey language. Perhaps it had been the Mapmaker's own invention.

"Quinn, there's something I'd like to ask you before we land," she said.

"You're insatiable. If you prefer, I can drop you off at the college in Astoria instead of the window once all this business is done with."

"Oh, that's just your way of trying to change the subject, but the truth is, I *can't* put a question aside. It's against my very nature. We're stuck together. If it's going to pester me, it'll definitely end up pestering you. The Aés-Caill…"

Quinn glanced back and saw her face was flushed and alert. Her hands were steady as they gripped the sides of the book.

"You want to know about the Aés-Caill? My mother is one, as you surmised, but most have moved on to other realms. The Ladies of the Lower World have survived this long because their queendoms exist beneath the earth, in flooded caverns inaccessible to most. I'm not surprised you're so concerned with her since you have Aés-Caill blood yourself."

She looked at her knees knocking against one another and did not immediately answer. "Your mother must be wrong."

"She's not. My mother has many... devious qualities, but the Ladies hear much from their caverns."

Quinn chose not to mention that he had a habit of ignoring his mother's jibs and warnings himself. There was another reason he'd wanted to steer this conversation away from the Aés-Caill, but she asked before he could change the subject.

"The light between us, then. You claim it's not your magic. It's certainly not mine. Could it be because of our Aés-Caill ancestry?"

Clever Lydia.

He swallowed, cursing himself for not rehearsing what to say when this inevitably came up. The best he could do was too busy himself with the sail, though the winds were in their favor and the river was bright and wide; an easy path to what might be the worst place in this world or any other.

"That's certainly possible," he said.

"You need me alive and whole, King of the Barrow-folk. And I have absolutely nothing to do except sit here and annoy you until we drop anchor again."

"I think I liked you better when you were afraid of the Green Country."

"Liar," Lydia said, with a smile as if it were a term of affection.

The wind whipped her hair into a frenzy. Quinn imagined using his fingers to smooth out the tangles and had to force the thought out of his mind. She'd be gone from this place soon enough. Still, he smiled back; an expression at odds with the feeling of dread like a wolf's teeth were ready to tear into his throat.

"You won't like the answer," he said.

Lydia rolled her eyes. "I've heard that before. Stop deflecting."

"Fine. You're right. This is merely a theory, so don't read too much into it," he told her, then considered his next words. It was as if he and Lydia were standing on opposite ends of a raging river. If he said the right thing, perhaps it would build a bridge. A rickety, shaking bridge, but enough to connect them. However, if she was horrified, there was a chance she would take off and he would be swept away trying to chase after her.

"Modern fey society has been influenced by the Green Country's relationship with the human realm, and vice versa. The Aés-Caill ruled this world long before either humans or fey wrote stories, let alone told them. They likely had very different standards in terms of things like morality, justice, and courtship."

The raven made a noise that sounded something like a growl, but Lydia ignored him.

"Best get to the point before Isst pecks at you," she said.

"Give me a moment. It's just a folktale, and you haven't been in the Green Country for more than a few weeks. I'm trying to figure out how to explain it. There are old stories that suggest some of the Aés-Caill had a sort of mark. Like a tattoo. One that helped identify their mate. As I said, it's only a thought, seeing as the light makes patterns—"

"Oh. *Oh*," she said, eyes darting to the water. Her cheeks reddened, but he couldn't tell whether it was because of embarrassment or too much sun. Quinn was torn between annoyance that she seemed so put off by the idea, and annoyance that he felt so upset by it. Another emotion rushed through him. Guilt. Lydia had been brought to the Green Country against her will, and ever since, she'd been imprisoned and abused by men who wanted to use her. Was he any different?

"I wasn't implying anything," he said quickly. "I'm probably wrong, and even if I wasn't, there's nothing to suggest that sort of bond has to be anything other than platonic. Maybe it's a good sign. We're two descendants of the Aés-Caill, setting off on an impossible task. Perhaps it means we'll succeed."

The words sounded hollow, even to him. She brushed the hair from her forehead and met his eyes again.

"I... I suppose it's one more thing I'll have to research when I get home." She looked at the journal again. "We'll need to travel south until we reach a clearing, empty aside from a single willow tree that looks as if it has been struck by lightning. Then, we bank west," she said, running her index finger along a line of text.

"Is that a literal translation?" he asked. The abrupt subject change rattled him, and it didn't seem like enough letters to convey what she'd explained.

"No. This language is interesting. It makes pictures in my head, instead of words. I'm guessing that's why Belimar's translators had such a difficult time with it. What's strangest is that it gives instructions *from* Astoria, as though he had traveled this way, or knew I would."

Quinn sighed. "All this death over a map."

"A map to a window between worlds. One that might potentially control the Sorrowood," Lydia said, after a few moments. "I see why Belimar would want it. You told me he gained power because the previous king appeared weak against the threat."

"Politics in Astoria has always been complicated and bloody. The Sorrowood was the excuse for a regime change, this time. Next, it will be something else. I prefer to stay out of it. Once we close the window, what happens after has nothing to do with us," he said.

Lydia turned her gaze to the hills, where the stands of fir and birch had been replaced with the forest's twisting monstrosities. "But Belimar is a dictator. Perhaps the rebels would unite behind you—"

"We'll dock here," Quinn said, steering toward a clump of reeds that would obscure their boat from anyone passing on the river.

She was on the shore before him, planting her boots firmly into the ground as if trying to take root. The raven, whom his mother had called Isstulmanad, swooped down, playfully taking a strand of her hair in his beak before catching an updraft.

Quinn wondered if this was the last time he would see Lydia smile, considering what lay ahead of them in the woods.

"How far, do you think?" he asked, passing her the last handful of berries as he caught up. They had ripened farther in the sun, and a streak of juice smeared across her lower lip, looking like blood.

"To the tower? Maybe twenty miles. The book uses landmarks rather than exact distances."

"That makes sense. The wood distorts things. It took us a week to reach your window, but a couple of days to get back out," Quinn said. He'd rolled up the canvass and one of the hides, strapping them to the bottom of a pack he'd found in the Avalon's hull. There had been some other useful items; a few rations of smoked salmon, a kit with simple medical supplies, and a vial of saltpeter for preserving fish.

Carrying both the pack and the bardiche was unwieldy,

but the weight of the weapon against his back was a comfort.

"Something is strange," she told him, taking a last look back at the river. A group of mallards paddled across it, green feathers bright against the sun-washed water. "Isst said that his friend was already here, but I don't see anyone."

Quinn surveyed the landscape himself, and like Lydia, he saw nothing but trees. Even the river had disappeared, though they'd traveled less than a few yards. Fish bones littered the forest floor along with rusting tide markers and overturned rowboats covered in moss. A grim reminder that the river was all that remained of an ocean that had once lapped against the shores of Brittlerun.

"Perhaps he'll catch up to us," Quinn said. Still, the way his mother had spoken to Isst—like an old friend dropping by for tea—made him wonder if Lydia should trust the raven as much as she did.

There were many kinds of monsters in these woods. Most were beasts, normal animals corrupted by the wood and driven by hunger and instinct. Some had grown old and clever enough to trick even the fey, who prized riddles and wordplay above all else. And some were like Isst and Quinn's mother; ancient beings that existed when the fey had still huddled together beneath the hills with hardly a way to defend themselves.

"Did you hear something?" Lydia asked, after another few minutes of hiking. Time had passed without Quinn realizing how long he'd been staring at the wispy strands of hair stuck to her nape barely visible above his cowl.

He hadn't been prepared for how much the thought of her wearing his clothes made him want to squirm.

They paused, but all he heard was the distant river and the songbirds' voices distorted by the heavy tree cover.

Their titters echoed strangely, as if they were surrounded by four high walls.

"No," he said. "Nothing unusual."

Lydia turned and gave him a tight smile. "Sorry. It must be my nerves getting the better of me. We should hurry, right? Someone is going to spot our boat, eventually."

"Let's try for ten miles before nightfall," Quinn said. "It's easier said than done in these woods, even for my kind. Camping will be dangerous, but it's better than trying to travel in the dark."

"Camping," Lydia repeated, "Well, at least it's not the tower."

She turned away, and Quinn allowed himself to wince. Their night on the boat had been terrifying and exhausting, yet he couldn't deny how much he wanted to ask her to let him touch her again. *Professional curiosity*, he told himself.

After all, she seemed intrigued about it, too.

Walking helped put it out of his mind. He let Lydia guide them, occasionally pausing to consult the book, while he checked the ground for animal tracks. The massive elk that'd attacked Belimar's company had come from the darkness silently, goring the nearest soldier before anyone had the chance to shout.

Fortunately, the trek was uninterrupted until he and Lydia stopped to take gulps of river water from their flask. They jumped at a rustle in the bushes, but it was only a chipmunk; a little larger than the ones in Astoria and with two sharp fangs where its buck teeth should be. It scampered off as soon as it had their attention.

Lydia pinched the bridge of her nose.

"Headache?" he asked. "You're dehydrated. Have some more water. Plenty of creeks run through this wood.

Most of the water is brackish, but I know the magic to cleanse it."

"It's nothing. Let's keep moving," she said, and he had the feeling the extra slug of water she took was for his sake alone.

Quinn did not suspect they were being followed until they came across the wreck of an old frigate that Lydia noted as a sign they were headed in the right direction. This was one of the most impressive ruins he had ever seen in the woods. It had clearly been one of his father's ships, with a kelpie for its figurehead. Crates stamped with the royal seal spilled their contents onto the forest floor; deep green wine bottles, jars of red and yellow spices, finely spun wool enchanted to retain its vibrancy even after decades in the dirt.

He swore he saw a shadow darting from one tree to another. Despite watching the space for a long time, it didn't reemerge.

"Isst says that's his friend," Lydia said when the raven landed atop the kelpie's moss-covered head. Her hands were clutched against her chest.

A friend that probably wants to eat us, Quinn thought. The raven may have been commanded to serve the changelings, but the old creatures of the Green Country were clever and patient and no spell was fool-proof. There was always a loophole, a turn of phrase, to be exploited for those who wanted to get around their commands.

"What is it?" he asked, as the raven relayed another few caws to Lydia.

"Something ancient. Not Aés-Caill, but he says it existed here before the wood. It's agreed to help us once in exchange for——" She cut herself off, seemingly shocked by the raven's words.

"For what?" Quinn snapped. A bargain with one of his

fey kin was dangerous enough, but with a creature of the wood...

"For a proper meal," she said with a shrug, pulling his cloak tighter around her shoulders. "That's all he'll tell me."

"Let's hope the meal won't be *us*," he muttered. It did not take much longer for Quinn to realize he was sensing something other than Isst's friend. As they passed the scattered bones of a dolphin pod, he caught a scent on the wind. Wood smoke, blowing in from the direction of the river. He motioned for Lydia to stay quiet, then scrambled to the top of the largest tree he could find, hating the way its bark felt like burned flesh beneath his hands.

It was enough height for him to catch sight of Belimar's flags waving above the riverbank. The deer with an arrow in its eye, flying high over a fleet of ships that rarely left the harbors of Astoria.

Lydia seemed to understand the look on his face as he climbed down to the ground.

"Can they track us in this wood?" she asked. He could tell she was attempting to keep any quaver out of her voice.

Brave Lydia.

"The King's Cleaver must be on that ship. Cithral is an excellent tracker. He got us through the forest by following game trails the rest of us couldn't spot. I didn't think they would get here this fast. We should have done more to cover our tracks."

"It's too late now," she told him. "The book shows another route. Shorter, but more dangerous. It banks that way, following a steep hill. If the trail isn't too rough, we could be at the tower by morning."

He nodded. They'd been lucky so far, but more

urgency meant more attention. "Can you take the pack? It'll get in the way of me drawing my weapon."

She held out a hand and took it with a look of surprise. "It's so light."

"You can thank the fisherman whose boat we stole for the enchantment. It fits more than it looks too, but it's not as if we had much in the way of supplies. Can you lead us?"

She nodded and raised her head to address Isst. "Caw three times when they enter the woods. Four times if they're headed in our direction." Then she shouldered the pack and headed back to the dolphin bones. Quinn hadn't noticed the narrow trail, too small for any deer. Perhaps it had been made by hares, raccoons, or the other small, vicious things living in the undergrowth.

Lydia took care to duck under cobwebs and avoid breaking any half-dead twigs that dangled from the trees. Quinn knew he shouldn't speak, not when they didn't know how close Belimar's scouts might be, but he whispered, "You can move in the woods without leaving a trace."

"I'm a librarian. You'd be surprised what you pick up when you're surrounded by books all day."

"I'll do my best to get you back there," he said.

"Thank you. Let's try to survive the journey to the tower first."

He realized she may have been understating the difficulty of the trail when they came to their first obstacle. After another half mile, the trees butted up to a high cliff, continuing as far as the eye could see in either direction. The rock was partially covered by layered tiers of moss and dangling vines, but none looked sturdy enough to use as a climbing rope.

"Dammit," she said, pounding a fist against the stone.

"The book didn't mention this. There must be some way up or around nearby, or the Mapmaker would have given instructions."

"Perhaps he was wrong, or the woods have shifted somehow. As I said, you can't always rely on your senses here."

At that moment, three caws sounded overhead. Quinn's eyes shot up, but the canopy was too thick to see the sky.

"Everything else has been accurate so far," she said, also squinting through the trees. "We need to find a way over these cliffs. I'll search to the left and you to the right."

"No. We stick together. The wood is denser than you think, and it will be easier for the trees to trick us if we're apart."

They went left, traversing over dead logs and bulging tree roots. Faint glyphs peeked through the moss on the cliff side whenever it was thin enough. Old hunter's marks, perhaps, from when the wood was smaller, and folk in the fishing villages might have tried to hold their ground against it.

It wasn't the marks that disturbed him, more their subject matter. Wolves. Redcaps. A wyvern with curved claws. Something resembling a fey, apart from the enormous teeth in an otherwise featureless face.

"There," Lydia said, drawing his attention away from the pictographs. She pointed to a set of thick tree roots dangling over the cliff's edge. "They look sturdy enough. If you give me a boost, I think I can climb them."

Quinn twined his hands together and let her drop her heel in, just as he had done on the path to visit his mother. He tried not to be aware of the way her new trousers stretched around her hips, or her soft grunt as she pulled her body up, reminding him of the night he'd spent beside her, turned away so she wouldn't notice how hard her touch had made him.

They were alone in the woods with one weapon between them, pursued by the king's men, and if the trees hadn't tried to lure them into danger yet—he knew they were watching, waiting. But Quinn couldn't stop his thoughts from drifting to Lydia again and again.

It was going to get them both killed.

She found a stable place to perch and dropped a hand. It was enough to get a grip on the roots and climb to the next ledge as she had.

"Let me go first," he told her, eyeing the next path up. It was easy to access, and perhaps another ten feet up before the cliff's sheer edge gave way to a slope. "Need another boost?"

"I'm fine," Lydia said. Her expression was distant again, as though she was caught in a memory. A fine sheen of sweat made her hair stick to her forehead. There was no way they'd make it to the tower tonight. This trek was hard enough on him, and he'd spent years training both with Rai and the army.

She kept going before he could suggest they find a place to hide and rest, scaling the last few roots with surprising ease.

"My ex used to teach at this rock-climbing gym in Portland," she said, once Quinn reached her at the top. He understood almost none of her sentence, and Lydia didn't elaborate. She pulled the book from the inside of her jacket and turned to a dog-eared page while he scanned the area.

It was devoid of even that strange, echoing birdsong.

Odd, Quinn thought, before his eyes locked with another pair.

Gold, ringed in darkness, nestled into the face of a fox

as tall as him. What would normally be a white tuft of fur around its muzzle was black—a color that extended into the inside of its mouth and its teeth. It looked as though he could fall endlessly into that mouth, tumbling and tumbling without ever reaching the fox's stomach.

He heard Lydia cry out. The thud of the book hitting the ground. Then four caws came from the raven overhead.

Quinn had barely enough time to draw his weapon before the fox leaped, wild hunger on its face.

He was knocked to the ground by the blow, the fox's paws landing on his chest with such force it felt they might go through his sternum. Quinn struggled for a breath, barely dodging the fox's black teeth as they made for his throat. Somehow, he jabbed his bardiche into the creature's shoulder.

It was a sloppy shot with little momentum behind it, but at least the fox was momentarily distracted from its attempt to eat Quinn's face.

He tried to scramble away as the fox's left paw ground into his chest. The thing was too heavy for Quinn to heave off by himself. He attempted to shift the bardiche in his right hand, to get in a strike at the fox's throat or stomach.

A copper tang hit his nostrils, but there was no way his first hit had been deep enough to get through the fox's thick fur. He hoped it was his blood and not Lydia's.

The fox repositioned itself. The brief motion was not enough to give Quinn a chance to wriggle away. It did, however, offer him an opportunity to swing his right arm, striking the fox on the side of the neck.

It yowled, black spittle smelling of mulch, of rot, and of the corpses he sometimes had to tend when Brittlerun's undertaker was too hungover with fairy wine, flying into Quinn's face.

He struck again before the fox had the chance to recuperate, but a dreadful thought sunk into him. The beast's fur was good as armor, and he could not strike properly with most of his body pinned to the ground.

The fox's tongue darted out to taste the skin of his neck, but before it could take a bite, something hit its temple. It turned its attention to the left, eyes narrowed.

"Lydia, don't," Quinn wheezed. Another rock flew through the small clearing and hit the fox on the muzzle. The animal looked torn between the current prize beneath its paws and the attack from the side. It was enough to give him the chance to kick the fox in the stomach.

It growled, rearing up as Lydia sent another rock flying in its direction. "No! Stop!" she cried, her voice reverberating strangely.

The fox did.

For a moment, Quinn wondered if they were still on the boat. If they had fallen asleep beneath the makeshift tent, and he was simply dreaming of the horrors they'd encounter once they entered the forest. The fox huffed. Though it did not move from its perch on Quinn's chest, it stared in Lydia's direction, as if waiting for her to speak again.

"Get off him," she said.

Once more, the fox did as she commanded.

Not that it didn't display its frustration. It snorted and growled, sending another fine spray of black saliva into the air. Once Quinn dragged himself away, the fox pawed at the dirt as if to release the unspent energy in its muscles.

Quinn held the bardiche in front of him, circling the fox until he was between it and Lydia. The beast dropped back onto his haunches, black tongue lolling out the side of its mouth.

"What did you do?" he whispered.

"I don't know. She was growling about how starved she was. I thought I'd try to speak to her," Lydia said.

Before he could answer, Lydia raised her voice and addressed the fox again, "If you're hungry, soldiers are pursuing us. They won't be far from the cliff's edge."

A ripple of shock moved through him. It was a good idea, and the sharp edge in Lydia's voice made him forget he was bleeding through his undershirt. The fey might heal quickly, but there was a decent chance he'd need to stitch himself to get the skin to close.

The fox made a high-pitched noise, sounding more like a human whine than an animal cry. Then it lumbered back into the woods. Its tail was the last thing to disappear, tipped in black as its muzzle had been.

Lydia's knees gave out as soon as they could no longer hear twigs breaking beneath the fox's stride. He reached out to catch her without thinking, but she steadied herself before hitting the ground.

"Fuck, I'm sorry," she said, with a breathy laugh. "The adrenaline… I… I didn't think it would work."

She made no effort to move away from Quinn's arms. Her white hair tickled his cheek. Though it had been days since she'd escaped from Belimar's tower, it still smelled faintly of jasmine soap from her washing tub. It would have been enchanted, much like everything else in the Green Country, to hide the decay beneath.

It was only when the hand with which she held his forearm began glowing that she moved away, and brushed the dried leaves from her trousers. "So much for Isst's friend. We need to get going. Those scouts…"

"Lead the way," he said, missing the weight of her in his arms as soon as it was gone.

The Same Mote of Stardust

She was glad her muscles burned so much it was almost as if they were eating through her bones. It forced her to focus on navigating the narrow trails, giving her mind no time to wander to the way the forest came alive with whispers whenever she attempted to listen.

It wasn't simply the birds screaming to each other, or the fox, who had wept about hunger in a tender voice at odds with her monstrous body. The trees spoke slowly, though they mostly repeated a few messages. The first: *The Barrow King has returned.*

The Barrow King; Quinn. The trees spoke the words with no emotion or sign of why they were so interested in his presence.

Speaking of fey kings, her soreness was a decent distraction from the way it had felt to collapse against him. It wasn't just the solidness of his arms and shoulders, no doubt the result of swinging that bardiche around for years. She hadn't been able to wrap her head around that damn light between them, and it frightened her to admit how much she wanted to feel it again.

It was the one time she'd felt calm since coming to the Green Country and the only time she'd felt safe. Especially considering the other thing the trees liked to whisper was *her* name.

They'd heard the fox's high-pitched scream an hour ago—a piercing cry that had meant FINALLY, FINALLY, FOOD—but since then, the woods had been quiet and Isst hadn't sounded his alarm again.

"Lydia," Quinn said. She tried not to look at him unless absolutely necessary, but the breathlessness in his voice made her turn. An owl with glittering emerald eyes watched them from a low branch.

"I need to… the fox got in a good blow. I need to stitch myself up," he said. "There are some medical supplies in the satchel."

The pallor of his face was startling. Lydia was used to the beauty of the fey by now, even if she secretly preferred Quinn's features, which were less angular than his cousin's—a softness and roundness that were a gift from the Lady of the Lower World. But this was the first time she had seen one of the fey look ill. Pale blue veins spread across his throat like a spiderweb, and Lydia remembered the fox's black spittle. Could it have been venomous?

"My mother's blood gives me some extra resilience. I'll be fine. Truly. I just need to tend to the wound," he said. Lydia was beginning to resent the way he always seemed to know what she was thinking.

"There's a creek a few yards ahead. It might give us a chance to speak with Isst," she told him, having checked the book a few moments ago to make sure they were on the correct path.

Quinn nodded, his mouth fixed in a straight line.

The creek was wider than expected, offering a decent view of the sky. She tried to focus on searching for her raven as Quinn unbuttoned his shirt to examine the damage the fox had done.

"I don't suppose you learned how to stitch a wound in your library," he said, opening the satchel in his lap.

"In theory," she said, looking anywhere except for his exposed torso. Lydia had expected the toned muscle, but not the pale scars crisscrossing it. She knew Quinn was well-trained, considering how he'd stood his ground against Belimar, but this made her question exactly how many fights he had been in.

"Lydia?" he asked, as she realized her silence had gone on for too long. "It's fine if you don't want to. I can get most of it done myself."

"No. It's okay. I can help. I've read about wilderness medicine, and maybe you can talk me through it."

"I'll show you."

She rinsed her hands in the creek as he summoned a sphere of fire to sterilize the needle. That was another surprise. Lydia knew the fey used magic, and she'd seen plenty of spells cast by the Guild of Lightkeepers, but she'd never seen Quinn do anything more than mix herbs for tea.

"Hold the wound closed with your left hand, and suture with your right. Push the needle in at a ninety-degree angle, then twist your hand clockwise," he said, performing the motions on himself as he spoke. She realized too late she hadn't asked to borrow his gloves, and this meant their bare skin was about to touch.

Black streaks ran around the edges of his wound, and she could tell he was struggling to keep his hands steady. The odd angle wasn't likely to be the reason.

"Are you sure you're okay?" she asked, taking the needle from him once it was obvious he could no longer reach.

"I'm fine. I told you. My mother's blood gives me a few advantages over regular fey."

She tried not to let her hesitation show as she attempted the first stitch. It was more difficult to push the needle through his skin than she'd expected, but he muttered, "Good. You're doing good. Just repeat that another few times."

The glow started quickly this time; incomplete runes and sigils dancing beneath her fingers as she worked. She could feel Quinn's eyes on her, but had no idea if he was examining her stitches or the shimmering light. The warmth was achingly familiar, even if they'd only done this on purpose once before. It did not take long before the festering blackness around his wound receded, but she didn't know if it resulted from the light or Quinn's innate healing abilities.

At last, she tied off the final stitch. Her end wasn't nearly as neat as the ones he'd done, but at least the wound had closed. It was difficult to pull her hands away, though they were covered in blood. Lydia looked up to find Quinn staring at her with something like wonder on his face.

"I want to know more about it," she said, her voice a shaky whisper.

"About what?" Quinn asked though she had a feeling his obliviousness was a ruse. He was clever, she knew, and there were times their thoughts seemed to synchronize like a flock of birds navigating a storm in perfect formation.

"This light. These marks. You haven't told me everything because you're afraid of what I'll think. I need to know."

She finished wrapping his wound with a roll of cloth they'd found in the Avalon's stores. The light flared whenever her fingers met his skin, dancing in a flurry of circles and triangles—half-formed symbols as meaningless as an unspoken word.

"I told you, I'm not sure," Quinn said. He winced as he moved, but his voice remained steady.

"Stop trying to protect me. I already have Isst to tell me my curiosity is going to get me killed someday."

Quinn sighed as he rolled his tunic down, and Lydia realized she should have taken more time to look at the pale scars on his torso, the lean muscles of his abdomen, and the trail of dark hair disappearing below his trousers.

"I told you almost everything I know," he said, after some consideration.

"Almost everything?"

"It isn't actually an appropriate conversation to have with a woman you've just met. A woman who isn't with you of her own accord."

Lydia sat back on her heels. She'd always assumed the Green Country was a place of excess. The books in her library were filled with tales of fairy wine, food, and seduction. Quinn's reticence unnerved her.

"Whatever it is, I'll be fine, I promise."

He leaned over to re-pack their supplies as he spoke, voice clinical. "The Aés-Caill were about as hedonistic as my fey cousins. The mating bond is supposed to be… unique, even among the dwellers of the Green Country. A connection unlike any other."

"You mean sex?"

He shrugged, but she didn't miss the way his hands flexed around the satchel. "Sure, but not merely that. There's a phrase for it, even among the modern fey. Ia hai ves-ka gain aber-la elvesalai."

"We were born from the same mote of stardust," she said, recognizing that he had briefly switched to what was perhaps an older dialect.

"Two halves of a whole, reunited after an eternity apart," Quinn went on. He'd gone back to what she thought of as his sawbones voice. Distant. Unaffected. As if he was delivering the grim news of a diagnosis.

"But…" Lydia began, already knowing there was nothing Quinn could say next that wouldn't cause her pain. And why? Because she would either die in this realm or leave it? The library had always made her feel safe, but this wouldn't be the first time she wondered what her life would have been like if she'd made a different choice. She could have stayed in Portland, blissfully unaware of the fey realm. Or she might have demanded a different job at the compound. Surely, with her skills, she would have qualified for one of the teams Francesco was apparently sending into the Green Country.

Everything could have been different had she come here of her own accord.

"I don't know anything else, I swear. If we ever make it back to my mother's lake, we can ask her. Right now, we have to keep moving."

Lydia nodded, then she realized he hadn't mentioned taking her back to the window, and worse, she hadn't thought about it. He paused, looking at the sky.

"What is it?" she asked again, her voice so low it was nearly lost among the rustling trees.

"I'm not sure…"

Four caws sounded from above, and Quinn was on his feet before she dropped the needle. It bounced into the creek to be swept away by the current. He didn't bother to button his shirt, only grabbed his bardiche and the satchel, slinging the latter over his shoulder.

"This way," Lydia said. A part of her hoped the fox had killed all of Belimar's soldiers, and another wished its high yips of joy simply meant it'd found a deer. She had never expected to have to kill anyone, even after being brought to the Green Country. Sending the fox after them had been as good as murder.

LYDIA REYES WILL KILL THE FEY KING.

No time to think about that now.

Isst swooped beside her as they ran, weaving through the trees low and deft, as he used to fly between bookshelves. "I'm sorry! They have scholars with them—they used a glamour to hide this time."

There was not enough breath in her lungs to speak, but she told herself again that she trusted Isst. He had been her closest companion for years. The Guild's enchantments prevented him from causing the changelings any harm, though stories of fey trickery ran through her mind. Quinn had warned her of their skill with wordplay, with evading the terms of a binding, but she had known that even before coming to the Green Country.

Lydia had never doubted Isst before. His wings sounded a heavy beat as he disappeared again.

She knew without having to check that she'd led them in the wrong direction. The woods looked relatively uniform until now, matching the images the Mapmaker's guide conjured in her head, but the trees here were larger than any she'd seen in the book. Their upper branches tangled together to form a massive dome, blocking out the sky.

"Quinn," she whispered, but he urged her on— forward, in any direction.

"It doesn't matter. Just go."

They passed the first structure that was not a shipwreck. A small cabin, so covered in climbing vines it was hardly noticeable among the trees. A sprawling pumpkin patch surrounded it, full of plump gourds gleaming with dew. A sudden pull in her gut urged her to kneel in the dirt and tear into one of the pumpkins until she could get to the sweet flesh underneath, but a hand encircled her wrist before she succumbed.

"Enchantments. It's a trap. Keep moving," Quinn said.

"Wait! This would be a good place to rest," Lydia told him, horrified by the words as they came out of her mouth. She had felt fairy magic in the tower and again on the bridge, but this was the first time her bones seemed to move on their own.

A speckled pair of golden eyes watched them from the window.

"*Keep moving*," he snapped.

She tried to yank her arm away, so she could kneel in the curled vines of the garden, but he held fast. "We'd be safe here. Can't you see that?" she cried.

"My mother's blood protects me from glamours. I'll show you how to do it too. Let's go! I'll carry you if I have to."

The light between them shimmered at Lydia's wrist and she blinked, the dreamy warmth replaced by panic. She cast another glance at the cabin and saw it was nothing but a rotting tree stump, atop which an enormous toad watched, its long tongue wagging with anticipation.

"Gods," she muttered, finally able to get her feet moving. She couldn't leave without telling the toad to go fuck itself.

"Oh, very nice. You're the ones who wandered into *my* clearing," the toad answered.

They were moving too quickly. Every broken branch and footprint in the mud would be another way for Cithral to track them. Even if this company failed to catch her and Quinn, Belimar would send in more men.

"We can't outrun them forever," she panted. "We need to confuse the trail. Let's double back to the creek."

"What? We'll be heading *toward* them," Quinn said.

"We're lost. Running water will throw off their trackers. The creek is a good landmark, and we can walk in it without leaving footprints."

She hadn't spent as much time with the library's naturalist guidebooks as she should have, although to be fair, she'd never expected to be kidnapped by the fey and set to wander in an enchanted forest.

Quinn looked at Lydia for a long moment, his darkgreen eyes locked with hers. She had no idea why it *ached* so much to maintain eye contact with him. Why every time she wasn't worried about dying, her mind drifted to the warmth spreading through her whenever they touched. It was his grip on her wrist that'd chased the toad's magic from her mind.

She'd wonder about that later.

"Fine," Quinn breathed. "I can remember the way back. Let me lead."

It was only a few steps before a voice cut through the woods.

"Kill the sawbones! We need the girl alive," someone shouted.

An arrow whizzed past Quinn's head.

Lydia barely processed what happened before his body was over hers. The small clearing where they'd paused made them easy targets. They ducked into the forest together, Lydia's hand clasped around Quinn's forearm. A thin trail of blood seeped from the wound on his side, but thankfully, the stitches held.

They ran without direction, weaving through the forest in zig-zags. She felt a tug as they again passed the many-eyed toad on his stump, but with her hand on

Quinn's arm, there were no gleaming pumpkins to tempt her.

She couldn't keep track of how many voices were in the woods behind them. Perhaps a few soldiers would be snapped up by the toad, but Belimar had sent a full company of men to chase them. Even if Quinn could stand against the king in single combat, one fey with a bardiche could never hold an army back.

She pictured the library. The books on tracking. On army tactics. The section about forestry that October visited frequently. But it was her self-taught chemistry lessons that caught Lydia's attention.

An arrow hit one of the trees behind them with a thud.

"I have an idea. Are we moving back to the creek?" she managed.

"I think so."

"I saw saltpeter and sugar in our supply bag. The fire you summoned. Can you do it again?"

He nodded, as though he didn't need to hear more.

Isst cawed overhead, but the forest was still too dense to spot him. They passed a familiar tree resembling a withered old man, leaning on a cane near where the fox had attacked them. The glimmer of wet rocks glistened like stars in the forest's darkness.

The soldiers' voices faded. It was harder to move through dense forest in a large group, but she knew it would not be long before they caught up.

"Give me the satchel," Quinn said. "You get a head start. Stick to the creek and don't stop, no matter what. Don't head into the trees. I'll be right behind you."

The thought of separating made her jaw clench, but she would not be able to move as easily as Quinn once the chemical reaction began.

It was quicker than she expected. She heard the spark

of magic, and a billowing cloud of white smoke mush-roomed from the place he'd stood. Her damp boots splashed into the water, and she heard a voice that did not belong to one of the soldiers.

"I'm here. Let's end this," Quinn called through the mist.

Idiot, Lydia thought. She kept moving. The improvised smoke bomb engulfed the forest behind her and expanded quickly. Soon she was surrounded by the thick cloud, and only able to navigate by the water rushing beneath her.

Confused shouts rang out from behind. Her heart raced, and not merely from the effort of traversing the creek. Quinn might have abilities beyond that of a normal fey, but this wasn't an enchantment. He'd be just as hindered.

"Lydia, where are you?" she heard from overhead. Isst wasn't visible through the dense smoke, and she bit her tongue to keep from calling back and giving her position away.

She ran until her lungs were too exhausted to keep pumping. Ran until her legs shook and were as brittle as matchsticks. She'd outpaced the smoke bomb with her head start, and could barely see a handful of trees when she looked back. Even those were misty and wavering like ghosts.

Lydia finally allowed herself to fold and attempt to get her breathing under control. She was too exhausted to react when Isst landed on a stump beside her and clicked his beak.

"Where's Quinn?" she panted.

"I don't know. The smoke was too thick. I was only able to follow you because I could hear the creek."

Are you lying to me? she wondered, feeling both guilty and panicked at the thought. Isst had been her closest confidant for so long. He would look for Quinn if she asked, but then what? Would he lead Quinn to her or Belimar?

"This friend of yours hasn't made an appearance," she said instead because it gave her another moment to think. Lydia was alone in the Green Country, alone in this wood full of terrors, and the one fey she might be able to trust was missing.

"He's been with you the whole time. I told you, he's shy."

"We were attacked by a fox. Quinn was badly hurt. We've been pursued by soldiers. I was nearly eaten by a toad. You said he would help us," she snapped, anger leaking through.

"Only once, when he believes the time is right. His judgment of what constitutes danger differs greatly from yours," Isst said.

She glared at him.

Isst ruffled his feathers, a shudder going through his small body. "I'm sorry. I've been doing my best, but this wood doesn't like the bindings the Guild put on me. It's been testing my defenses, if you will."

"You can go back to the window if you need to. Find some way to tell Francesco I'm alive," she said. The thought of being here without Isst was terrifying, even if she was no longer sure how much trust to put in him.

"No. You're my changeling. I'll be by your side until you're safely home, and then you can find me a nice dead squirrel for all my trouble. Keep moving. I scouted ahead and there's a small cave where you may camp for the night. You shouldn't travel in the Sorrowood after dark. I'll find Quinn."

The raven took off before she could protest. Lydia forced herself off a small boulder and took a few shaky steps in the water. It had been a long time since she'd heard shouting. There was nothing except for the persistent whisper of the trees.

"Don't you ever shut up?" she muttered and was surprised when the trees answered.

No.

She whirled at a splash from behind her to find a reasonably sized frog chasing a dragonfly. Lydia wished she had a weapon, even just a stick, but hearing the trees whisper made her hesitant to break a small branch from one.

The sound of someone chuckling came from nearby.

"There she is. The princess who escaped her tower."

Her stomach dropped. It was not Quinn's voice, but she recognized it all the same.

"Belimar was so angry when you were snatched out from under his nose. He blamed me for not anticipating the rebel attack."

Cithral stepped from the forest's dappled shadows. His eyes were a cold blue, rimmed with red from smoke. His face was swollen and a healing bruise the color of seawater spread across his left cheek, obscuring the scar.

Lydia shuddered, but gave no other indication she understood him.

Run, she told herself, but the facts were depressingly obvious.

Cithral was faster, stronger, and had sharper senses than she did. He also had more experience traveling in the woods.

"It was a neat trick, the smoke," he went on, drawing a short sword from the sheath on his hip. "Did you or the sawbones think of it? I want to know who to thank. It was a good excuse to send my men off in the wrong direction, so I could have the pleasure of chasing you myself."

She shook her head as if she had no idea what he was

saying. *Could I call the fox back?* she wondered. *And even if I did, would she get here in time?*

There was no choice but to run. Cithral laughed as she stumbled away, tripping on a damp log across the creek. He showed no urgency as he followed her, his polished sword reflecting the teal of the water.

Lydia forced herself upright, abandoning the creek in favor of the woods.

"Go ahead, run. I serve the Hunter King. The chase makes the catching all the sweeter," Cithral called after her.

Lydia Reyes, the Sorrowood whispered, as mocking as ever. *Whatever will you do now?*

Branches cut into her skin. A flock of magpies, cackling in delight, followed her path, eager to feast on what they thought would soon be a corpse.

The sizzling anger inside of her was not directed at Cithral or even Belimar. It was directed at this fucking forest.

You wouldn't be here if it wasn't for me. It was my pain that created you. This place took me from my family and turned my hair white. I've spent nearly all my life hiding in a library, she thought, trying to ignore the sound of Cithral's boots crushing dead leaves. He was right behind her. If he wanted, one swing of his sword and she'd be dead.

Oh? How shall we repay you? the trees answered. It was the first time they'd said anything other than Lydia's name or Quinn's title, but the stink of Cithral's traveling clothes and the sound of his sword cutting through brambles was much more pressing.

He caught her by the ponytail, yanking her back. In a desperate attempt, Lydia reached for his sword, hoping he might be surprised enough by her boldness to let it slip, but there was no such luck.

"Enough of that," he said, breath hot against her neck. He brought a hand to her hips, then her chest, letting it linger even after he reached for the book beneath her armor.

Binds wrapped around her chest and ankles, shimmering with golden magic. Struggling against them was futile, for they tightened as she fought. She cried out as Cithral spun her and tossed her over his shoulder, hoping someone would hear. Quinn. Isst. Even the fox. But there were only the trees.

A wild thought came to her.

"You're right, you owe me a debt!" she managed in English, though Cithral's shoulder ground into her stomach. "

"I told Belimar this girl was mad," he muttered, readjusting his grip as he took a step toward the creek.

She ignored him. "You exist because the Mapmaker used *my* blood to open his windows. You owe me. I've come to collect."

Is that so, little changeling? the trees whispered. *There are so many other things you could ask for. We could reunite you and the Barrow King. We could send you an elk that would carry you safely home.*

"My captor! Kill him!"

She rarely had control over which language she was speaking unless she focused. Lydia did now. She used the language of the fey. Cithral had done all he could to strike fear into her heart. It was time to pay back that debt as well.

"Who are you speaking to, girl? Your sawbones is already captured. They've likely lobbed his head off with an iron sword already," he said, with a soft grunt as she attempted to knee him in the chest.

Are you certain? the trees whispered.

"*Yes*. Kill him."

She didn't see the reason Cithral stumbled, but Lydia went with him, falling over his shoulder onto a patch of rotten leaves. Although the bindings on her wrists and ankles held fast, she wiggled to her knees and spotted the fey attempting to do the same. A tree root took hold of his legs, but his sword arm was free and he plunged it into the bark. A mass of oily black sap welled to the surface.

"What is this? What have you done, witch?" he gasped, as a branch lashed out to wrap around his throat.

Lydia forced her eyes to stay locked on Cithral as she backed away. It was different with the fox. She had only sent it in the direction of the soldiers and hadn't been there to see the blood that spilled as its black jaws clamped down on them.

"Wait," she said to the trees. "Stop. I changed my mind."

Cithral's short sword fell, landing with a soft thud. With his free hand, he pulled a hunting knife from his boot and drove it into the branch constricting his throat. Although it released another spray of sap, it did not loosen.

We liked you better when you were a savage little beast, the trees said. *What's done is done.*

She reached for the sword, but with her hands twisted and bound, it was difficult to lift. A hole in the nearest tree, which looked like an animal's burrow, began expanding. Cithral seemed to realize he was being dragged toward it and thrashed against his binds. His lips were pale blue. The hunting knife tumbled from his fingers and joined a cluster of white mushrooms on the forest floor.

Lydia watched as the hole expanded like a gaping mouth. Cithral's scream was abruptly cut off as the roots dragged him in, and the hole closed. Then came a horrible crunch—like an axe plunging into a tree or many bones breaking at once.

After that, silence.

The gap shrank back into something no more innocuous than a woodpecker's nesting hollow.

Even the trees lapsed into a satisfied quiet.

The only sound was Lydia's ragged sobbing.

Debts and Balances

The enhancement spell he whispered as the reaction began worked far better than Quinn expected.

His father's blood was to thank for that. Quinn always had a talent for magic, though he rarely used it himself. Magic was finicky, and nothing was free in the Green Country. Plenty could be achieved with a rudimentary knowledge of chemistry or alchemy. A vial of Quicksilver might be dangerous, but it didn't *mean* you any harm.

Magic could. That was the difference.

Smoke engulfed the forest. He dropped to all fours, but it was impossible to see past his outstretched arm. A part of him had hoped, with little reason, that his talents for seeing and breathing underwater would somehow extend to this situation.

They hadn't.

Quinn tried to focus on the sound of the creek, as the soldiers who'd surrounded him moments ago were thrown into a panic. They called to each other, shouting names and instructions no one heeded. All he needed to do was to locate the water and follow it until he caught up to Lydia.

The thought of her alone in the woods made him feel like he'd been hit in the stomach. Keeping her safe was a vow he'd known he wouldn't be able to keep in the Sorrowood, but it hadn't stopped him from coming up with a thousand ways in which he might torture Belimar if she didn't get out of this alive. A good medic knew *so* many interesting things a body could endure.

A sphere of green light glowed through the smoke, closer than he would have liked.

"She went that way. Follow the flare," Cithral called.

That couldn't be right. He'd *seen* Lydia follow the path they'd agreed on. Had she doubled back for some reason?

A silhouette drifted past, but Quinn went unnoticed. He groped ahead, hoping for water, but only dirt and wood rot and a fleshy pile of shelf mushrooms knocked from their log lay in his path.

Finally, his fingers met damp rocks, and someone drove their boot into his back.

"Found the sawbones!"

Rai's voice filled Quinn's head. It was a younger Rai, who'd arrived unexpectedly in the small town of Brittlerun and shoved a bardiche into Quinn's hand. "Learn to use this as if your life depends on it because someday, it might."

He drew his weapon and rolled onto his back. The smoke was so thick, Quinn did not see the face the soldier made when the bardiche struck his ribcage. The fey crumpled to the ground with a spray of blood. It was a good hit and the soldier cried out before falling.

I have to move, Quinn thought. The company's silhouettes were close enough to make out their bows and swords. His one relief was that it was unlikely they would release arrows while in the cloud of smoke. Or so he thought until one thudded into the decaying log to his right.

"Idiots," he muttered. He'd been with Belimar's army long enough to know how well-trained the king's soldiers were. They might not all have experience in the Sorrowood, but they'd sparred in almost every condition.

The thought that something *made* the archer loose an arrow urged Quinn to crawl faster. He'd known the smoke would agitate the trees. He'd always felt connected to the Sorrowood. Perhaps it was his mother's blood. Even these trees needed water to grow, and she had been born in a puddle from the first storm to sweep across the Green Country.

"Where is he?"

"The trees are disrupting my magic. We need another flare!"

The latter voice was that of a scholar Quinn recognized from the king's inner circle. Allinus, a war magician. One of the few men Belimar considered too valuable for their previous expedition into the woods.

If he was here now, Belimar must be angry.

Good, Quinn thought.

He stood, wondering if he was now far enough away to run without being noticed. Another arrow flew over his head, but this time, Quinn was certain it hadn't been aimed at him. The soldiers continued to shout in a layered chorus of words that made no sense.

It did not pay to be curious in this forest. Better to run now and live to wonder about what had happened in the smoke.

"There you are, sawbones," a voice said.

Quinn whirled. Although he had never seen Allinus in person, he recognized the black robes with the glowing red crest the war magicians in Belimar's company all wore.

The magician's ears were long, even for a fey, though one had been torn off in battle, leaving a scarred stump, and his pale green hair was tied back in elaborate braids.

Quinn's heart beat once, but not again. It felt like the blood in his chest had hardened. He couldn't move. Couldn't swing his bardiche. Couldn't blink the smoke out of his eyes. The magic he'd inherited from his mother strained to push off the spell, but it was like trying to shake off his skin.

"I'm a scholar before a soldier, half-breed," Allinus said. "Your mother's blood can't save you. I look forward to studying it."

Allinus did not turn at a sudden bout of screaming from the smoke, but he raised a slender eyebrow. "A pity I won't have time to interrogate you about *that* little trick. At least I get to test out one of my newest projects."

The magician raised his hands and silver strands of magic wove between them like thread. Allinus separated one and with a nod sent it flying in Quinn's direction. It pierced Quinn like a needle, burrowing into his veins. As the fiery pain flared inside him, he realized exactly what Allinus intended to do: tear Quinn to shreds from the inside.

No, Quinn tried to say. He knew he might die on this mission, but not like this. Not until he'd gotten Lydia to the tower and then safely home. Gods, Lydia. Out in the woods on her own. His friend. His—his…

The pain stopped, and Quinn attempted a strike. Even though it was a clumsy attack, the magician was less than a few feet away. It should have hit.

Instead, Quinn's bardiche only parted smoke.

Something had struck Allinus from the side, knocking him to the ground.

The smoke here was thinner than where he'd set off

the bomb. A shadow emerged, but he had less than an instant to register its towering height and long claws before it sank them into Allinus's shoulders and dragged him away.

Was this the friend Isst had promised? With its speed, the creature could have taken Quinn out as easily as he did Allinus, but it hadn't.

A raven's caw came from above as Quinn stood there, gaping at the space where Allinus had stood half a second before. The pain of the needle rushing through him returned, but the sensation was like being woken from a dream by a slap across the face.

He needed to move.

An idea came to him. The creature was obviously an ancient thing, bound by codes of honor and rules that were a mystery, even to the fey. Making a bargain with it would be wildly foolish, but if the thing was rational enough to obey Isst's requests, perhaps it would reason with Quinn.

"Wait. I need to ask something of you," he called. "I know of your bargain with Isstalmanud. I wish to make another. One that will lead you to a feast even greater than this."

The shadow paused to listen. After Quinn said his piece, it nodded, long claws clicking together like an affirmation.

Quinn grabbed the satchel torn from Allinus's back, ignoring the distant screams. The smoke cleared as he ran, searching for a sign of Lydia's trail along the creek side.

The raven flew low beside him. When Quinn cried, "Take me to her!" a glimmer of understanding flickered in the bird's eye.

IT WAS NOT LYDIA'S TRAIL HE FOUND, BUT CITHRAL'S.

A soldier's heavy footprint left in the mud. Scars on trees where a sword was drawn in a tight space.

Then he heard her. A choked cry that made him feel like Allinus's needle had made its way into the valves of his heart. He ran, no longer following the raven, but the sound of her voice. If Cithral had touched her… if he'd hurt her…

Her sobs stopped abruptly, but Quinn did not. He pushed through the woods, not bothering to watch for any creatures that might be nearby. He found her alone, kneeling, with her hands and feet bound. The jab of panic returned, but he realized two things. One, Lydia was holding a sword between her tied hands. And two, it was Cithral's.

"Quinn," she breathed, and though her eyes were still pink from tears, her words were steady. "Get me out of these binds."

"Where is he?" Quinn asked, rushing to her side. It was simple magic. A few snips with his fingers and the golden threads unraveled and dissolved. Lydia wiped her face with the back of her hand, smearing mud across her forehead.

"Dead," she said. "He's dead, I… *Oh.*"

She let out a puff of air as he embraced her. Her shoulders tightened.

Quinn drew away, realizing what he'd done, how rashly he'd acted, but Lydia's hands were on his arms a moment later, pulling him back in.

"Sorry," she muttered in his chest. "There was a sword between us. A really sharp sword. I was afraid it was going to…"

She laughed, a slightly delirious noise that Quinn wasn't prepared to analyze in either the medical or personal sense. He reached for her face, tracing the soft line of her jaw as golden light danced between them. The warmth eased the pain in his arm and side.

We're alive. We're both alive.

Lydia moved her head away and drew her hands back. She reached for the short sword wordlessly and tucked it into the empty scabbard that'd come with her armor.

Just what had Lydia done to Cithral?

It was a question for later. "You don't have to carry it," he said.

"Yes, I do. We should get moving. Isst told me there's a place to camp up ahead. The other soldiers…?"

Quinn swallowed unsure what the bitter taste in his mouth meant. "Gone. Belimar will send more, but they won't want to travel in the woods at night any more than we do."

Lydia nodded, meeting his gaze again before turning to the forest. Blood stuck to her face and her white hair. Her dark eyes shone as brilliantly as the sword at her side—the sword of a fey general, baptized in the blood of a thousand battles, taken as a prize by the mortal girl who'd felled him.

Quinn realized he was almost as afraid of her as he was of the window, the wood, and the army at its doorstep.

It thrilled him.

"ISST SAYS HIS FRIEND HELPED YOU," LYDIA TOLD HIM, settling down on a soft clump of moss. They were in the mouth of a shallow cave, no more than twenty feet deep. The sounds the wind made as it curved and curled around the rocks reminded Quinn of the muffled cries of soldiers falling one by one in the smoke. Still, it was a decent place to camp and at least their sides and back would be protected by a wall of stone.

Whatever had been in the smoke with them had been quick and stealthy in a way he'd never seen, even among the creatures of the Sorrowood. In the calm of this moment, he wondered if the bargain he'd struck with it would cost more than what he was willing to pay.

Quinn couldn't see Lydia's raven now. The forest was too dark and the bird's feathers too black, but he heard the occasional rustle as Isst dozed in the trees.

"He wasn't lying. His friend *was* with us all this time," she went on.

Quinn bit his tongue. It wasn't fair to argue now, not after she'd told him the full of what had happened to Cithral. He remembered the first time he'd been responsible for a death.

There'd been a young expectant mother in Brittlerun, who'd gone into labor three months early, while his mentor was away. She'd bled and bled, and nothing he'd tried—even magic—could stop it. In the end, he'd had to make a choice. Save her or the child. He'd spent the night pressing a cool rag against her feverish head, assuring her nothing could have been done to bring her son into the world alive.

"I'm sorry. You must think I'm so naive," Lydia whispered, perhaps catching his skeptical expression. "I have to trust Isst. I *have* to."

A small fairy light hung between them, bobbing like a will-o-the-wisp. Quinn wished for the warmth of a fire, but Belimar was sure to send out another company at dawn, and the wood smoke would travel in the wind. Thankfully, Allinus's satchel was well-stocked and contained a canteen of fresh water that never seemed to get any lighter. Strips of elk jerky. A few small flasks of oil, liquor, and a shimmering substance Quinn promptly stashed away, recognizing it as a sleeping draft.

"I don't think that at all. If it wasn't for you, we both

would have died," he said.

"You're hurt. Do you want me to redo your stitches?"

He shook his head. "It's all right. The wound is nearly healed."

"There's something else I need to tell you. When Cithral grabbed me, I panicked. I called out to the trees like I did to the fox, and it *worked*. The forest listened."

Quinn sat quietly with this revelation, hoping she would spare him the pain of having to choose which of the thousand questions in his mind to ask next.

"Before you ask, I already told the Sorrowood to stop spreading, but it won't. Nor will it stop the next wave of Belimar's men for us. I'm half-convinced it only killed Cithral out of some strange sense of gratitude for the curse we…"

She paused, watching her hands as she absently picked dirt from beneath her fingernails.

"Best you don't ask the trees for anything else unless it's absolutely necessary. Remember, nothing is free—"

"In the Green Country," she finished. "I know. It's just the strangest thing. I don't think the Sorrowood is the curse. No. I think the Sorrowood *is* cursed."

They sat in silence until Lydia asked, "Tell me about your home."

The question surprised him. She always seemed eager to learn what she could about the Green Country, but she hadn't pried into his personal life, even after he revealed he was technically the rightful king of Astoria and the North-western Court.

"Brittlerun was a kind place, and my mother was less than a few hours' hike away. I enjoyed living there. Liked hunting and fishing and learning about herbs. When my friends left to join Belimar's rebellion against my father, I didn't blame them. Llewel was weak. Not a cruel ruler, but an ineffectual one—the farmers and foragers outside the city suffered most from the way he ignored the Sorrowood."

"Did you ever know him?"

"I met him once when I was a child. He came to Brittlerun, disguised as a nobleman seeking an elixir for his wife's infertility. It was a short conversation. He pushed a satchel of coins into my hand, told me I looked like my mother and warned me that if I ever came to Astoria to claim my birthright, I'd be beheaded. I have to admit, I'm curious about you as well. What sort of human woman lives near a window into the Green Country with a raven for company?"

Lydia dropped her chin onto her knees and looked up at him. The fairy light danced across her face, illuminating the softness of her jaw. Quinn's mouth felt dry and an odd ringing drummed in his ears. He had been truthful when he said his wound was nearly healed, but that didn't mean something inside of him didn't *hurt*.

Till the king drives his sword
Through his queen's beating heart
And the wood and its mother
Are no longer apart.

Why in all the hells wouldn't that song leave him alone? Even after she had commanded the fox, he'd convinced himself the old prophecy was meaningless. But now...

Lydia began to speak. "You already know I was a changeling. One of thirteen girls, stolen from their homes in the night and taken to the Green Country. The following year, twelve of us returned. The parents of the missing girl—the Onners—were desperate to study us. They built a massive home near the window, where they poked and prodded until they realized we didn't hold the secret to bringing their daughter home."

"I'm sorry," Quinn said.

"Don't be. It was a fine life, for the most part. I had the library and Isst, and after the Onners died in a sailing accident, the man who took over was more concerned with the window than us changelings. He gave us money and identification papers, then said we were free to join the rest of the world."

Quinn wasn't sure what identification papers were, but Lydia mentioned it so casually he was embarrassed to ask. "And did you?" he said instead.

"For a while," she went on, with a throaty laugh that made something in him tighten. "I guess I wasn't cut out for it. I drank too much, had my heart broken, and less than a year later, I was back at the Guild's doorstep, begging for a job. Pretty pathetic."

It was his turn to give a low chuckle. "Hardly. You tricked the king of the fey *and* you defeated his high general. You have influence over these woods, which have kept the Green Country in fear for decades."

Although her smile seemed genuine, there was a distance in her eyes, visible even in the dim glow of the fairy light. She pulled his cloak more tightly around her shoulders, but her hands were shaking too much for her to fasten the pin.

"May I?" he asked, feeling foolish. It wasn't as though the army had afforded him time to chase after potential partners, but he had never felt so laid bare in front of anyone before. The worst of it was, he wasn't sure *what* he wanted. There was an urge to touch her, to feel that warmth again. He wanted to know what her hair felt like, and if she would give another throaty laugh if he pressed his mouth against hers.

But then what?

Lydia wanted to return to her world. She'd made that very clear. And if the song was indeed a prophecy, a real prophecy, it meant...

No. He wouldn't dwell on that now. He'd reach the tower and find some other way to close the window.

It was a surprise when she captured his hands before he pulled them away from the clasp. Her palms were rough, but wonderfully so, dotted with writing calluses. She watched the glow slowly appear, her shoulders relaxing as warmth flooded her body.

"Sorry," she whispered, without pulling away. "I'm so cold. It's the only thing that helps."

"It's okay," he said, well-aware of how choked his voice sounded. Lydia didn't react.

"It's not. I'm about to do something foolish," she said.

"You are?"

"You're absolutely ridiculous, do you know that? A prince-turned-sawbones with a mother who lives at the bottom of a lake. I don't know if I'll ever make it back to that window, Quinn. I might end up dying here after all, and... I've been thinking about what you said. Ia hai ves-ka gain aber-la elvesalai. The same mote of stardust. If I'm going to die, then I need to *touch* someone and you're the only one who—Gods, I'm rambling, aren't I?"

Runes moved across her skin like strange, incomplete tattoos.

"Funny," she continued in a ragged voice that made Quinn's cock tighten. "Like this, I feel like I might... *control* the light."

He understood what she meant. It felt like there was a massive golden bell hanging in front of him, begging to be rung, and if he just reached out, its rich tone would sound out across the Sorrowood, driving all the monsters away.

"Don't try. Not here. It's too dangerous."

"Then, kiss me. It's all that will chase the notion from my head."

He couldn't say who moved first. Their hands stayed entwined as he pressed his mouth against hers, running his tongue along her lower lip. When he finally found the strength to let go of her hands, it was only so he could cup the back of her neck, tilting her head for better access.

Quinn closed his eyes. The shimmer between them still danced in the darkness, now brighter than the fairy light and almost hot enough to sear his skin. He wanted to know what it would be like if he pulled both of their clothes off and pressed their bodies together.

He was half-hard beneath his trousers, and Lydia gasped as she pulled herself onto his lap. As Quinn wondered if he should apologize, she rolled her hips, grinding down on his cock with delicious pressure. He hesitated to lower his hands from her waist to her ass, but she reached for his wrists and pushed them down herself.

They'd laid the thin bedroll from Allinus's satchel on the cave floor. Both he and Lydia laughed when they fell onto it as she straddled his hips. Quinn suddenly wished they were back on the Avalon, or even in his medical tent. She deserved better than a quick screw atop hard rocks.

"Maybe we should—" he began, but Lydia only kissed him harder and moved against him in a steady rhythm. Her voice was hypnotic as she whispered against his mouth. "Tomorrow. Tomorrow, we can both come to the conclusion that this was a bad idea and never speak of it again. Today, I killed a man. I commanded the woods, and they obeyed. We might both be dead before we see another sunset, and I need to feel something good."

It was lucky she couldn't see his eyes. Quinn knew the words hadn't been meant to hurt. She'd been clear this was merely a distraction from the horrors of the Sorrowood, but why did it feel like the warmth rushed out of him?

Still, when he looked up, their shared light surrounded her like an aura, tangled in her pale hair, illuminating the two freckles on her left cheek, her kiss-bruised lips, and the small scar just below her hairline he hadn't noticed before. Runes and sigils swirled across her skin. Her words didn't matter. He would give her anything she wanted, even if it destroyed him.

"Lay on your back," he said roughly. A look of confusion crossed her face, but she allowed herself to be pulled down so he could reverse their places. Her tunic was nearly translucent in the light emanating from beneath her skin. He took in the softness of her stomach, the lower curve of her breasts, picturing how they would move as he fucked her.

"May I?" he asked again, this time running his thumb along the button of her trousers. It was an effort to keep his voice easy, casual, as he reminded himself she wanted nothing more than release.

"Gods, yes. Please," she said.

His smile was more genuine than he cared to admit. "So eager. You've just won your first victory in battle. I thought you might try to challenge me next."

She smiled too, and Quinn was certain the warmth filling his heart had little to do with the shimmer dancing between them.

"Only when you least expect it, Barrow King."

He helped her wiggle the trousers off, and his cock ached at the sight of her full thighs and the tuft of pale hair between her legs. Now that she was half-naked, the glow moved across her like moonlight shimmering on a lake. Quinn wondered if it was happening to him as well, but he was distracted from asking by the way she arched her back when he ran the back of his hand up her inner thigh.

Till the king drives his sword
Through his queen's beating heart

No, he told himself. Don't think about that now.

An involuntary moan left his mouth as he discovered how wet she was already. Her hips lifted at his touch, demanding more. He'd intended to make her come with his hands, but as his fingers slid into her, he realized he wanted something else.

"May I kiss you here?" he asked, surprised at his voice. He sounded less like one of the fey and more like one of his mother's people—the half-beasts lurking in the world's remaining shadows.

"That's the best idea you've had all evening," she said.

Quinn could agree with that.

Her nails slid against his scalp as he kissed his way down her stomach, pausing to deliver a gentle bite to her hipbone. Then, he sank lower and was delighted to learn she tasted as lovely as he'd imagined. There was her warm human scent, but also something like rain, like wildflowers, and all the promise of spring. He wanted to bury himself in it.

This is an act of worship, he thought, feeling slightly delirious. They moaned together as he pressed his tongue against her clit, again and again.

"Quinn, I'm going too—"

The sound of his name in her mouth, full of desperation, was almost enough to get him off on its own. He gave a satisfied hum, slipping two fingers into her, just in time to feel her clenching around them as she climaxed.

He didn't stop until she clutched his hair and dragged

him upward, her body twitching against his. Lydia's free hand made its way to the bulge in his trousers. It made him feel off-balance in the sweetest way possible.

"Nothing in the Green Country is free. Let me return the favor," she said between kisses, using his waistband to drag him closer. As her dark eyes met his, he forced himself to rise, coming to sit back on his heels. Every part of his body screamed in protest. It had been so long since he'd been touched like this. For it to be Lydia, her eyes wild and wanting beneath pale eyelashes, was nearly enough to shatter him.

"Another night. I want to savor you properly," he told her, careful to keep any malice out of his voice.

This wasn't her fault. She'd been clear about her intentions, and Quinn had thought he could tuck his traitorous heart away for long enough to please them both. But looking at her now, he realized something very important.

What bound them was something even more ancient than the fey. If he allowed this to continue, he'd let the damn forest take over the whole of the Green Country if it meant she'd never ask him to return her to her world again.

"There might not be another night," she said. He hated the doubt in her voice.

"Don't worry about me. You need to rest," he told her, tucking her into the bedroll. He lay on his back, not wanting her to feel how desperately, painfully hard he still was.

Though it made him feel like a ship splintering against rocks, he did not protest when Lydia curled up beside him and rested her cheek against his chest. Quinn stayed awake until dawn, listening to the woods, an old song running through his head again and again and again and again.

An Endless Forest,
An Endless Ocean

LYDIA REYES WILL KILL THE FEY KING.

She woke with a start, the words running through her mind, and immediately reached for the book tucked beneath her shirt. It hadn't moved from its hiding place last night, while Quinn...

Gods, Quinn.

Lydia took a wild glance around, but the cave was empty and the fey man was nowhere to be seen. It was a relief to see both satchels against the stone wall. There was a dull ache between her legs—it was more than a year since anyone had touched her the way he had last night.

Regret flooded her stomach as Isst landed on a nearby boulder and ruffled his feathers.

LYDIA REYES WILL KILL THE FEY KING.

No. Quinn was not the king. He was an army medic with clever hands, who was good with a bardiche and even better at talking her into entering a cursed forest. Lydia had already killed Cithral and she'd kill Belimar too if the Mapmaker's prophecy needed fulfilling.

"You foolish little changeling," the raven hissed. "He's

gone off to hunt for breakfast, if that's what you're wondering. Everything I've warned you about the fey and the Green Country, and you still invite the King of the Barrow-folk into your bed."

"Oh, Isst, tell me you didn't watch," she said, certain her cheeks were about to blister from the heat beneath them.

"And witness two foul creatures slapping their wet bits together? No, thank you. My friend and I shared a riveting conversation about carrion. Do not let Quinn touch you again, Lydia. If the promises and debts of this country frighten you, then you should be even more wary of *that* sort of bond. It is nothing to be taken lightly," Isst said.

The raven glanced away. "If you accept it, and then choose to leave, you will turn into something like the Gyfoal. A creature that burns from the inside, aching and aching, until there is nothing capable of smothering the flames."

It was one of the rare moments when she let a question die in her mouth. Isst was forbidden from speaking about details of his life before the compound, but those words made her wonder if he had a fire of his own that could not be doused.

"Is that such a bad thing?" Lydia whispered.

"If that's what you think, then clearly the Green Country hasn't scared you enough. Get your things together. Belimar's second company is preparing to enter the woods, and this time, their false king will join them. By now, the rebels should have reached the woods as well, and I can't track both at once. Let's hope the forest feels wicked toward your enemies. Since you've strayed from the Mapmaker's path, you'd better tell me what landmarks to look for, and I'll scout a way."

Lydia opened the book, careful to avoid any pages that

mentioned her directly. "We'll need to follow the creek, then bank north again. The Mapmaker mentioned a graveyard of ships, a few miles before the tower."

Isst nodded. "I know it."

"Tell me the truth, Isst. What were you before you came through the window into my world?"

"Something monstrous," he said. "Something that would have looked at the fine flesh on your bones and wondered how it tasted. But no need to worry—I have more refined interests these days. I'm not sure why my friend lingers. His hunger has been sated and our bargain fulfilled. Let's hope it's a good thing." He turned his gaze to the trees. "I'll be back as soon as I can."

She watched the raven take off, then searched for the woods for a sign of the shadowy figure Isst claimed was trailing them. There was only Quinn, fully dressed, with a large fish slung over his shoulder. Lydia decided to keep it to herself that she didn't like seafood.

"Hi," she told him, unsure of what else to say. There was always: I'm sorry about last night, and I'm not sure if I want to leave, and the book that everyone is willing to kill for says I'll be the one to murder you. Somehow, none of those things seemed appropriate.

"Hello," Quinn said, setting the fish down. He looked everywhere apart from Lydia's face. A striking contrast to how he'd stared at her last night—full of need and hunger, like all the other beasts of the Sorrowood.

"I spoke with Isst. He said Belimar is entering the woods with a new company of soldiers. We should get out of here," she told him. There was no graceful way to search for her trousers in the messy bedroll.

Quinn gave a low hum and drew his hunting knife. With a well-practiced motion, he slid it into the flesh near the fish's tail and removed the skin in a few easy pulls. "I

thought that might be the case. Did you sleep well? Ready
to hike again?"

No mention of the previous evening, she noted.

She watched Quinn cut a block of pink meat from the
fish's belly and attempt to hand her a slice. "No, thank
you," Lydia muttered. "The jerky is fine for me."

He shrugged and popped it into his mouth, then rose
to help break down their camp. She gathered their
remaining supplies; it was a decent distraction from the
way Quinn's throat flexed as he ate, or his long fingers
fastening the satchels.

Lydia packed the book into the straps below her armor,
but it was no longer the comforting pressure it had been.
Instead, it felt like there was a sword pointed against her
breastplate. If she so much as stumbled, it would drive
into her.

On the subject of swords, Cithral's leaned against the
cave wall where she'd left it last night. It felt heavier now
that the rush of adrenaline had cleared her body, but its
weight was less burdensome than the book's. She slid it into
the scabbard and wondered just how much the Lady of the
Lower World saw from the depths of her lake.

"If we can make it back to the trail without interrup-
tion, we should be able to reach the tower today," she
murmured.

He looked up from where he was burying the remains
of the fish. Lydia was certain her face was greasy and her
hair a mess, but his eyes focused on her hand resting on the
sword's hilt.

"Do you have any idea how to use that?" he asked. His
bardiche was tall and imposing over his shoulder.

"You use the sharp part to cut people." In truth, Lydia
had read a few books on medieval weaponry but hadn't

bothered to delve into any technical details. She had never expected to find swordplay a skill she needed.

"Well, there's a bit more to it than that. I'm no expert, but I can teach you—" he said, seeming to lose his train of thought a moment later. "You look rather terrifying with a sword at your hip, changeling."

"You say that like you're flirting with me."

Natalie is going to laugh her ass off when I tell her about this, Lydia thought, barely able to stop herself from cringing.

"Perhaps I am," he told her, giving an audible swallow. "I'm sorry. I shouldn't have said that. It's your connection to the woods we might need to take advantage of, but only if we have no other choice."

Lydia managed a nod. The woods had stopped their whispering last night when it became impossible to concentrate on anything other than Quinn's hands on her body. She'd lain awake for a long time afterward, listening to his slow heartbeat and wondering if the glow between them had eased her mind as it had healed his wounds.

She paused to listen, but heard nothing except for the forest's usual conversation with itself. Songbirds asking one another other about breakfast. The trees and their quiet repetition of hers and Quinn's names. There was none of the power she'd felt surging through her as she'd commanded the woods to do their wicked work on Cithral.

Wait. That wasn't entirely true. Something had shifted yesterday as the general's body was dragged into the tree trunk. Lydia realized that listening was not all she could do. She could command.

Just as she'd always been afraid of.

She was well-aware of Quinn's eyes on her as she stood on her tiptoes to reach the lowest branch of the closest tree and whispered, "Fall."

Its leaves shuddered and dropped all at once as if a cold autumnal wind had swept through the forest. Lydia caught one of the leaves in her hand, still not quite believing what she had done, or that it had actually worked.

"You *are* a witch," Quinn said.

She shook her head.

"No. I'm just a changeling. But maybe that means more than I thought."

"TELL ME ABOUT THE MAPMAKER," QUINN SAID.

They made their way back to the path with a caw from Isst, telling them Belimar had entered the forest. Quinn briefly touched her shoulder as they looked up—the first time they'd made physical contact since last night—but there was none of the intensity she'd experienced before.

"I don't know much. He was a human mage. I'm not sure how he arrived in the Green Country or why he opened a window as the Aés-Caill used to. I'm surprised you haven't asked before."

"You didn't seem ready to talk about it. A window to where?"

"The book doesn't say. I think he was ashamed. To be honest, there's not much in it, other than the maps, and when he makes notations, it's usually an apology. He feared the Sorrowood would spread into my world."

And said that I'm supposed to kill you.

They reached the top of the hill and paused for a moment to catch their breaths. Lydia's muscles ached in places she'd never used even when hauling book stacks around the library.

"A human mage kidnaps thirteen human girls with

Aés-Caill blood to power his ritual. Yet, only twelve return; all with white hair, as if they'd been put through some unimaginable trauma. Now, his damn forest is going to take over both our worlds. You must be angry with him," Quinn said.

She wasn't sure what he was getting at, but this was still a safer topic than whatever the hell was going on between them. Lydia took a slug of water from the canteen when he handed it over and imagined she could still taste his mouth on it.

"Yes. I am angry, but reading his words now, he seems so... sad."

"Sad isn't an excuse for what he did to you."

"I know. It's complicated," she said, remembering why Quinn sounded so furious. Even though the forest was just starting to make its appearance in the human realm, it was already eating the Green Country alive. "Francesco, the master of the Guild of Lightkeepers, always says there's no use in being upset over the things you can't change."

"Hm. Perhaps it's a coincidence, but it always seems to be the people who hold the power to change things, saying that to those with no recourse at all."

Lydia didn't know how to answer, and thankfully, he didn't press.

They continued on their way. Once, before stopping for a few bites of the jerky, she spotted a spider as big as a mastiff, spinning a web decorated by gem-like dollops of dew. Its pincers clicked as they approached, but Lydia only had to mutter, "Leave us alone," for it to return to its weaving.

Power thrummed through her veins. Maybe Quinn was right. Aside from the year she spent away from the compound, it never felt like her life was fully under her control, except in the small world of the library. But here, the Sorrowood and all its monsters bowed to her command.

She did not miss the glance Quinn shot her, filled with both caution and awe. For a moment, she wondered if this was how the Mapmaker had felt. His blood singing as he realized the whole of time and space might be his to conquer.

"Lydia, perhaps it's best you don't exercise that power unless completely necessary," Quinn said, as the trail widened enough to allow them to walk side by side. "The forest might want revenge if it feels slighted."

She understood Quinn's caution, yet didn't know how to explain that this was *her* forest. Its soil was fed by the blood of the changelings, who'd been dragged from their beds in the middle of the night. This wood resulted from their fear, their pain, and their anger.

"You're right," she said, reaching out to take his hand on impulse. He did not pull away and within a few seconds, an uncanny light danced beneath their skin, full of warmth and comfort. She watched the half-formed patterns between them, just as unreadable as ever.

Quinn squeezed back, an uncertain smile on his face.

Every metaphor in the Green Country was over-wrought.

A thing could not simply be blue—it had to be the blue of a bride's tears after being made a fool on her wedding day. Red was the blood of a groom-to-be's heart, stabbed by the person he betrayed. Ice was as cold as the thoughts of a jilted lover committing a murder.

But... there *was* something about Quinn's eyes, Lydia realized.

They were the color of a deep lake. A lake that had drowned many swimmers. A lake no one had ever touched the bottom of, except as bones.

Only the blood of the Aés-Caill can close the window, Lydia thought, turning the words in her mind again.

LYDIA REYES WILL KILL THE FEY KING.

She stopped herself from flinching, knowing Quinn was watching.

Fuck you, Mapmaker, she thought.

The graveyard of ships arrived slowly at first. Bits of wood, dotted with long-dead barnacles. Green bottles, nearly invisible among the moss on the forest floor. Even several anchors, covered in rust, spiderwebs, and bird nests.

"What was this?" Lydia said, as the trees cleared and the whole of the graveyard came into view. It reminded her of the Green Country's Astoria, with its wooden tree-houses and towers, haphazardly arranged like someone had tossed a city into the sky and allowed it to fall where it may.

This place was a chaotic mess of hulls, masts, and figureheads of every design—dragons, winged fairies, dryads, deer, foxes, bears. A few magpies tormenting a squirrel fled as she and Quinn approached.

"Either a shipping lane or a battlefield, I suspect," he said. "This must be the oldest part of the wood. It would have been deep ocean."

"Is this where you learned to sail?" she asked.

"No. The wood was already spreading by the time I was old enough. It was on the river, with the man who taught me medicine. He liked to fish, and it turned out I had a knack for it. Must be my mother's influence."

Lydia realized he hadn't let go of her hand. A part of her wished they could go back to the Avalon, to sail and keep sailing, until they found a place in the Green Country not even Quinn knew about.

How she'd hated the ocean and its whispering, but... perhaps it wouldn't be so bad to see it again. She might be less afraid, now that she'd spent so much time in the Sorrowood.

Something in her settled, like an animal pawing and pawing at the ground, unable to get comfortable until now. But she understood what the animal didn't. It had wandered into a trap.

She forced herself to release his hand and sank onto a nearby stump, not caring that Belimar and his men grew nearer every moment. They were near the Mapmaker's tower, of that Lydia was certain. If she didn't share the truth with Quinn now, she might not get the chance.

"There's something I have to tell you." She tried her best not to look at Quinn's face, which was devastating in this dappled light.

"Go on," Quinn said when Lydia didn't speak. He rummaged through one of the satchels, producing a tin flask. To her surprise, it contained a slightly bitter herbal tea.

"The book. It doesn't only have maps in it. The Mapmaker believed whatever rituals he'd performed gave him the ability to see through time. I'd bet anything that the reason Belimar's translators told him to drag me out of that tower early was because of the... prophecies."

"Prophecies?"

"Only two that I could find, and they're both pretty cryptic. One states that the wood will spread into my world, just as it has in the Green Country and it will devour them both."

Lydia wondered if she was about the hyperventilate. For a moment, she imagined that the ocean had come rushing back to this place and she was staring at Quinn through a wall of dark water.

"The second says... Lydia Reyes will kill the fey king."

Quinn was silent.

"Even the scholars put little stock in prophecy—" he eventually began.

"They must have believed this book was accurate enough to want to execute me before I'd finished my translation."

"You killed Cithral. We're going to do everything we can to avoid Belimar, but—"

"Quinn. *You* are the fey king. The rightful one."

"No, I'm not. Why didn't you tell me this before?"

"I never knew how."

"That prophecy might mean anything. They're always intentionally vague, left open to interpretation." His expression was complex and unreadable. His eyes darted to the left as if he was remembering something.

She sighed, knotting her fingers together. "I know. The mages on my side of the window feel the same. I couldn't keep it a secret any longer. It wouldn't be fair."

Quinn's hand moved against her hair, the sensation disappearing so quickly, she was left to wonder if it'd been a breeze. He looked as though he was about to say something and she closed her eyes, knowing whatever it was would make her feel like she'd fallen onto a sword.

But there were only his lips against hers. Soft and fleeting.

"You don't have to do this," he said in a ragged voice, pulling away from the kiss. "I lied. Forget the tower. I'll take you home now if that's what you want."

"Not a chance in hell," she said against his mouth. "Being here has made me realize something important. I want what's been taken from me. I want the life I never had. I want this armor. I want this sword. I want... this *power.*"

"All right. All right. Then let's hope his maps are more accurate than his ravings. Are you okay to continue?"

In truth, she wasn't. Isst had been silent since his warning caw this morning, and his friend had gone back into hiding. The clouds overhead looked too heavy to hang in the sky.

"Yes," she told him. "We're not far now."

They walked on, but not before Lydia found an old scallop shell, laying outside a ring of bright red mushrooms. She tucked it into her satchel, wondering if she would ever get the chance to place it on her mantle at home, and whether or not the events of the past weeks would seem like only a dream.

The sound came gradually. A steady rush rising and receding.

How could it be? Lydia thought, recognizing it as the sound that'd haunted her at the compound for twenty-two years. The ocean should have been gone from this place. The scattered bones of ships and sea monsters were proof of that.

As the forest thinned, Lydia smelled brine and seaweed. Crabs and jellyfish rotting on the beach. Her stomach clenched and she thought she might retch up the last dried strips of elk she'd forced herself to eat this morning.

"I didn't expect this," Quinn said, as they stepped onto a beach of gritty black sand.

Lydia attempted to force her feet to move forward. This ocean whispered as the one in her world had, but unlike the forest, this one, she could not understand.

"Do you see it?" Quinn asked, finally snapping her out of the daze.

He pointed to a rocky lump less than a quarter mile out.

It was covered by a garden that, even from a distance and in its overgrown state, looked as though it had once been meticulously planned. Pink and yellow roses gave a touch of color to an otherwise gray landscape. A tall structure stood atop the island, but not a lighthouse. No. This was a tower.

A tower out of a fairy tale, Lydia thought. Tall and made of marbled stone, with narrow slit windows. Climbing vines covered the structure until mid-way, from where a few continued, swirling in artful patterns.

"The Mapmaker's tower," she breathed, remembering this was not the first time she'd been here.

Had he kept her in a room at the top? Had her screams echoed through the spiral staircase as if they were trying to escape on their own?

Quinn touched her neck, moving aside a strand of hair stuck to her jaw. "I'm sorry. I'm sorry we have to have to be here. I'm sorry you have to do this."

"It's not your fault."

"That doesn't matter. Lydia…"

It was difficult to turn her back on the ocean, but she looked at him; the King of the Barrow-folk, with his feet in two worlds, just like her. Last night, she'd thought perhaps he didn't want her in the way she wanted him. That he'd done his best to appease her with his hands and mouth, because she was a human who got cold and scared and couldn't sleep, and Quinn-the-Sawbones compulsively took care of people.

But he looked at her now like she was the lone star in an endlessly black sky.

"I have a confession too," he whispered.

His voice was barely louder than the tide.

"There's a prophecy about the fey kings. A song that predates the Sorrowood. Words so old that they only live on as a children's rhyme, but everyone in Astoria knows them. Maybe everyone in the Green Country. For years after the forest sprung up, everyone thought it was about Llewel."

Quinn began singing in a low baritone, and though Lydia knew the fey were talented musicians, she was still surprised at how even the scrubby beach grass seemed to perk up at the sound.

Here comes the Sorrowood
Gnarled and dark
Bane of the pauper
And the monarch

Here comes the Sorrowood
Where once were our seas
To chase us, to eat us
Our blood for its trees

Here comes the Sorrowood
And it won't go away
Because our king and his mate
Have a debt to repay

It's the mother's blood
Her tears and her pain
That made the wood grow
And it won't stop again

Till the king drives his sword
Through his queen's beating heart
And the wood and its mother
Are no longer apart.

This is ridiculous, Lydia thought, a completely inappropriate laugh bubbling up in her throat. She wanted to be afraid, knew she should be afraid, but she was too tired. "So, we're destined to kill each other?"

"I guess so. If you believe in that sort of thing," he said, looking at her with something like medical concern.

Lydia wondered if she should sit down. The laughter was making her light-headed. "Well, let's just agree we won't."

"An easy bargain to make," Quinn said, hooking an arm around her waist when Lydia's knees wobbled beneath her. She let herself sag against him; her forehead pressed against his collarbone. But it was less than a moment before the rejection from last night stung.

He'd wanted her too, she knew that. Was the song why he'd stopped them from going any farther?

"There's a dock over there," he muttered into her hair. "Might be a boat."

"I hate boats."

"I know."

"I'll still go with you."

"I know."

They stumbled through the sand together, and Lydia quietly confirmed that this beach was no more natural than the forest. She'd figured the Mapmaker was a powerful magician, but this... Lydia doubted even the whole of the Guild of Lightkeepers could manipulate a landscape as he had.

No, she told herself. The Mapmaker hadn't done this by himself. He had used her. Just as he'd used Amelia Onners, Natalie, October, and all the changeling girls the Guild so meticulously documented. This was her tower as much as his.

"It must be difficult to see," Quinn said. His hand was entwined with hers, the glow between them gentle and warm.

"It is. It'll be satisfying to end this once and for all."

"Where do you think he was trying to go?" he asked.

The dock came into view. That it had taken her so long to see it made her wonder how good fey eyesight was. Two dinghies bobbed, tied to the pillars, both smaller than the Avalon. Lydia had never expected to miss the sailboat that'd carried them so swiftly from Astoria.

Lydia knew who Quinn meant, but they were distracted by a raven's caw. Four in quick succession.

"Never mind. We need to go," he said, moving his hand to her forearm, just below the elbow. "Listen, there's something I need to say first. I never believed in the prophecy, even before I suspected it might refer to *me*. Then, you… You made me wonder. You made me doubt. And even when we were being chased by Belimar and every damn monster in these woods, it was that which made me afraid."

"Quinn—"

"Shh. Let me speak. You are brave. You are brilliant. You are powerful beyond what you know. I hope one day you'll understand why I have no other choice but to do this…"

She opened her mouth to speak as Quinn looked at the tree line. She followed his gaze. All she saw were swaying branches as if a flock of birds had taken off in a flurry a moment before.

"Ollmos, friend of Isstulmanad, I've offered you a feast, and you shall have one. Remember our bargain. Keep her safe."

"Who are you talking to?" Lydia asked. Quinn gripped her chin, forcing her to meet his eyes.

"I'm sorry, Lydia Reyes."

A bitter taste flooded her mouth followed by another wave of light-headedness. She tried to think back. They hadn't eaten berries on the trail, only the elk, which had left her fine yesterday, and…

"You poisoned the tea," she managed.

The last thing Lydia heard was Quinn saying, "It's only a sedative…"

It was a slow fall to the ground followed by a soft landing. The sand was warmer than anything else in the Green Country. This was as comfortable as her bed back at the compound.

She caught a last look at the sawbone's face before falling unconscious. He was mouthing something, but she could no longer understand.

There was the steady thrum of the ocean.

The heat of the sun.

Then… nothing.

"LYDIA. LYDIA," SOMEONE CALLED.

Her eyes fluttered open, but it took several minutes for her body to catch up. Every limb was heavy and filled with static that might have hurt if the rest of the world didn't seem so dream-like. She was in fairyland, Lydia thought, and wanted to giggle, but her vocal cords were slack. When she could finally turn her head, Isst perched nearby with his talons digging into a rotten log.

Whatever words she tried to say—she wasn't sure—came out slurred.

"Belimar's men are nearly here. Quinn hid you, but even so, you need to be quiet and stay down," Isst said.

The water flask and both satchels were propped up on a tree stump beside her. She could feel the weight of Cithral's sword pressed against her hip, but her body still wasn't entirely under her control. The grogginess gave way to anger she had no way of releasing. What the hell was Quinn thinking? How dare he drug her?

Struggling into a sitting position, she tried to think about what he could have dosed her with and how long she'd been unconscious.

Isst gave an irritated click. "I told you. You need to stay out of sight."

At last, she managed to speak. "Quinn went to the tower alone. He could die."

Gods, she hated him right now, but she was also irritated she hadn't thought of the idea first.

"And so might you, if you don't shut up. Belimar wants that book, and now he's about to discover the Mapmaker's tower; he'll want that too. You're the key to both. So stay down and stay quiet. You humiliated him in front of his city. You killed his general. It won't simply be a prison waiting for you in Astoria. You can command the forest now. It will guide you home if you survive this day."

"Your friend… Quinn's bargain," she said, hoping Isst would understand. Every breath hurt as if the surrounding forest were in flames.

"The Barrow King offered him a feast the likes of which he hasn't eaten in years. Ollmos is waiting for the soldiers. Don't get caught between them."

Lydia tried to think. The rational part of her understood Isst was right. Perhaps Quinn would succeed and she'd return to her world, safe in the knowledge that the few trees dotting the lighthouse's island would remain a monument to the lost fey king who'd given his life to stop the Sorrowood.

She could forget and return to the library, or perhaps try the outside world again—somewhere inland, where the sound of waves couldn't reach her. In time, the Green

Country would become a distant dream. A half-remembered fairy tale.

Lydia already knew she wouldn't. Every leaf would remind her of the color of Quinn's eyes. She was so angry, she actually *might* kill him, fulfilling the damned Mapmaker's prophecy after all.

Her toes wiggled in her boots. At last, some progress.

"Isst, I need a favor," she said, pleased her words were no longer slurred. "Get to the island. Do whatever you have to do to stop Quinn from trying to close the window by himself. Peck his eyes out for all I care."

"No. I am *your* raven. I'll be by your side until you're safely back in Oregon."

"There won't be an Oregon if I can't make it to the tower. If you love me, you'll go."

Isst stared at her. It was impossible to read the emotion in his small, black eyes, but the rest of his body seemed to sag beneath the weight of a decision. "There is more to it, Lydia. That tower is full of strange magic. It could break the Guild's binds on me. When I find Quinn, I may no longer be a raven."

"You'll still be you, won't you?"

"Perhaps. Perhaps not. I have spent so much time in this body that the monster beneath it may have been tamed. I cannot say for sure."

Although she had pushed herself upright, her legs were still anchored to the ground. Lydia wondered if it was the drug making her feel reckless, impairing her judgment. That was a problem for her future self.

"Quinn's a good fighter. He'll be able to hold you off if it comes to that. Please, Isst. I know I've asked you for so much…"

"And yet, not a single rabbit in return. You owe me,

child of the Sorrowood. Do not move until I come back. My friend still stays to watch over you."

It was the last thing Isst said to her before taking off in the direction of the beach. Lydia wished she'd had the chance to correct him.

She was not the child of the Sorrowood.

If anything, she was one of its mothers.

"Help me up," she said, and to her surprise, the ferns that had been her resting place unfurled, pushing against her back with more force than she'd thought possible. Once upright, she took stock of her situation. Quinn had left her with Cithral's sword—no. *Her* sword. The reward of her first victory in battle. The book was still against her chest in its makeshift sling.

That was good.

Her legs tingled; another positive sign. It meant the feeling was returning to her limbs. Lydia reached out to massage her thighs, and for a long moment, let herself think about how *furious* she was at Quinn.

She would survive this if only to chew him out for drugging her and leaving her to languish in the forest. If she managed to grab his bardiche, she'd clobber him with the dull end. Maybe she'd kiss him after, but that would be a brief intermission before another clobbering.

They'd trusted each other. At least, she thought they'd trusted each other. But as she'd been keeping her secret from him, he'd been keeping the same one from her.

Later. She'd have to process that later. Right now, she needed to figure out a way to get to the tower.

"Give me a branch," she told the Sorrowood, and it complied. One of the trees leaned toward her, and she used the lowest offshoot to pull herself upright. A wave of dizziness washed over her, passing quickly. A thought came. Had the Onners known of her distant ancestry? Did Francesco?

If they didn't know now, they never would. The changelings had suffered enough.

She took a few shuddering steps, pleased her legs didn't fold beneath her, and tried to walk toward the sound of waves. Quinn would have taken one of the boats, but she would figure out a way to force herself into the other once she got to the shore. First, she needed to get her body back under control.

Lydia realized she must be groggier than she thought when she took another few steps and found herself face to face with an arrow drawn and pointed at her throat.

Belimar. His army. They'd snuck up on her.

No. Not them. Her heart stilled when she saw the face behind the bow. He was no longer dressed in army clothes and instead wore traveling leathers covered with clumps of moss to hide their color.

Rai looked like Quinn, her brain supplied unhelpfully. They had the same sharp cheekbones and almond-shaped eyes. There was even a dark freckle above Rai's jawline almost perfectly mirroring one of Barrow King's.

"Arms up," he said in a fierce whisper. "Don't move, or I'll shoot. Do you have the book?"

"No. Quinn stole it from me," she said, knowing the lie would fall flat as it came out of her mouth. The sawbones she'd met at the army camp didn't seem like a thief, and his cousin would know it. Still, Quinn *had* drugged her and left her to fend for herself in the woods. There was a ruthless streak in him she hadn't seen until today.

"Humans lie. I suppose you found that sword in your scabbard, didn't you? Was it Quinn who killed Cithral or you?"

"I did," Lydia said. "And I can do it to you, too. *Please.* Let's talk."

Her voice shook, but Rai remained expressionless. "We have translators of our own now. Put the book on the ground and back away slowly."

Where the hell is Isst's friend? Quinn had made a bargain with it. Ollmos should have been here to protect her.

Unless it didn't think she was truly in danger.

"I can't do that," she told him. "The book was written for me. It's mine by birthright. You can help me, Rai. I need to get to the tower. If I don't, this forest will consume not only the Green Country but also my world."

Rai lowered his bow a fraction, keeping the arrow still aimed at Lydia's chest. At this range, the point would have no trouble piercing her sternum. "So, Quinn's been filling your head with that nonsense, too. The scholars will find a way to push the Sorrowood back. Belimar cannot be on the throne when that happens. It would cement his power in Astoria forever."

"The scholars *can't* push it back. How many years have they had to reckon with the wood? Has anyone been able to diminish it by even an inch? Belimar was right. The book tells how to stop the spread of the Sorrowood, but only I can do it. If you care at all about your home, *help me.*"

A twig snapped behind them. Rai looked unconcerned. Lydia realized why Isst hadn't been able to warn her about the rebels. Belimar's army was full of bluster and might, but these fey knew the forest probably as well as their ancestors, who had lived in barrows under the hills before building their towering, wooden cities. They were as connected to this land as she was.

"I do care about my home. That's why Belimar must

be deposed. I won't ask you again. Give me the book or I'll take it off your corpse."

"I can't do that, Rai. So shoot me if you must."

It was a gamble. One Lydia regretted immediately. Rai leveled his arrow at her throat but did not release it. She didn't think Quinn would be willing to go to such lengths to protect Rai if he was the kind of fey who'd kill someone who wasn't fighting back.

A thundering horn echoed across the forest before he could respond. Lydia whirled too quickly, her unsteady legs nearly giving out, but the king's men were hidden by the thick trees.

She turned back to Rai and saw he'd lowered his bow after all. "Please," she said again. "Belimar is coming. I need to get to the tower. You can have the book afterward. Trust me. Trust Quinn."

Rai nodded to someone over her left shoulder. "I will hold you to that promise, human. Come with me."

An arrow struck Rai in the shoulder before he could finish the last word. He staggered back and in one motion, wrapped his hand around the shaft and yanked the point from his flesh. She recognized the arrowhead's metal. Meteorite iron. The same metal as Quinn's bardiche. The metal used to kill fey.

"Let's go." Rai groaned, his face contorted in pain. "Get in front of me."

She obeyed, stumbling forward. There was no more time to wait for her body to recover. She needed to move fast and to move now.

A loud crash came from the trees as Belimar's men met the group of rebels, but Lydia did not look back. Rai's hot breath brushed the back of her neck, and a stink of sweat and adrenaline emanated from within the forest.

"Protect us," she told it, and the Sorrowood dropped

vines and branches as they ran, obscuring her and Rai from view.

He did not ask what she'd done, and she didn't dare look back to see how he was faring with his wounds. If they survived, Quinn could tend to him later.

They reached the edge of the forest. The beach's black sand simmered with heat beneath the sun. Lydia turned and saw a pale Rai clutching his shoulder with a blood-soaked hand. Soldiers and rebels emerged from the woods, some with bows drawn, others already locked in sword combat.

It took one glance to understand the rebels were vastly outnumbered. Several were already strewn across the beach, limbs twisted unnaturally. Rai made a choked sound.

"There was a dock," she told him, "Maybe—"

She didn't finish her sentence. The forest parted as the Gyfoal came leaping through, mounted by Belimar. He carried a red banner emblazoned with his crest: a deer head with an arrow stuck in its eye.

The king's gaze found hers as if he'd known where she'd be standing. A tremor went through her already weak legs as Rai reached for her arm. "Come on," he urged.

She nearly gasped when she saw Rai's face, with black veins spreading across it. His blue eyes were covered by a milky sheen. By the time she forced herself to move, their path was blocked by fighting. It was impossible to see blood on the dark sand, but she smelled its tang over the ocean brine.

Rai shifted, drawing his sword. He took a swipe at a soldier in their immediate path, landing his blade in the fey's torso, but the blow was weak. The soldier stumbled a few feet to the side before righting himself.

"I'll hold them back. *Go*," Rai commanded, pushing Lydia forward.

There was no chance to argue. Two more soldiers advanced on them, and Rai dodged, then counter-attacked. He seemed steadier in combat, as if his muscles were responding to a surge of adrenaline in the only way they knew how.

Lydia tried to obey. Tried to run. But the last of the rebels had either been killed or driven back into the forest to regroup, and she heard the Gyfoal huffing in pleasure as it stepped onto a battlefield strewn with fresh meat.

There was nowhere to go. She would not let herself be taken. It was better to die here than let Belimar drag her back to whatever hell awaited her in Astoria, and she would go down fighting.

She drew Cithral's short sword. It was still awkward in her hands, but she mimicked every action movie October had ever forced her to watch and swung at the solider advancing on her.

Lydia missed, but not because her aim was off.

Something wrapped its claws around the soldier's feet and sent him flying through the air. He landed with a thud several yards away and did not get up.

She nearly screamed at the sight of the creature before her. It was impossibly tall and covered in short, black fur the exact color of the forest. The only hint of a face was a dim reflection in otherwise hidden eyes. Ten impossibly long claws scraped against the sand.

Isst's friend. Ollmos.

The creature was gone before she took her next breath, somehow disappearing into the crowd. Lydia's brain had trouble keeping up with the scene in front of her. Blood sprayed in arcs across the beach. Soldiers exploded into piles of limbs and armor. She was distantly aware of an urge to throw up, but the destruction was so unexpected, so nightmarish, that time seemed to slow.

By the time Ollmos stilled, none but she and Rai were left standing, his sword in shaking hands. The creature regarded Rai. The only indication of its mood the disappearance and reappearance of a reflection as it blinked. In the distance, the Gyfoal's hooves pounded into the sand, but she couldn't turn away.

Ollmos was not bound by magic as Isst was. If its bloodlust hadn't been satisfied, she and Rai were the two closest targets. Lydia raised the sword again, wishing she'd at least asked Quinn for a few pointers.

Ollmos's impossibly dark eyes swept across the beach. Rai took a step closer to her, though he could barely stay upright. His face was smeared with blood, but she could not tell if it'd come from his mouth or if it had splattered across him in the chaos.

"Get behind me, changeling. Do whatever you have to do to get to the tower," he whispered, but neither of them moved. The creature lunged in a blur, the scant details of its body losing form as it dashed across the beach. She swung, missing by several feet, and the weight of the sword drove her blade into the sand. Her muscles burned as she yanked it out of the earth and turned to see what the creature's actual target had been.

The Gyfoal.

It scarcely had time to snort, releasing plumes of red smoke, before Ollmos latched onto its neck. If the Gyfoal was injured, the blood was invisible against its onyx fur. It screamed with a human voice; the sound distorted by another rush of smoke spilling from its mouth. As it shook, Ollmos's claws dislodged.

Belimar struggled to get control of his mount. Lydia knew this might be her last chance to run, but her feet were stuck in the sand. She watched the Gyfoal's jaws open. Belimar was again nearly thrown as the Gyfoal kicked its front legs, knocking Ollmos to the ground.

Isst's friend scurried away. It could run into the forest now and avoid a fight it was outmatched for, but perhaps the bargain it'd struck with Quinn compelled it to stay.

Ollmos attacked again, but this time, the Gyfoal was waiting for it. The Gyfoal's jaws unhinged. Teeth snapped once Ollmos was in range, tearing into its flesh. Ollmos thrashed, its shoulder trapped in the Gyfoal's bite.

"Finish it," Belimar ordered.

The Gyfoal reared, lifting Ollmos along with it. There was another screech from Isst's friend. The sound was nearly enough to make Lydia drop her sword and clap her hands over her ears. She imagined it was like the sound of a star dying—a massive boom shifted all the beach sand at once.

The Gyfoal could not hold on to Ollmos for long, but by the time Ollmos wrenched free of its grip, it was missing an arm and a chunk of its torso. Wounds that would not have been survivable had Ollmos been a human or perhaps even a fey.

Go, Lydia told herself. You need to go now.

There was a movement beside her.

From the corner of her eye, she saw Rai run forward, ready to take advantage of the Gyfoal's brief distraction. Belimar was shouting too, perhaps orders to his mount or a word of warning. Ollmos did not stop fighting, clawing at the Gyfoal's eyes with his remaining hand.

Belimar swung, but Rai had the advantage of solid ground. Even injured, Rai moved with a fluidity Lydia had only ever seen in Quinn, pirouetting past Ollmos's struggling form and plunging his sword deep into the Gyfoal's neck.

The horse-like creature reared, forcing Belimar to abandon a strike mid-motion and reach for the reins. This time, when the Gyfoal tried to scream, blood spewed from its mouth instead of smoke.

"Go," Rai shouted.

It was all Lydia needed to snap out of her daze. Her feet sank into the sand, slowing her progress, but she did not turn to see what had become of her allies. She had no idea what she would do when she got to the dock. Quinn was the sailor, not her, and even at the library, the one subject she'd always avoided was anything to do with the ocean.

The whispering ocean, that she'd been able to ignore when the beach was still full of living soldiers.

"Lydia!" a voice boomed.

Belimar, not Rai.

Hot tears came to her eyes, blurring the last stretch of beach before her.

The Gyfoal was silent, but the king had survived.

Something wrapped around her ankles, and her body fell. The sword slipped from her hand. Before she could reach for it, the same vines that Cithral had produced curled around her wrists, pinning her in place.

"Help me," she cried to the Sorrowood. The trees nearest the edge sent out long, root-like tendrils, but Belimar chopped through them as if they were ribbons.

If monsters watched from the tree line for their chance to devour the corpses piled around her, the Hunter King made them wary. She caught sight of the place from where she'd run. Three dark lumps on the ground, one as large as a van. The Gyfoal.

Fucking good riddance, Lydia thought.

"All this blood shed for your sake, little changeling. And you're carrying one of my high general's swords. Don't worry, I won't try to take it from you. Its magic hums to the beat of your heart. I can tell you've won your right to it in combat," Belimar said.

His black boots shoved aside the fallen fey and weapons to reach her. The book was still secure against her chest, and she wished she'd had the forethought to throw it into the damned ocean.

"Sorrowood," she called, spitting sand and blood. "This is my forest. Grown from my blood, and the blood of my sisters. You will do as I say. *Kill him.*"

Belimar crouched beside her. His heavy armor obstructed her view of the woods, but Lydia knew in her heart she was too far away. The trees could not help her here.

"Cithral's death. I can forgive you. He was crude, hot-headed, and used to steal wine from the royal cellars when he thought he could get away with it," he went on as if she hadn't spoken.

Lydia spat on Belimar's boots. He laughed, but there was no mirth in the sound. Anger radiated off him like magic.

"And my soldiers were granted the honor of a warrior's death. One of the highest aspirations in the Green Country. My Gyfoal is the one you must answer for. Get up."

"You need me. For the book," she attempted, even as the binds on her wrists and ankles went slack.

"So you *can* understand our tongue. That's hardly true. My scholars decoded the Mapmaker's language in time. Even so, I'm afraid their work was in vain. You led me to the heart of the Sorrowood all on your own. Now, *get up.* Pick up your sword. Let's find out if you're really destined to kill me."

She struggled to her feet, not bothering to reach for the weapon. Lydia couldn't delude herself; she had no training and little strength left. Would Belimar leave her here for Quinn to find?

She resisted the urge to close her eyes and let death come.

Instead, she thought of Isst. She thought of Natalie and October and Francesco and Zoya, and the Guild's record collection, and tacos. She thought of dancing to Cuban music, and Patsy Cline's melancholic voice. And Lydia thought of Quinn. His dark-green eyes and clever hands and the warmth that spread through her every time they touched.

"Pick up your sword," Belimar demanded, blocking her view of the sun. Black armor gleamed like obsidian, except for the bright red crest on his chest.

She did, pleased to find her hand was steady enough to wrap around the hilt. Faced with the inevitability of death, the fear left her. Even the ocean at her back was no longer the looming presence it had been her entire life.

In fact, there was something peaceful about the steady back and forth of the waves, and the whispering...

The whispering.

"What are you trying to tell me?" she asked aloud because Lydia didn't much care if Belimar thought her mad.

"You've agreed to a duel by drawing your weapon," he said, perhaps thinking she'd been addressing him. "Get into a fighting stance. It is an abomination that a human should be granted the glory of a warrior's death in the Green Country, but even I will admit you deserve it."

Your ancestors nurtured this world. The ocean is made of their tears. The soil is made of their blood. The Aés-Caill and the Green Country are tied more deeply than you can imagine.

"I can understand you," she muttered.

Belimar's shadow fell over her. "This is your last

chance. Get in your fighting stance and die with honor, or I drag you back to Astoria and let my scholars have their way with you."

You always did. It was simply your fear that made you think you couldn't.

A wild thought came to her. An idea that would surely get her killed, but might buy Quinn more time to close the window.

"I will fight you, Belimar," she said. "Not for my honor. For the honor of the rightful King of the Barrow-folk. May your name be soon forgotten in this world and every other."

Belimar grinned. He dragged his right foot back into the sand and raised his weapon. The blade caught the sun and there was a burst of light as bright and sharp as the sword's edge.

Lydia turned away from him. She faced the water, knowing that a king as cruel as Belimar wouldn't be satisfied by simply plunging his blade into her back. He wanted her to suffer. He wanted to see the pain in her eyes as she died.

"What are you doing, you foolish—"

She didn't speak. It wasn't necessary. Lydia simply showed the ocean what she wanted in her mind and a wild power rumbled through her. It was as forceful as the waves and just as impossible to stop once she let it into her veins. Her vision filled with a brilliant blue-green. At that moment, she forgot Belimar and the Green Country altogether.

There was only water. There was only power.

"What—" Belimar began, but the word cut off.

Lydia opened her eyes in time to see what had caused the tremor in his voice.

An enormous kelpie rushed out of the waves. Though

the water forming its body was translucent, there was no doubt the two hooves pounding through sea foam could crush anything beneath them. Fish swirled in the kelpie's chest, their scales reflecting sparks of red and orange like jewels.

She heard Belimar turn to flee, but there was no outrunning the ocean. Lydia took in a deep breath, trying to fill her lungs with as much air as possible. As the kelpie galloped onto the beach, the water parted around her and jellyfish flew past in shimmering, incandescent colors. She had always imagined the ocean to be filled with darkness, but now she knew this was not the case. It was pink. It was gold. It was blue and green and silver, all at the same time.

A scream cut through the roar, and she turned to see Belimar swept off his feet by the blast of water. It was not the fear on his face Lydia relished, but the surprise. She could practically hear his thoughts. How *dare* a changeling, stripped of her family and her past, barge into the Green Country and command it as even the fey king could not?

The last she saw of him were the soles of his boots, as black as the rest of his armor. She nearly reached for his sword as it flew from his grip into the mass of swirling water, but it was gone before she could lift her hand.

Too bad. It would have been a nice prize for her collection.

LYDIA REYES WILL KILL THE FEY KING.

She nearly sobbed with relief.

It took a long time for the water to recede, and when it did, the forest was flooded as far as she could see. The kelpie had washed away most of the sand and corpses, but the Gyfoal was pressed up against the trees, its legs jutting out at odd angles. She searched the wreckage for Rai, but the man had either been swept away with his comrades or pulled into the ocean as the water receded.

"Do whatever you have to do to get to the tower," he'd said.

The words didn't make her heart ache any less. Rai may have wanted to use her as Belimar did, but he was Quinn's cousin. And in the end, Rai had sacrificed himself for her. There was no time to cry for him now, even though she felt the weight of the loss. Another brick in the house of sorrow she was slowly building within herself.

Quinn. Right now, she needed to get to Quinn.

It was easier to reach the dock without an army in her way, but as she arrived, the hope inside her was swept away as everything else had been. The small structure hadn't survived the kelpie. All that was left were a few shards of wood floating in what puddles remained, and the second rowboat was nowhere to be seen.

Lydia turned to the tower, hoping to catch sight of Isst, but the raven was missing. It was a shame. He would never believe what she'd done.

There was only one direction to march, and that was toward the forest. The trees hummed with renewed energy, their trunks fat with the blood of soldiers and the fey king. She remembered the winding roots they had attempted to send for her, while she'd been too far up the beach to help. They had been thick and sturdy. Just not long enough.

"Listen," she told the Sorrowood. "I hope you saw what I brought up from the ocean. Don't think I won't do it again if you won't help me properly this time. I need to get to the tower, and I can't have any more excuses from you. You're spreading throughout the Green Country at a breakneck pace. I need you to do that here. Move as close to the water as you can and build me a bridge."

And stunningly, miraculously, the Sorrowood did.

Red Roses, Red
Candles, Red Blood

He might have dreamed about this tower once.

Or perhaps it merely looked like the tower in every fairy tale, where a queen or treasure was stashed away in the top room, waiting for a foolish knight to attempt the climb.

Only he was neither seeking a treasure nor a queen. Lydia and the book were not in the tower, but back in the forest, a place rife with danger. Though hopefully not as much danger as here.

Quinn had a difficult time keeping his eyes off the structure as he docked his boat and found a path leading to the entrance. The surrounding garden was lush and overgrown, smelling of roses so heavy they weighed down their branches. Someone must have taken great care to plant this garden, but like the Sorrowood, it had been left to its own devices for too long.

He expected to find wards surrounding the tower—wards he'd hoped his mother's blood would allow him through—yet there was nothing. Quinn guessed the forest had proved an effective deterrent until today.

For no one had counted on Lydia Reyes.

Gods, Lydia. She'd been brought to this tower as a child, hadn't she? How far had her screams carried across the water?

The door swung open as Quinn fiddled with the latch, but before he could step inside, he heard a rustle of wings coming from the garden. He knew what he would see should he turn, knew he should ignore it, but… had something happened to her?

"What is it, raven? You know I can't understand you," he said, finding the black bird hopping from rose bush to rose bush, unable to find a place to perch not beset with thorns.

To Quinn's surprise, the raven began to croak. Not in the fey-tongue, but the ancient language his mother used any time she captured Quinn by the ankle and dragged him under her lake to sing lullabies while he tried to remember he wasn't drowning.

"You must stop. Wait for Lydia. She's coming."

"That's not possible. I sabotaged the other boat," Quinn said. So, he'd been right. Isst was one of the creatures that occupied this land before the fey. Not quite Aés-Caill, but liars and tricksters all the same. The bargain he'd struck with Ollmos had been dangerous enough, and Quinn half-suspected he too might get eaten if he ever made it back to the beach.

"Go away, Isstulmanad. You hold no power over me."

The raven gave up on the rosebushes and landed atop the open door. "You must listen. The magic in this place is loosening the binds put on me by the Guild. I will not be your friend or hers for much longer. You *cannot* close the window on your own, Barrow King. It was a changeling who started the curse. Only a changeling can end it."

"She'll die if she comes here. The prophecy made it clear."

"*You* will die if you attempt it, and the Green Country will be left kingless. As much as that would please me, it would sadden Lydia, and that is something I cannot abide."

"Then try to stop me," Quinn said as he attempted to slam the door shut behind him.

Isst's claws tripled in size, which might have been comical were it not for the transformation happening to the rest of his body. His beak elongated into a sharp curve, almost like a sickle. What were once wings now resembled arms with feathers, ending in large hands that tapped against the wooden doorframe impatiently.

"I told you once," Isst croaked. His voice no longer had any of the jovial sarcasm it usually did. There was only desperation and anger. "You will *not* enter the tower alone."

Quinn did not expect the attack and didn't even attempt to dodge as one of Isst's feathered hands grabbed Quinn's shoulder and tossed him back into the garden. The bardiche pole dug into his spine—there'd be bruises in the morning if he survived that long.

Isst crawled down the door as Quinn pushed himself to his feet and drew his weapon. If this creature was as fast as Ollmos, Quinn didn't think he'd escape a fight unscathed. Still, all he needed to do was to get around Isst. Get into the tower and hope the door bolted from the inside.

Besides, he didn't think Lydia would ever forgive him for killing Isstulmanad, even if Quinn had no other choice.

"It's your turn to listen," Quinn said. "If there is anything inside of you, anything that still cares for Lydia or the human realm, you need to step aside. Every moment we delay, the forest spreads into her world and mine."

"Lydia," Isst said, drawing the last syllable out as if the taste on his tongue was too delicious to relinquish. "My little changeling, who speaks the language of all things."

"Exactly. Lydia. Remember her and step aside. She wouldn't want me killed."

"Oh, but a Green Country without a Barrow King. What a lovely thought. My cousins and I could drive your folk back under the hills, where they belong."

"Isst," Quinn began, unsure how to continue. The creature, which no longer resembled a raven in any way, apart from its inky feathers, stood directly between him and the doorway.

"You like riddles, don't you?"

The creature that used to be Isst paused in its advance and clicked its curved beak. "What of it?"

"How about we play a game? I ask you a riddle and if you can't answer, you step aside and let me pass. However, if you guess right, you may ask me one in return. If I fail, I'll give you permission to take this bardiche and sink it into my head. Imagine; the last King of the Barrow-folk put to death by his own weapon. Wouldn't that please you?"

"What a foolish game you propose. You forget I am much older than you. I know a trick when I see one," Isst said. A thin black tongue darted from his beak and slapped away a gnat.

"Consider a group of three. One sits and will never get up. The second is hungry, no matter how much it eats. The third leaves and never returns," Quinn said, hoping Isst would feel compelled to reply. In truth, it was the only riddle he knew.

"Oh, I'd at least hoped you had something interesting in mind. The answer is simple—a stove, a fire, and—"

Quinn's attack caught Isst off guard, and the bardiche

pole made contact with the creature's neck, sending him flying to the side. It took less than a moment for Isst to right himself, but Quinn had no interest in a proper fight. Kicking dirt in the raven's direction, he lunged for the still-open door.

Isst's claw sliced through the air inches from Quinn's neck.

"You cruel trickster of a fey," the creature snarled, as Quinn's bardiche punched into its stomach. The blow was strong enough to send Isst back a few inches, giving Quinn the chance to dive past him for the tower.

He wasn't fast enough. Even his mother's blood did not give him the speed to match something so ancient. The creature caught him by the leg, sending him sprawling. Claws raked into his flesh as he tried to propel himself forward, closing the last few inches to the door.

Isst looked as though he would follow, but a shimmering wall of magic sprung up in the doorway and the creature's body was thrown back with a hiss that might have come from it or the wards.

I didn't cast that, Quinn thought dimly. The pain in his leg was distracting, but he was too nervous to see what damage had been done. His shoes were already filling with blood. Isst released a string of expletives Quinn couldn't follow.

"Is she really coming here?" Quinn asked when Isst was forced to take a break from cursing him to breathe.

"Yes, you miserable wretch. I told her I would stop you from entering the tower."

Quinn felt like he'd swallowed a mouthful of ocean water. Isst's voice was not the hissing, feral growl of a monster. It was rational, if angry. Had Isst kept his mind—or, at least, parts of it?

"You failed. If you see her again, promise me you

won't hurt her. They're important to your people, aren't they? Promises?"

Fury blazed in Isst's eyes as he glared at Quinn, but then his shoulders slumped. Black feathers disturbed the garden dirt, sending beetles scuttling away. "Of course, I wouldn't hurt her, you idiot, promise or not."

"Then go to her, if you can still fly. With both Ollmos and you protecting her, she'll stand a chance."

"It's too late," Isst said, with what Quinn interpreted as self-satisfaction. "She's already on her way."

BLOOD TRAILED BEHIND HIM LIKE A MACABRE WATERFALL trickling down the stairs.

Quinn took the steps two at a time, though it felt like the skin of his left leg was barely hanging onto the muscle beneath it. Pain shot through his nerves each time his foot struck the hard, stone steps but Isst's words had rattled him.

If Lydia made it to the tower before he could close the window, then... the song still had a chance of coming true.

The tower was so full of magic, he was surprised the walls were not bulging as they attempted to contain it. Now was not the time to wonder why the wards let him pass and not Isst. His one thought was to reach the top.

The tower may not have expanded in diameter, but it'd certainly carved room for itself vertically. Quinn's thighs were already trembling, yet when he looked up, he couldn't see the end of the spiral staircase. Perhaps he'd wandered into a trap, after all, and the staircase extended infinitely. He would spend the remainder of his life in this place, vainly traveling up and down until he died.

He stopped to breathe and thought of Lydia. Unspeakable things happened to her in this tower. Rituals that stripped her of her memories and turned her hair white. So much pain had emanated from this place that the forest which was meant to protect it had grown corrupted and become a Sorrowood.

Quinn kept climbing.

As he did, he repeated the old song over and over to himself. It helped to keep his feet moving to a steady rhythm.

Here comes the Sorrowood
Where once were our seas
To chase us, to eat us
Our blood for its trees

All of Belimar's army had been schooled in the basics of magic, whether or not they showed an aptitude for it. Quinn could detect curses well enough, and he'd always had a talent for dispelling magical traps. He hoped it would be enough when he reached the top floor. After all, he was the rightful King of the Barrow-folk. His blood ran with all the magic of the Green Country.

"Oh, you're here early," said a voice from overhead.

Quinn nearly lost his footing in a smear of his blood. There'd been no indication he wasn't alone. He drew his bardiche, not failing to note how tired his body felt already.

He didn't wish Lydia was here, and yet…also he did.

"Who are you?" Quinn called, as he kept climbing. It didn't matter what was waiting for him. Only that he got to the top.

"Seeing as you're the one in *my* home, that question seems a bit entitled. Still, you've come a long way and you must be tired. I am the Mapmaker, and you are the king of the fey. Come on up. I've been waiting for you."

The man spoke Quinn's language with a stunted accent, as if each syllable burned his tongue. Another sound became obvious as Quinn spotted a platform above him. Music. Strange, crackling music, seemingly both near and distant.

He glanced down as he cleared the last few steps to the platform. The trail of blood that trickled down the stairs showed no sign of slowing.

This room was circular. Both the paintings and shelves curved to accommodate its walls, giving Quinn the impression the world was bending and stretching around him. Only magic could explain how so many books were lined neatly on shelves that shouldn't have been able to house them.

A human male stood before a work bench covered in a myriad of small objects. Quartz spheres, a string of vertebrae from some unknown creature, and so many vials and bottles that it would be impossible to pick one up without knocking the others over.

He turned as Quinn arrived on the landing. His graying hair was swept back into a low ponytail, and he wore clothes Quinn assumed were from the human realm —strange blue trousers made of some rough material, and a dark jacket that would offer little protection from the elements. There was a gaunt look to his face. The look of someone kept alive by magic alone.

The Mapmaker looked at a round medallion on his wrist. "Hmm. Lydia is late."

"Lydia isn't coming," Quinn told him, unsure if the Mapmaker would see through the bluff.

"She *is* coming. Any moment now, I'm sure of it. I'm never that off," he said, finally moving aside to reveal a single window.

Quinn forced himself not to react. He had never seen

the lighthouse window himself, but Rai had done his best to describe it to him.

It doesn't actually look very magical at all, Rai had told him. *Just an unbroken pane of glass, perhaps unusual in a ruin, but not unheard of. At least, until you peer through it.*

This window did not lead to an ocean or a forest. There was nothing but darkness beyond the glass, and yet that word was not nearly enough to describe it. The blackness seemed... vast. Every few moments, a glimmer of light would dart across, gone before Quinn could follow its path.

"Oh, *that*," the Mapmaker said, frowning. "It never did quite work out. I suppose that's why you're here, isn't it?"

"What... where does it go?" Quinn asked. Without bothering to answer, the Mapmaker waved his hand.

"I've already heard the lecture you're going to give me about meddling with the magic of the Aés-Caill, so I assure you, there's no need. Ah, there is our honored guest now."

Quinn heard the slap of boots against blood and stone and gritted his teeth. The kelpie etched into his bardiche seemed to move in the candlelight.

"Close it. Close it now, before I make you," he told the Mapmaker.

"Close it? I wasn't even able to open it in the first place," the Mapmaker scoffed. "Why ever do you think *you're* here?"

The sound of Lydia's footsteps echoed louder from the spiral staircase. Quinn's heart beat in double-time against his chest, matching the rhythm of the children's song that informed him he was destined to murder the young woman with white hair who had forced her way into his heart like a dagger.

"Listen to me. If you don't close that window before she gets up those stairs, I am going to kill you. Do it," Quinn said.

"No, you're not," the Mapmaker told him.

"And how do you know that?"

"Because you don't. I hardly have time to delve into the whole of anomalous physics now. Just wait. Listen."

The music swelled and receded, like a tide. Quinn realized it was coming from a strange device, tucked between piles of books. A black disc spun beneath a needle. Perched on a small table beside it was a red pillar candle, burning so rapidly it must have been fueled by magic.

Lydia arrived on the landing, falling to her knees with exhaustion. Quinn rushed to her. Her clothes were soaked with seawater, but aside from the scrapes she'd picked up during their time in the woods, it didn't look as though she had any new wounds.

"There was so much blood. Isst told me...," she began through panting breaths. Her words trailed off as she realized they were not alone in the tower. The ragged tips of her nails dug into Quinn's forearm.

"It's you," Lydia said quietly. "You're still here."

"I'm afraid it's the only place I can be nowadays with that forest outside my window," the Mapmaker said.

Had this been the Mapmaker's game all along? To bait Lydia with a book and bring her here, where she'd faced a trauma not even Quinn wanted to picture?

"Enough," he said, rising to his feet and drawing his bardiche. "I don't care one bit about you or this place. We're here to close the window. Either do it yourself or tell me how. Or do neither, and allow me to swing this into your skull so I can find the answers in your workshop in peace."

"Patience, Your Majesty. Now that we're all here, we can begin," the Mapmaker said. Quinn had never heard the odd title with which he'd been addressed, yet somehow it sounded like an insult.

Lydia forced herself upright and their eyes met. He could not interpret the emotion on her face. He was desperate to ask what had happened on the beach—why she was awake, if Belimar's army had come, and how she'd made it to the island. But they needed to survive this moment first.

"Welcome back, Lydia," the Mapmaker said with a small bow. The wrinkles around his eyes deepened as he gave something between a smile and a grimace. "I wish our reunion was under different circumstances."

"You heard the king," she said, moving a hand to the sword in her scabbard. "Talk."

The Mapmaker rubbed the creases of his forehead. Quinn noticed the man's hands were well-callused, like his own. The palms of an alchemist or surgeon, who'd spent years with working caustic chemicals.

"Our time is short, however, I'll explain as best I can. You deserve as much as that. When I first came to the Green Country, I was nothing more than an ordinary mage, seeking to learn what I could from the fey scholars. This was before there was too much hostility between our peoples to make it out of the question. After a series of what were most likely foolish bargains, the Order of the Radiant Eye allowed me limited access to their college."

Lydia pulled the book from the sling beneath her tunic and held it in front of her chest like another layer of armor. "Get to the point. Why did you write to me?"

"After a few years at the college, I discovered what enthralled me most were the works of the Aés-Caill. What we in the human world might think of as elementals—

beings tied to the water, the air, the trees—often thought to be the first residents of the Green Country."

His mother had told him those kinds of tales, but it was difficult to trust any story so old. The bardiche pole burned between his hands as if it was aching to be swung and get this over with.

"I must admit, I did terrible things in pursuit of knowledge, even before I came to this tower. By the time the Radiant Eye decided I was a threat, I had already sequestered myself here, with what would become the Sorrowood to protect me. I thought I might escape them by learning to travel to other worlds, not merely the human realm and the Green Country, but there was no chance of a modern fey performing that sort of feat themselves, let alone a human mage."

"You stole us. Children with traces of Aés-Caill blood," Lydia sneered. Her grip tightened on her sword hilt. Quinn wished he could tell her to relax. It was unwise to start a fight when emotions clouded your judgment. He'd have to teach her about that later.

Later? If we survive this, I'm taking her back to the window.

"Aés-Caill abilities are easier to find among a species where magic is rare to begin with," the Mapmaker said. "Amelia Onners was the first girl I took. Unfortunately, I hadn't yet perfected the ritual to extract her power while causing minimal damage to her body. She didn't survive."

"You monster."

"I don't deny that. As I won't be leaving this tower, let me speak for a few more moments. I did better with the second girl. With each changeling I took, the window cracked open wider, but I should have realized there were vital differences between the Aés-Caill and myself. As the reality around the tower broke down, I heard snippets of the past and the future. I saw you, Lydia, and I understood the true horror of what I had done.

"And the window," the Mapmaker continued, with darkness in his voice. "I only opened it partially, yet the magic amplified with each girl I took, and every ritual I completed. Although it was I who created the first trees, the window's magic moved through the changelings, turning their sorrow into power and their magic into a curse."

"The Sorrowood will consume both our worlds," Quinn said, trying to swallow his anger. "You must tell us how to close the window. How to stop it."

The Mapmaker nodded. "It's not merely the Sorrowood. The window itself is a danger. The Aés-Caill were careful as they traveled between worlds. They may have opened windows, but they also knew how to close them. For all my research, I'm afraid both skills have eluded me."

Fear hit Quinn like someone had struck him in the back of the head. "If you brought her here for another experiment, you'll have to go through me first."

He *felt* Lydia's glance, though his eyes were locked on the Mapmaker. The bardiche in his hands—the weapon of his ancestors—burned against his palms with the promise of blood.

The Mapmaker gave a tight smile. "Well, I could hardly get away with that *now*, but you are correct in the assumption that the window can only be closed with the blood of the Aés-Caill. Blood that lives on in Lydia... and in you, Barrow King. I wish a few drops were enough, but nothing is free in the Green Country. The seed of the curse was planted by Amelia Onners's death, and only another death can end it."

The price of ending the curse will be the same as the cost of starting it. Blood for blood, Quinn's mother had said.

A tremor moved through the tower, rattling the dense collection of glass bottles on the Mapmaker's workstation. He frowned, hooking his index finger onto his lower lip. "This is it. The last moment I saw. I suppose that means one of you is about to kill me, or…"

No one moved. The Mapmaker turned to his window and stared into the vast blackness beyond it. "You may find this hard to believe, but I would like you to know I'm truly sorry. I have a brother in the human realm, and perhaps if you could tell him—never mind. I will not ask any more of you. Not when I have taken so much already."

"I can't forgive you. I won't forgive you," Lydia said.

"I know."

"Why did you choose me?"

He shrugged. "Because you were the only one who could decipher my codes and read the book. Now, do you see the candle behind me? I lit it when I began the ritual, just as your boat landed on my shore. The sigil on the floor here will close the window, but it requires the final sacrifice before the candle burns down. If you fail to complete the ritual, there will be no more chance of stopping the Sorrowood. I'm afraid you have only three minutes to choose who will die."

"What?" Quinn demanded. There had been something inside of him that suspected this was the case. The song. The Mapmaker's prophecy. He'd tried so hard to deny it, but he already knew the outcome. Lydia would be the one walking out of this tower. Quinn was certain Isst would guide her back to the window, even in his newly monstrous form.

The Mapmaker took a step back, and then another.

Quinn realized what the Mapmaker was doing too late.

The other man closed the gap between himself and the unlatched window. Before Quinn could rush forward and grab him, the Mapmaker hauled his body over the ledge and disappeared into the void.

Lydia shouted, the sound muffled by her hands. Quinn heard the cleaver of his bardiche slice into the floorboards. But the Mapmaker did not scream. There was no sound other than the creak of a windowpane that'd been closed for too long.

"Fuck," Lydia gasped. "Fuck. Fuck. Fuck."

Quinn didn't know what the word meant, but it felt appropriate. Like a slap when you least expected it.

She ran toward the window. Seawater trailed behind her, splattering the Mapmaker's sigil. Quinn didn't recognize the symbol, but it reminded him of the runes the army scholars used to brand their clothes and horses.

"He was lying," Lydia said, tugging her hair. "Belimar is dead. I *already* killed the fey king. I won't... I won't do it. And I know you won't hurt me either. So what do we do now?"

She pulled books from their shelves, examining each cover before tossing it aside. He was unable to tear his gaze away from the candle, dripping red wax over the table's edge.

"I'm a librarian, dammit. There's an answer here somewhere. Neither of us is going to die," she said. "How much time do you think we have?"

"Less than three minutes," he said, repeating the Mapmaker's words. At least his leg wound had started to close, he thought, though he wondered if the strange numbness inside of him was caused by blood loss.

I'm going to die here.

At least it would be with Lydia. Slayer of the King's Cleaver. Commander of the Sorrowood. Apparently, a

King-killer now as well. He had never desired a soldier's death, but if he was going to get one, there was worse company to do it in.

"It's all right," he said in a whisper. "I'll be the one."

Lydia found a book requiring more investigation. She shoved the Mapmaker's vials off the table, and they clattered to the ground in a discordant chorus of glass and metal. "This one. It's old and I don't recognize the script. It must be the language of the Aés-Caill."

Quinn circled the table. She was too engrossed in the book to notice him move, flipping through the pages so frantically he was surprised they weren't ripped from the spine. There was no magic in the sigil to greet him—at least, none he could feel.

"Come here," he said, louder this time.

This got her attention. She looked up, though her index finger continued trailing along the page. "What are you doing over there? Get off that thing. We don't know what the Mapmaker did to it."

"Lydia. Please. Come here. I want to tell you something."

She turned, her hair flinging droplets of water. "Think. Maybe your mother mentioned something. Blood to open, blood to close. Do you remember anything else?"

"Yes. Come here."

Her fingers twitched around the page, but she released it. He saw a skeptical look in her eye as she moved closer, and she tensed as Quinn reached for her and pressed his mouth against her own. Her lips tasted of the ocean, and her body softened around him as he deepened the kiss.

Gods, Quinn wished he could say everything on the tip of his tongue. That he'd never met anyone like her. That he hoped when she made it to the human world, she wouldn't return to the library. And instead, she'd take her armor and her sword and go on a proper adventure. One that didn't end in tragedy and death.

He wanted to tell her he cared for her, but it didn't seem fair. Not when he was about to steal the sword she had rightfully earned.

So instead, he said, "I didn't know it, but I have missed you all my life."

"We can do this later," she muttered against his lips. "Let's figure this out first, then we can—"

He kissed her again. This time, he closed his eyes and tried to feel nothing except for the way her face felt cupped between his palms. His right hand drifted to her waist and pulled her closer. Her heart beat against his chest like it was trying to break through his sternum.

"Do it. You have to, or both our worlds are lost," he told her.

"No. I would let this and every other world burn, just for the hope of finding you in the rubble."

That didn't sound like Lydia. It was too wild, too romantic, too impractical. But perhaps she'd noticed the way he'd looked at her and knew exactly how to stall.

"Liar," he said affectionally, smiling against her mouth.

Another minute passed.

Her hand encircled his wrist as he inched it lower.

"Nice try, Barrow King," Lydia said. "I won that sword, and you're not taking it. You are the High King of the Northwestern Court. The Green Country needs you. It's not over yet, there's *something* in these books—"

But she was not as quick as him, and it wasn't her sword he was going for. She jumped back as he lifted his bardiche between them, the kelpie scarcely visible in the fading candlelight.

"What are you doing?" she gasped.

"There are two prophecies, Lydia. Only one has to come true."

He anticipated her next move, yet even if he hadn't, she didn't have the strength to wrench the bardiche from his grip. Falling on the cleaver would work only if he managed enough momentum to send the sharp edge through his heart, and the iron alone would not kill him before the candle burned out.

However, something as precise as a sword...

Quinn knew the swipe he took at her was not believable enough. She barely jumped back, as if knowing he would stop short.

"I know what you're doing. This isn't—we'll figure something out—"

A bardiche was not a weapon made for small rooms. His next swipe missed her by inches and crashed into the Mapmaker's work table. Glass vials shattered, reflecting the nearly spent candle like a myriad of star bursts.

He realized the one regret he had about this whole sorry business was the fear in Lydia's eyes as she drew her sword, holding it across her chest defensively. It was all Quinn needed. He flipped the cleaver away, hoping to disarm her with the blunt edge of the pole. This time, it was she who anticipated his attempt. She clutched the hilt with both hands, pointing the blade at him as she readjusted her grip.

That was her mistake. Lydia could not match his speed as he tossed the bardiche aside and rushed straight for her. His first thought was to snatch the sword and drive it into himself, but from the corner of his eye, he saw the candlelight give a final flicker as it snuffed out with a curl of smoke.

He grabbed both her wrists and yanked her closer, angling the sword at his heart.

A blade of meteorite iron ran through him.

LYDIA REYES WILL KILL THE FEY KING.

Lydia Reyes will kill the fey king.

The last he saw was Lydia's dark eyes, wide with shock. His blood on her face.

She looked beautiful.

She looked terrifying.

SILENCE

Lydia could not move. She could not breathe. She could not think.

A Strange Loop

QUINN FELL.

She tried to catch him, but he was already slick with blood, and she could not support his bodyweight on her own.

This was the second time she'd seen a fey stabbed by meteorite iron, but with Rai, the arrow hadn't hit vital organs. Quinn was a medic. He'd known exactly how to make sure the blade pierced his heart.

"Quinn," she said with a sob. His chest was still, aside from the occasional spurt of blood, that slowed in time with his pulse. Lydia tossed her gloves to the side and pressed her bare palms to the stretch of exposed skin near his throat.

His blood seeped into the Mapmaker's sigil. A draft swept through the room, but she was dimly aware the candle was already extinguished. The pages of her forgotten book fluttered like moth wings. Lydia glanced at the window. The space beyond was still black, with drifting spheres of light passing more frequently.

His skin was quickly losing warmth, despite the soft glow that started beneath it.

"Come on, come on," she muttered. Her touch had helped the fox's poison recede. It had kept them both alive in the freezing Sorrowood.

This would work. It had to. He'd *tricked* her twice now, and she wanted revenge. Wanted to scream at him until her voice went raw. She repeated his name like a spell, but nothing answered. Even the constant whisper of the ocean outside fell silent, as if in mourning.

"It wasn't supposed to happen like this," she said, remembering what she could about first aid. He'd fallen to the side, the sword slipping out as he did. That was a bad sign. It meant there was nothing to keep his blood from pouring out. There was no CPR, no dragging him from this tower before his heart stopped permanently.

"I don't know what to do," she whispered. Quinn's song ran through her mind, although with none of the tenderness with which he'd sung it. Instead, it was cruel. Mocking. Delighting because her prophecy had come true instead of his.

The tower room lightened. She stared at the glow beneath her hands, careful not to look at his face, drained of color. When she focused on nothing else, a feint pulse fluttered beneath her fingers.

The light. It was magic, as she'd suspected, but not the magic of the fey. The magic of whatever had come before them. Magic powerful enough to open windows into other worlds. To peer through time. To grow a forest out of pain and sorrow alone. What was reviving a fey king, when you had all the might of the Aés-Caill at your fingertips?

She tried to speak with it as she had the Sorrowood and the ocean, but still, nothing changed. The glow beneath his

skin continued to fade as the room lost the oppressive darkness of a few moments ago. This time, a sea breeze rustled
the pages. A gull's shadow moved across the windowpane.

She was bleeding, Lydia noted dully. She hardly
remembered reaching for the sword, but her hand must
have shot out on instinct, the blade nicking the inside of
her palm. The king had pierced her heart along with his,
and he'd used her sword to do so. Perhaps she would make
another curse. Blood for blood for blood for blood. The
cycle could go on forever.

Think. Think, she told herself.

For the first time, her armor felt too heavy.

Nothing in the Green Country was free.

No, that wasn't the right phrase.

We were born from the same mote of stardust.

"I think I understand now," she said to no one. "I
accept this bond."

The fractured symbols dancing across their skin locked
together into something she could read. And Lydia pushed,
as she had the night Quinn kissed her, and made her question whether she'd ask him to return her to the window
after all. He was so weak, the light seemed to fill him like
an empty vessel. Healing runes danced beneath her fingers.

His pulse stirred beneath her fingertips, but her head
was already swimming as if she was the one bleeding out
onto the floor.

"Come on. Come on," she panted, knowing she
couldn't keep this up for much longer. There was no separating the magic from the rest of her body. As it drained,
so did she.

Let go, the ocean whispered. Or maybe it wasn't the
ocean. Lydia couldn't tell anymore. It could have been the
light itself, finally making its language known.

Let go. Let go. Let go. A steady rhythm, like the waves

hitting the shore and receding, as they had and would forever.

"No," she managed, searching Quinn for a twitching finger, a fluttering eyelid, any sign of life. "This is my power now. I intend to keep it. *And* him."

The room moved around her like a tide had risen high enough to engulf the tower. Her body slumped, but she righted herself. A foot hit the sword's hilt, sending it clattering across the floor where the Mapmaker's sigil was drawn. And as if this was enough to break the spell, Quinn took a single breath.

Lydia wanted to laugh, but she was too light-headed to focus on anything aside from trying to pull her power back. Pouring magic into Quinn felt like falling down an endless well with walls too smooth to grab onto. She couldn't stop.

Let go, something whispered, and she realized it was not the ocean speaking. It was a part of herself she had tried to ignore for so long. The part of her that heard the language of everything and understood it. What she'd thought was a gift from the Green Country, but was actually hers all along.

She tried.

Someone was calling her name, the sound distant.

Her vision blurred. There was simply the sensation of Quinn's skin, hot and alive beneath her hands.

Then darkness, as vast and absolute as the world beyond the Mapmaker's window had been.

HER MOUTH FELT LIKE IT WAS FULL OF DANDELION TUFTS. Lydia tried to speak, but there was something in her throat.

The lights overhead didn't look like stars. They didn't look like magic.

An antiseptic smell stung the inside of her nostrils.

Quinn? she wondered before she could think no more.

LYDIA AWOKE IN A HOSPITAL BED.

Three things made her realize she was back in the human world.

The first was the taste in her mouth. Bile, saline, and medicine. No herbs, none of Quinn's teas or tinctures.

The second was the sound. Metal on metal. Hushed American voices, whispering to one another.

She opened her eyes and there were Natalie and October, both with furrowed brows, standing over her bed. Lydia nearly wept at the sight of them, though her throat was still raw.

"You were intubated," Natalie explained, brushing Lydia's hair back from her face. "You may not be able to speak for a while. You're home. You're back with us."

Time was murky after that. Lydia could never quite tell her dreams from reality, and sometimes, she was back in the Green Country with Quinn, either in the Sorrowood or Astoria. The dreams were bittersweet. It was a relief to be back in a proper bed, with air conditioning and the record player October had dragged all the way to the hospital wing, but the world here did not *speak* as the fairy realm did.

At least, not as loudly.

It was another five days before Francesco came to her.

Lydia awoke from a nap to find him at her bedside, wearing a plain gray suit, with the Guild of Lightkeeper's crest stitched over the right pocket. His hands were steepled in his lap, and he seemed to notice her after she noticed him, looking up with both eyebrows raised.

"Sorry. I was lost in thought," Francesco said.

"Why didn't you come for me?" she asked. It was not the first question on her mind, but it seemed like the most logical place to start and Lydia was a librarian. She wanted the story from the beginning. If Francesco wanted *hers*, he'd have to play fair.

"The fey put wards on the lighthouse. The Guild wasn't able to break them for weeks," he said. Francesco had always given her the impression he was an honest man, and she couldn't tell if he was lying.

"We sent several scouts, but none returned. In the end, it was decided the life of one changeling wasn't worth sacrificing for half of the Guild's mages. That didn't mean we were giving up on you. I hope you understand. We needed time to rethink our strategy," he continued.

His voice reminded Lydia of someone. She tucked the idea away in her mind so she could return to it later.

"How did I get home?" she asked because her blood was on fire with rage and this seemed like a safer question to follow up with.

"A monster with raven wings carried you here in his talons. Your heart had stopped by the time you reached the window. Our doctors restarted it before any permanent damage to your brain, but you've been in this hospital bed for two weeks now."

"Isst," Lydia said, nearly choking on the word. "Where is he?"

Her blood pressure monitor began beeping.

"You need to stay calm. Isst consented to our mage's binding spells. Your library raven will be waiting for you as soon as you feel ready to go back to work," Francesco said.

She turned her head into her pillow to hide the tears filling her eyes.

Bring him here, she wanted to cry, but her time in the

Green Country had taught her how to be patient. How to wait for an opportunity to get what she wanted without needing to make a bargain.

"What happened to the book?" she rasped.

"I don't know. It wasn't with you when you came back," Francesco said.

That triggered a vague memory. Isst, in a monstrous form. The book slipping from her hands as they flew. She hoped it was dissolving at the bottom of the ocean.

"Before we turned him back into a raven, Isst told us you..." Francesco began, sounding more hesitant than Lydia had ever heard him. "Did you meet the man you call the Mapmaker? The one who made you a changeling."

Lydia tried to swallow, but her throat was still raw from the intubation tube. The motion made her want to gag.

"Yes. The book you wanted me to read—he wrote it for me. It was bait. To lure me to his tower in the Green Country, so he could absolve himself of guilt. There was a fey man with me when I... when I was dying. Isst must have seen. What became of him?"

Francesco shrugged. From the way he leaned in at the question, she could tell the gesture was meant to hide his interest. "You might be glad to know your Isst was infuriatingly tight-beaked on the subject of your time in the Green Country, and now that he's a raven again, his only talking will be through you."

"When can I see him?" she asked.

"The nurses won't allow a bird into the medical complex. He'll be waiting for you in the library when you return. The Mapmaker. What became of him?"

She studied the way Francesco's fingers tapped against the chair's armrest. "He's dead. Or something like it. The Mapmaker used the magic of the ancient fey to open a portal into another world. It didn't work and instead created a wound which bled, damaging everything around it."

"How did he seem when you met him?" Francesco asked, frowning.

It was not the question she'd expected. A realization swelled in Lydia's mind. Francesco and the Mapmaker shared the same crooked nose and thick eyebrows. They even looked to be about the same age, though that usually wasn't a reliable indicator when mages were involved.

"You knew him, didn't you?" she asked.

"He is—*was*—my brother, Gabriel. An uncommonly talented magician, but I'm afraid he was too ambitious, even as a young man."

Lydia had the urge to rip the IV lines out of her hand and slap Francesco across the face. "You *knew*? You knew he was the one who took us, and you said nothing?"

"I suspected it, based on the research he left behind when he traveled to the Green Country. It was never confirmed until a message came through the window, telling us about his book. What good would have come from burdening you with unfounded theories? After the Onners died, I tried to rectify my brother's mistakes. I cared for the changelings as best I could. I tried to give you all the chance for a normal life."

Anger burned in Lydia's stomach, but she wasn't sure who it was directed at. She thought of the year she'd spent in Portland, drinking, dancing, and having her heart broken. Even before she'd retreated to the compound, it had felt like this world wasn't meant for her. Her hair dye and fashionable clothes had never been more than a disguise.

The Lady of the Lower World's armor suited her better.

"Lydia?" Francesco asked when she'd been silent for a full minute.

"I want the clothes I returned here in. Was there a sword as well?"

"I'm afraid you'll have to pry it out of the hands of our researchers. They have so few objects from the Green Country, and you'll hardly need a—"

"Are you the head mage of this Guild or not?" she snapped. It hurt her throat to speak so loudly, but there was a powerlessness to being here, surrounded by tubes and machines that would not listen to her as the Sorrowood had.

Francesco sighed. She hoped the murky look in his eyes was guilt. "You should rest. I'll speak to the researchers. They'll be wanting to interview you as soon as possible. It's taken quite a few wards to keep them out of the medical center."

Lydia turned her face into the pillow and closed her eyes. She heard Francesco leave after a few minutes, perhaps believing she'd fallen asleep. The truth was, she didn't want him to see her cry.

Her vision swam with a particular shade of dark green. The color of the summer ocean. The color of Quinn's eyes.

Lydia Reyes will kill the fey king.

Would she ever know if she had?

"Lydia," Natalie sobbed.

Natalie's hair was dyed a soft shade of lavender. It still smelled of chemicals as she buried her damp face into Lydia's chest.

"Be careful," Lydia chided. "You're getting your mascara all over my sweater."

Those words really meant: Gods, how I've missed you.

"We were so scared we'd never see you again. I wish I could replay the moment October learned the Guild was going to stop sending mages in to look for you. I thought she was going to set the entire compound on fire. We even tried getting to the lighthouse ourselves, but the wards—"

Natalie's voice wobbled as she took another breath and wiped her eyes on the particularly nice cashmere sweater Lydia had chosen for her first day back in the library. Francesco had been partially true to his word; her armor and sword were still locked away, but he'd returned Quinn's mantle cloak to her. It was carefully folded and hidden in her closet—a dark, still space she thought might preserve the scent of the Green Country lingering in the fabric.

October burst through the door a moment later, disturbing the ravens on the coat rack. It was a popular roost when the library was slow, due to the small mouse hole behind the front desk no one had ever gotten around to plugging.

October joined the hug without a word, and Lydia was crushed and filled with warmth at the same time. The joy inside of her had only one outlet from which to escape—a tear-filled laugh she hoped conveyed how much she'd hoped for a chance to see them again.

"Tell us everything," Natalie muttered.

October shushed her.

"I'm sure she will in her own time, Nat. Let the woman breathe. Welcome home, Lydia."

Home.

Surrounded by the smell of books, furniture polish,

pine trees, and the sticky sweetness of Natalie's coconut-lime shampoo, the word felt true.

Natalie and October did not leave until Zoya shooed them out for disturbing the peace. The head librarian turned to Lydia and waved her off to the bookshelves, though not before briefly clasping Lydia's hands in her own.

Finding Isst was not a difficult task, as he was at his regular perch on the back of a chair near the esoterica shelves. Tiny talons dug into already well-worn rips in the upholstery, a far cry from the enormous scythe-like claws he'd sported when Lydia last saw him.

There were so many questions she wanted to ask that her mind reeled, but she'd already decided the first thing she would say.

"Thank you. You saved my life," she told the raven.

Isst bowed his head slightly. "And you saved the Green Country and the human realm, Mother of the Sorrowood. Because I quite like both, you can consider us even."

"I'm sorry about your friend," Lydia muttered.

"Ollmos is stronger than he looks. He may still be out there."

Her next words got stuck in her throat, but Isst seemed to understand.

"I don't know what happened to your Barrow King," he said. "He was very weak when he carried you from the tower, and by then, your heart appeared like it might stop at any moment. I flew you back to the window as quickly as I could, and never once did I look back. He didn't seem well, Lydia."

She sank into the chair, forcing Isst to take a few hops to the left. "*You* could go back and search for him."

"I tried," Isst admitted. "The Guild was shaken to learn their binding on me had broken. Many of the Lightkeepers argued it was best to seal me in an object or kill me altogether, but Francesco convinced them you'd never cooperate if I wasn't returned to my previous form. The new spells are stronger than before. They've commanded me to stay away from the lighthouse, and so far, I've been forced to obey."

Lydia dropped her face into her hands. Perhaps the nurses had been right, and she was still too weak to return to work, but this was better than lying in bed, thinking of Quinn's last words.

I didn't know it, but I have missed you all my life.

The speed with which she'd come to care for him had frightened her then and it still frightened her now.

"What did Zoya want us to work on?" she forced herself to say because a public breakdown in the library was all the evidence Francesco needed to send her back to the medical wing. Worse, the researchers would approach her any moment now for an interview about her time in the Green Country. Best to seem as uninteresting as possible.

Isst picked at her hair in the tender way the ravens groomed each other.

"Something about re-categorizing the manuals in the technology section. *Even the Guild of Lightkeepers needs to keep up with modernity*," he said, in a stunningly accurate impression of the head librarian's voice. "However, seeing as the Guild is currently desperate to keep you happy, I believe we could get away with doing something else."

Lydia uncovered her face. She knew it was a bad day for winged eyeliner, but squinting into her bathroom mirror as she painted on makeup this morning had briefly made everything feel normal again.

"Oh? You say that as if you have something in mind."

"Stop moping and follow me before Zoya notices

you've wandered off into the interesting aisles. There are some restricted books about the Aés-Caill, you know."

"Isst, I believe you're fond of using the word *interesting* when what you really mean is *deadly*," she said, feeling the first glimmer of happiness since she'd returned to the compound.

"And Lydia, I believe that is why we are such good friends."

FIVE MONTHS LATER, LYDIA SET HER PHONE ALARM FOR three in the morning.

Dinner was difficult that evening. After her interview with one of the mages, Lydia took her usual seat next to Natalie and October. She knew it was important she pretended to be in good spirits, especially since the cooks seemed to go out of their way lately to make her favorite foods.

Both a reward and a bribe. For being patient with the Lightkeepers, consenting to their questions, and assuring them she would continue to do so. It was easy to feign ignorance about most of the subjects they asked about, considering her version of events included much more time locked in a tower. But the Guild didn't need to know that.

Nor did Natalie and October, as much as it hurt Lydia to conceal the truth from them. She had barely mentioned the Mapmaker, or Quinn, as anyone other than the sawbones who'd briefly treated her wounds at the army camp. That didn't mean he didn't occupy every thought not already taken up by her research with Isst in the library.

Once in her bed, she didn't sleep. Though she now

understood the ocean, she'd learned to tune out the repeating rhythm of its words unless she was actively listening for them. Tonight, the water sang of moonlight and longing and endlessness.

She slapped her phone into silence before the first note of her alarm ended. The boots she pulled on were not as sturdy as the ones she'd worn in the Green Country, but October had been thrilled to lend her a pair when Lydia expressed an interest in hiking.

All she left behind were three letters—one each for Natalie, October, and Francesco. It had seemed impossible to summarize everything Lydia wanted to write into a few short paragraphs, so she hadn't tried. The letters were honest and concise, with Francesco's the shortest of all.

Isst waited for Lydia near the bottom of the wide staircase leading from the dormitories to the entrance hall. He was nearly invisible in the darkness, but his eyes caught the dim glow of the emergency lights and for a moment, she was reminded of the fearsome creature she'd found on the Mapmaker's island.

"Anyone awake?" she whispered.

"There are still lights on in the research department, but I saw all the mages leave, save one."

"Who is it?"

"Who do you think?" Isst said with a low click. "Francesco has hardly left those rooms for weeks."

She held back a sigh. There was a reason Francesco had risen to the head of the Guild after the Onners's deaths. He was an uncommonly powerful mage, just like his brother. His wards would not be easy to slip through. Thankfully, she'd planned for this contingency.

"Can you really do it?" Isst asked. "I know you're clever, and once you get an idea in your head, it's impossible to fish it back out again, but—"

"I can do it. This is not the time or place to have this conversation. Let's go."

The research department was in a small building east of the main house. They crept toward it, avoiding the cameras Lydia had carefully mapped, and she thought about what she'd told Isst. The easiest part had been persuading Zoya to let Lydia re-catalog all the library's literature on the Green Country. When tears filled Lydia's eyes as she explained how it might help her process the time she'd been away, Zoya was already nodding in agreement.

The thought of what her distant ancestors, the Aés-Caill, could do thrilled her.

That was the thing about power. It was hard to get and even harder to give up.

Even with unfettered access to the Guild's research, it had still been months before Lydia attempted what she was about to do now. And when she had, it was as if her cells were being ripped apart. She'd lain on her bathroom floor for hours, the cool tiles the only thing making her feel like her body wasn't burning up from the inside.

Lydia hadn't lied when she told Isst she'd eventually been successful in her experiments. She just didn't mention it had only been once.

"This seems like a good place. It's a straight shot from here," she said, as Isst landed on the branch of a nearby Douglas fir.

"Are you *sure* you want to do this, Lydia? Even the Guild's mages can't—"

"It's in my blood," she interrupted, not wanting any of Isst's doubts to creep into her head. The one time she'd been successful was the night she, Natalie, and October shared a few bottles of wine and listened to old Dolly Parton records until one of the Guild mages burst into the music room and demanded they go to bed. Lydia hadn't been thinking about every horrible thing that could happen to her body then. She'd simply been missing Quinn more than usual.

"Okay," she went on with a shaky breath. "I'll slip in, grab my armor, and slip back out. Francesco is probably in his office. He most likely won't notice me, but if you hear any commotion, don't let yourself be found."

"All right. Good luck, little changeling," Isst said.

She closed her eyes and listened to the world around her. The trees here murmured as the ones in the Sorrowood had, though more quietly. Mushrooms delivered messages about earth and rain through vast networks in the dirt. The owls engaged in a strange conversation about kings and scribes, something she would normally be ravenously curious about. Tonight, she put even that thought out of her mind.

It took Lydia a moment to find what she was looking for—a small spot of quiet, of clarity, as if someone had cleaned a sliver of an extremely dirty window. She took a step toward it and then another, and when she opened her eyes again…

Lydia was in the Green Country.

Her previous tests had shown this was a decent enough point to move from her realm into this one. The Sorrowood was thick, and though the oppressive malevolence of the forest had disappeared along with the Mapmaker's window, she doubted there was a high chance of running into any fey here.

Hello, mother. We've missed you, the trees cooed.

Lydia waved. They'd said the same thing to her when she'd come through from her bedroom, and in her surprise, run face-first into the nearest trunk. It had been a difficult bruise to explain in the morning.

"Please don't call me that. It makes me feel weird," she said, searching for the flashlight in her backpack.

Whatever shall we call you? the forest asked.

"My name is fine. You haven't been expanding, have you?"

There was a murmur through the trees that she swore was them bristling.

Of course not. The blight on us is lifted. The fey don't fear us as they did. They've begun chopping down our cousins at the edge of the wood.

"I'll—" Lydia began, but her words failed as soon as she realized she had just been issued a *complaint*. "I'll talk to the King of the Barrow-folk about it once I find him. I promise."

The trees seemed satisfied with her answer and said nothing else.

She'd calculated this part of the plan a thousand times, poring over blueprints stolen from the library. Twenty steps and she'd be beyond the walls of the research center, and with another ten, in the room she believed her armor was kept.

Toads dodged out of her path, none with the fearsome size or intelligence of the cursed animals that had roamed this wood months ago. It was difficult to count her steps when navigating over stumps and fallen logs that didn't exist in her realm, but she moved slowly and carefully, trying not to consider what would happen if she slipped back into the human world and found herself stuck in a wall.

This should be the place, she told herself, and cleared her mind again. The return trip had been harder last time, too. Lydia wondered if that had less to do with anomalous physics or whatever Francesco would call it, and more with the fact that without a homicidal usurper chasing her, the Green Country was quite… nice.

She found the quiet spot, took a step, and returned to a world of florescent lights and white walls. Heavy magical wards surrounding the building hummed like insects. Her calculations had been close enough. Lydia spotted her armor and sword laid neatly beneath a glass display case.

The sword that'd pierced Quinn's heart. The one he must have put back in her scabbard.

"I thought it would take you longer to figure out how to get in here," someone said. Lydia jumped and whirled to face the speaker, the flashlight raised like a club. Francesco sat on an upholstered chair, looking out of place in this otherwise clinical room.

"But you always were clever," he went on. "I was surprised when you returned to this compound after setting off for the outside world. I'd figured there wasn't enough here to keep your mind occupied, even with the library."

Lydia said nothing. She tried to think. There was no chance of her overwhelming Francesco physically or magically. Perhaps she could drag him into the Green Country with her. The Sorrowood still listened to her, but she didn't want him hurt.

He looked down at the book in his lap. It wasn't one from the library's collection. Their copy of *The Faerie Queene* was much newer.

"It was my brother's," he said in explanation of a question Lydia hadn't asked. He traced the filigree on the cover with his index finger. "He became obsessed with fairy tales as a boy, and never grew out of it—if anything, his fixation only increased with age. Speaking of fixations, our researchers are having a hard time figuring out what sort of leather your armor is made of. One of your interviews stated that you're not sure yourself."

There was an accusation in the sentence, as if he knew she had lied, yet he didn't sound angry.

"Kelpie," she told him, hoping the truth would stall the conversation for long enough to come up with a plan. "It was a gift to me from one of the Ladies of the Lower World."

Francesco's face softened into a smile. "My, my. It sounds like there's quite a story there. It's a shame I'll never get to hear it."

Lydia tensed, preparing to return to the Green Country, but he only fished a key out of his pocket and tossed it in her direction.

"For the display case," he said. "I figure you'll need armor wherever you're going. Do you know how to wield that sword?"

"Not yet," she said, but her attempt to sound threatening was dampened by her confusion. "You're going to let me take them?"

"I'm not sure I could stop you if I wanted to, and besides, after flipping through this book, I've remembered it's unwise to meddle with fairy gifts. I meant what I said before. I tried to give the changelings the lives Gabriel stole from them, or at least, the option of it. Some girls merely needed a little money and a new identity. Others found a home among the Guild. And you—well, all you had to do was kill the fey king."

The last sentence stabbed through Lydia's heart. She knew Francesco meant Belimar, but it was Quinn's face that came to mind.

"Then why didn't you simply *give* my armor back to me? It's been five months!" she snapped, letting her anger bubble to the surface.

"And risk getting usurped as High Mage of the Guild? My colleagues would never have forgiven me. No, it would have been a terrible idea. Besides, it seems it gave you time to learn an important skill. One that will be useful to you wherever you choose to travel."

Lydia made a show of turning away, knowing she was acting petulant by stomping toward the display case and not particularly caring. Francesco continued speaking as though she'd been perfectly polite.

"That being said, this is as much of a head start as I can give you without the Guild getting suspicious. I suggest you take the armor and *run*."

With this last word, she heard a button click and a wave of magical energy passed through her. A repeating, high-pitched wail sounded through the building. Lydia's palms dampened as she scooped the armor and sword into her arms, and slipped back to the Sorrowood.

Isst was already in the parking lot when she returned to the human realm.

"Why not stay in the Green Country?" he cawed, struggling to be heard over the blaring alarm. His feathers puffed up with worry, making him look uncharacteristically cute.

"I had to come back for you, and I needed a car," Lydia said. She fumbled for the keys she'd stolen from Zoya's desk. The compound was now awash with light, creating a strange effect—night and day, competing to exist in the same space.

"Whatever for?"

"I'm not walking all the way to Astoria. The other Astoria, I mean. You can follow or you can get in, but either way, we are leaving right now."

She tossed the armor and sword onto the backseat, cringing as the blade nicked Zoya's upholstery. Mageflares approached from the direction of the house, but Lydia started the car and peeled onto the driveway. She'd had the forethought to discretely slash a few tires belonging to the Guild while most of them were at dinner.

"Have you ever done this before?" Isst called from above, as she took a sharp curve at high speed. She was grateful he probably hadn't seen the way she'd scrambled to keep the wheel under control.

"Once or twice, when I lived in Portland. I thought reading the driver's manual a few times would have been more helpful," she shouted through the open window.

It was easier once she joined the highway. The road smoothed, and occasional small homes and storefronts glowed through the trees. Twenty-two years she'd lived here, and it had been so long since she'd been gone into town with Francesco and the other changelings, that this stretch of coast seemed unfamiliar. The ocean smelled of brine and rotting wood, but for the first time, she found it pleasant.

The Astoria of the Green Country was further inland than the one in her world. When she felt she'd gone far enough, Lydia searched for a place where she didn't have to parallel park. She'd done enough damage to Zoya's car.

Isst landed on a nearby fencepost as Lydia surveyed her work. The car was in the lines—mostly—and the spot was opportune. Nearby was a public restroom, with a trail of sand leading to and from it on the sidewalk.

"Wait here a moment," she told him. It was surprisingly difficult to change into armor in a bathroom stall, all while trying desperately not to cut herself with a sword, and when she finally emerged, Lydia gave a sigh of relief into the night air.

Something about the weight of the leather was comforting. It meant this was actually happening.

"Ready?" she said, holding out an arm for Isst to perch on.

"Are you sure you want to do this?" he asked again. "We could stay here. You're practically the princess of the Lightkeepers now. They'll give you anything you want in exchange for a snippet about the Green Country. Or we could travel. You've already stolen the car. I'll go with you —humans keep ravens, don't they?"

She scratched Isst under the chin, and he stretched his neck to give her better access. "I need to find him first, Isst. Maybe we'll bring him to Oregon someday, now that the curse of the Sorrowood is lifted."

Isst nodded, his tiny eyes reflecting the yellow streetlamp.

It was easy to find the quiet place this time, the little gap between worlds, like pulling aside a curtain. When she opened her eyes again, she was surrounded by the bustle of an Astorian night market, held in a wide square lined by impressive wooden towers.

THE JOURNEY TO BRITTLERUN WAS DECIDEDLY MORE difficult than her escape from the compound. Lydia's first plan was to acquire some sort of mount, hoping the stash of fine jewelry she'd taken from the Onners's wardrobe would be enough to entice a trade. She knew she was not the only human in the Green Country. Unfortunately, the stable master had looked at her round ears and declared the gold in her hands must be false.

Eventually, she persuaded a courier headed to the edge of the Sorrowood to let her squeeze into the back of his carriage for a Cartier bracelet worth several thousand dollars. He'd examined it, muttering something about a gift for his daughter, and tossed the bracelet into a bucket filled with other trinkets from the night market.

Dawn crept in as the carriage rattled out of Astoria. She watched the city disappear through the door slits, with Isst balanced on her shoulder. He'd been the thing the fey seemed the least interested in whenever she approached someone, although that may have had to do with the myriad of strange mounts and pets accompanying the city's residents.

There was another odd thing, she realized. The flags over Astoria did not bare Belimar's stag or Llewel's kelpie, but rather the symbol of the three hares adorning her armor. She recalled the Lady of the Lower World's explanation: the armor once belonged to an ancient warrior. Perhaps that woman hadn't been the only one of her line?

Lydia would have to ask Quinn about it. Better not to bring it up when she was trying to escape into the country unnoticed.

Several hours passed before the driver tapped on the door to let Lydia know it was her stop. She emerged from the protection of the carriage to a late morning, obscured by lingering fog. Belimar had ridden her through a stretch of farmlands, but this carriage had taken her and Isst farther south. Here, the landscape was rugged. Hints of old fenceposts stuck out of heavy brambles, and it looked like everything except for the road was being reclaimed by nature.

"This is where I head east. Brittlerun was eaten by the Sorrowood a few months ago, but with the curse lifted, I heard some folks moved back. You'll find a trail leading from the road," the carriage driver said, as he took another slow look at Lydia in her armor and sword. "Be careful. It's dangerous land for humans, even with a weapon like that."

"Thanks for your concern. Hope your daughter likes the gift," she told him.

Hello, mother… Lydia, the forest said as she stepped into its cool darkness. Even though it had not rained since last night, the air still smelled of petrichor and mist.

She stopped herself from asking after Quinn, just as she had the first time she'd slipped back into the Green Country. The trees would tell her the truth, but if they confirmed the worst, then… Lydia didn't want to know. If that meant she would spend the rest of her life searching, well, perhaps it was not the worst that could happen.

"Hello," she replied, still unsure how to speak with a forest. "How have you been?"

The trees began a monologue about the politics of rabbit warrens in its northern meadows, and the names of all the fox cubs born last spring, and confessed they weren't certain whether the sprites that'd fled the curse would ever return. It was a comforting, constant murmur that helped Lydia ignore the way her hands shook.

As she rounded a bend, the first signs of a village appeared. The carriage driver had been right; the outskirts of Brittlerun certainly looked abandoned. Animal's eyes flashed through the broken windows of homes consumed by vines. Whatever had happened here, happened quickly. A set of knitting needles with yarn still tangled around them sat next to a teacup, overflowing with mold.

Near what must have been the town square, Lydia spotted a couple of fey men trying a wrangle a goat with elaborately decorated gold horns that made the remaining jewelry in her pocket seem insignificant.

"Excuse me. I'm looking for the sawbones, Quinn," she called, keeping to the other side of the square. She had no interest in being rammed in the hip by a goat excited for a new sparring partner.

Only one of the fey looked up. The other had lassoed the beast, but it was attempting to chew through the rope and almost succeeding.

"The sawbones? He's been gone a while now," the man said. He didn't seem to realize Lydia was human until after he spoke and looked her up and down. If he noticed her eyes were filled with tears, he said nothing.

"Oh," she breathed. Once all the air was out of her lungs, it felt impossible to fill them again. She stood, unable to focus, the world around her a blur of green and gray.

"What's a human doing in Brittlerun?" the other man muttered beneath the sound of the goat's happy bleating.

Lydia couldn't move. She was nothing more than a freshly broken mirror, held together by physics and luck. Once she took a step, she would shatter.

"She ain't a human. Look at her armor. Some of the old things in the woods used to disguise themselves like that. Best we offer help and maybe we'll get a blessing," another muttered to his friend.

He turned to Lydia. "Miss, are you hurt? We may not have a proper medic right now, but Aymar fixes up animals all the time. If he can stitch up an ornery bull, he can certainly help you."

Isst's head brushed against her cheek, soaking up a tear. Lydia wanted to run back to the safety of the Sorrowood but found she couldn't move. The cloak around her shoulders still smelled of Quinn's herbs. If she could only stop time from progressing and stay in this moment, it would be like putting a book down before she got to its tragic end.

"I'm... I'm fine. I don't need a medic. I was just looking for someone. Thank you for your help," she told them, her voice cracking around the final word.

Through blurred vision, she saw the men glance at

each other. Even the goat had settled, blinking curiously in her direction.

"Quinn, you said? He's been gone for a while. None of the towns swallowed by the wood have a proper medic, and he takes a whole day to make the rounds between them. He won't be back till late tonight if you've got an issue that needs looking after now."

"Wha-what?" Lydia asked. The word fell out of her mouth involuntarily. Isst shifted on her shoulder.

"I think she *is* only a human, Fiodor. If she were an old thing, she would have said something clever by now," the fey named Aymar muttered. "Miss, are you all right? Quinn set up a makeshift clinic down the road. You're welcome to wait there. He always leaves the door unlocked."

Unable to speak, she nodded. The goat, apparently having grown bored with the newcomers, wiggled in his binds and rammed his horns into Fiodor's stomach.

The fey man gave an oof and pointed toward a relatively well-kept cabin. As Lydia approached, she caught the sharp smell of antiseptic, mingled with the more pleasant fragrance of herbs—rosemary and mint, yarrow and rosehips. She pushed the heavy curtain over the entrance aside and stepped into the darkness.

The cabin's fairy lights gave off a dim glow, enough to see the cot and rectangular apothecary cabinet. They were not the same size or shape as the ones at the army camp when she'd first been brought through the window, but the sight of them made something inside Lydia shudder as if a bone had rattled out of place.

The emotions were so overwhelming, she couldn't even speak to Isst. She didn't know what else to do.

She sat on the cot.

She waited.

Night fell and Lydia was still alone with Isst in the makeshift clinic, but she'd restarted some of the fairy lights. Speaking with magic was certainly not as easy as speaking with the trees, and Quinn's spells had no reason to obey. Still, she was pleased when she convinced them that flickering back to life would be easier than listening to her complain about the dark.

The success thrilled her so much, she briefly forgot to be nervous and wondered what else would listen. What else she could do.

"Don't get a big head," Isst murmured sleepily. "It's just a fairy light."

"Pfft. I killed two fey kings and brought one back to life. The fairy lights are only a start," she said.

"I don't think I like where this is going," Isst said, but there was fondness in his voice.

It was another half hour before she heard footsteps on gravel, and Lydia's blood came to a stop in her veins. Should she stand? Should she sit? She was certain her hair was a mess from the carriage ride. Then again, Quinn had seen her lurching stiffly out of a bedroll after days with nothing but a creek to wash in. Still, she wished she'd packed some eyeliner in her satchel.

"Stop messing with your hair and calm down. The fey have a keen sense of smell. He'll already know you're here," Isst tutted.

But the footsteps didn't hasten. If anything, they hesitated. The pebbles on the trail bounced against one another as if caught underfoot at a dance.

Then the curtain slid aside and she saw him.

Belimar's sawbones. The rightful King of the Barrow-folk.

No.

Quinn. Just Quinn.

She was the first to break from the daze, having the advantage of several hours alone to contemplate their reunion. To be fair, it was only a blink, but Lydia had been frightened to do it, in case he would be gone when she opened her eyes again.

He stood, mouth half-open, until with what seemed like great effort he said, "I don't believe it."

Lydia didn't know what to do, so she tucked her hair behind her ears, despite Isst's earlier admonishment.

"Are you real?" he asked softly.

She nodded.

Time seemed to both speed up and slow down. Quinn disturbed the layer of sawdust beneath them, causing a thick cloud to rise as he dragged her body against his. His hair was slightly damp and smelled of the woods, warm animal fur, and mushrooms pushing through rich soil. She breathed it in, too afraid to speak, in case it would break the dream and she would find herself back in her dorm at the compound.

"Lydia, say something," Isst told her. "This is all getting very annoying."

A laugh escaped her, though the sound was mostly swallowed by Quinn's broad chest. His bardiche was strapped to his back, making the medical satchel hang unevenly against it.

"Yes," she finally whispered. "I'm real, and Isst was just leaving."

The raven bristled and took his time waddling out of the room.

Quinn backed away enough to grip her shoulders so he could look at her face. "You... how... how did you get here?"

"It's a long story. I'll explain later, just—"

He put his hands on her face, and even though she could not see it, she *felt* the glow beneath her skin. A sudden heat overwhelmed her, despite the cool night air drifting in when Isst disturbed the curtains.

"I don't know what to say," he told her, and Lydia decided that since neither of them seemed particularly coherent at the moment, they could attempt a conversation later.

She stood on her tiptoes and pressed her lips against his jaw, feeling a fine grit of stubble she hadn't been able to see in the darkness. Blood ran hot beneath his skin, and he made a soft sound. It was nothing more than a sigh, but it awakened something Lydia had spent so many months trying to keep buried.

"I thought you might be dead," she muttered, without pulling her mouth away.

Quinn turned his face into her hair and took a deep breath. "Your heart was barely beating when Isst flew with you to the window. There was nothing I could do to help you. I thought maybe in the human world... but I didn't think I'd ever see you again."

Lydia pulled back and met his eyes. In the glow of the fairy lights, they were the same color as a tidal pool. "There's a lot of catching up for both of us. And normally, I'd be forcing you to tell me every last detail about what's happened here since I left. However, I believe there is a matter of greater importance to attend to first."

He gave a half-smile, suddenly looking so young and vulnerable that she couldn't help but smile back. "Oh? And what's that?"

"I owe you a debt, sawbones. I mean to repay it."

THANKFULLY, QUINN'S HOME WAS LESS THAN A FEW YARDS away because he started kissing her on the street and didn't pause until they stumbled through the door into a dark room. A few fairy lights flared to life with his return. Though Lydia was distracted by the way his teeth gently tugged her lower lip, she saw this cabin was sparsely decorated. There were even fewer personal effects here than at the clinic.

"You can rest if you need to. Or we can talk," Quinn said, as he moved his mouth to her neck.

Lydia shivered beneath the ghostly touch of his breath. An ache throbbed between her legs; the same one that, at the compound, she had tried so hard to ignore. It had been painful to remember wanting Quinn when there was little chance she'd ever seen him again. She'd only touched herself twice in those long months, and both times, there had been tears in her eyes before she could bring herself to climax.

"Talking. Yes. We'll do that later," she told him, slipping her hands beneath his tunic. Her nails were still glossy from the manicure Natalie had given her yesterday. Lydia figured they'd be ragged before she knew it and took what might be her last opportunity to drag their sharp tips against Quinn's stomach.

This time, he shuddered, before drawing back a moment later, brow furrowed. The green of his eyes, a color to drown in, reflected the remaining fairy lights.

"Wait. I need to tell you—our bond. It's not fate. It's not destiny. It's not a prophecy or an ancient song. It's a choice. One you don't need to make tonight or tomorrow, or ever, if that's what you prefer. I'll be glad to know you either way."

"Tonight, I choose this. Tomorrow, I'll choose to sleep until noon and have you feed me berries until my teeth ache. The day after that, who knows? Maybe I'll slay a monster, make a bargain with a crone in the woods, or learn to cheat at cards, or steal another boat. But I have a decent idea of whose company I'd like to do it in. Besides, there's something I owe you," she went on. "I couldn't allow the honorable sawbones of Brittlerun to go unpaid."

He pulled back and smiled again. Lydia felt as though the light dancing between them would soon be bright enough to burst out of her.

The armor was significantly more difficult to get out of than his medic's clothes, but his deft hands made quick work of the straps. Lydia realized she was being backed toward a narrow bed scarcely large enough for Quinn let alone a second person.

At least there's a rug, she thought, dragging him to the floor with her.

Quinn was still infuriatingly overdressed when he landed atop her, but the hardness pressing into her hip made something inside of her clench. She wanted too much, all at once. Wanted to know what he felt like in her hand, in her mouth, between her legs. A fire raged inside of her, with no room to grow, and so it just kept burning hotter and hotter, building pressure that had no way to be released.

She gave a throaty laugh that didn't seem as though it should come from the sharply dressed librarian of the Guild of Lightkeepers. The sound appeared to stun Quinn, who didn't resist as she hooked a leg around his hip and used the momentum to roll them over.

"You don't owe me anyth——" he began, but the words were cut off as she tilted her hips to increase the pressure on his erection. She wanted to drink in the strangled sound coming out of his mouth. Force him to make it again.

As it turned out, he made that noise whenever she ran

her fingernails along the inside of his thighs, and again as she trailed her tongue up the underside of his cock before taking it fully in her mouth.

He doesn't taste human, Lydia realized. She'd noticed a hint of it in their kisses, but it was more pronounced like this. Trees, cool river water, and hayfields littered with wildflowers. He wound his hands through her hair and she let herself be washed away by the sensation, stopping only when he gave a tug firm enough to draw her attention.

Later, she'd let him know just how much she liked that.

"You're incredible," Quinn said breathlessly.

Just as she no longer sounded like a librarian, he no longer sounded like a humble medic from a town devoured by the woods. His voice was firm, insistent, and for a moment, she was reminded the body beneath her belonged to a rightful king of the fey.

Quinn smiled as she straddled him, an expression filled with tenderness and awe, and the man she knew was back. She leaned forward as he filled her, capturing his mouth in a deep kiss. His hands gripped her hips, but he let her set their pace—deep and slow, even as her body yearned for more.

"You're the most beautiful thing in this world or any other," he murmured into their kiss. "Sit up. I want to watch you."

Lydia obeyed. A tremor of fear passed through her as she moved upright on his hips. The glow between them was fading. She could see the faint trail of her hands on mouth on his torso, but even that was being absorbed by the room's shadows.

"What's happening?" she gasped, flattening her palms against his chest, desperate for the light to return.

He captured her hands in his own and planted a rough kiss against her knuckles. "Do you trust me?" he said.

She nodded, her mouth dry.

"It's our bond solidifying. The light is disappearing, because... it's not needed anymore. You still feel it, don't you?"

The warmth was inside of her. In her throat, in her chest, in her stomach, and the tips of her fingers. *Glow,* she told it, and the runes flared, illuminating the sparse room around them. *Connection,* they said. *We were born from the same mote of stardust.* Her body clenched involuntarily, and Quinn gave another ragged sigh as she tightened around him.

"Nice trick," he moaned, which earned him another rake of her fingernails down his chest.

"Mm, just wait until you see what else I can do."

The only speaking they did after that were breathless declarations of want and need and desire. She came while on top of him, moving her hips as if she were dancing, then again as he flipped their bodies and entered her from behind.

In that position, he seemed to lose the half of him that was fey and became one of his mother's people—the beasts that roamed this country before it was tamed. His teeth sank into her shoulder, leaving marks she knew she would relish come morning, and when he finished, it was with a low growl rumbling from his chest.

They collapsed together on the rug, his cock still buried inside of her. He didn't pull out, even when he rearranged their bodies and curled around her like a shell.

"We have a lot to talk about," he murmured against her shoulder, but there was no urgency in his words. "Promise me this isn't a dream. That you'll still be here in the morning."

"I promise," she said, already half asleep. The rug was surprisingly comfortable once she got past the fact that it was likely the hide of a monster from the Sorrowood. The human realm seemed even farther away, though it was only early this morning she had laid in a bed in another world.

From elsewhere in the village, she heard music. The melody was unfamiliar, with a reluctant joyfulness to it, as if some hope long ago stored away was ready to be dusted and brought back into the world.

Quinn said something else, but the words blended with the cricket song and the chirping of nightjars—the same sounds that had been her lullaby in the human world.

All Things in Cycles

Three Weeks Later

"I think we should go to Astoria," Lydia said, with her hands on her hips. Her armor was tucked away in a chest in Quinn's home, and today, she wore clothes scrounged out of the abandoned cabins. The tunic was too long, so she'd tied it around her waist, revealing a stretch of tan skin above her skirts. The small crease above her belly-button was distracting.

He'd gotten so worked up watching her drink morning tea in nothing but his tunic, that he'd already fucked her once today, bent over the kitchen table.

Quinn looked up from the patch of lemon balm. The medicinal garden had mostly been overtaken by the Sorrowood, but since he returned to Brittlerun, the new sprinkling of mushroom-rich soil meant this current crop was growing faster and better than before.

All things in cycles, his mother used to tell him.

"Did you read through all my books already? There's a very fine library in Malhill. Although it's a bit of a ride from here, the new doctor from the college will arrive tomorrow. We could take a few days off."

Lydia had become his de facto assistant these past few weeks, mostly because neither seemed keen to let the other out of their sight. She went with him on his rounds, clutching his waist as they rode through the Sorrowood on the back of an aging stag named Landseer.

While she had initially taken an interest in his medical work, she now usually wandered off to speak with the townsfolk. Any suspicions they held about her round ears and human scent were dispelled once she asked the Sorrowood to pull its vines away from a salvageable home or help returning farmers come to an agreement with the wolves—a weekly portion of meat in exchange for a vow to keep clear of the goats.

"New books would be nice. There's more research I want to do about the Aés-Caill," she said, hooking her index finger around her lower lip. "But after the Mapmaker, I doubt the scholars would welcome another human student. Those aren't my reasons."

Isst's shadow moved across the garden. The raven usually kept a close watch on Lydia's whereabouts, but his distance from Quinn. She claimed Isst felt embarrassed about what had happened on the Mapmaker's island. Quinn suspected the raven's motives were rather more complicated.

"The couriers tell stories of violence in the streets. Belimar's old supporters can't decide on a new leader, and the remaining rebels are no more organized. Those who have the means to leave the city already have, and those who can't live in constant fear," Lydia said, dark eyes boring into his. She'd taken to wearing a crown of bluebells in her white hair, as was the fashion of the young fey women in Brittlerun.

"I have no interest in claiming my father's title, or in politics for that matter," he said, as he did anytime the subject of his birthright came up. The words were neither fully true nor false, and he and Lydia had shared enough nuanced conversations on the subject for her to understand. Still, she was never shy about bringing it up.

"Besides, with the Aés-Caill bond, you'll be considered my mate. If they see me as king, they'll see you as queen, and I can promise there'd be nothing but danger for a human who attempts to take a throne in the Green Country," he continued.

"I know that, sawbones. Believe me, my ambitions in the fey realm are solely academic. Perhaps a bit romantic too," she said, with a smile that made him feel like he'd been drinking fairy wine. "Maybe you could... appoint someone. Someone good, someone who cares about Astoria. Bring an end to the bloodshed."

"They'll work things out between themselves eventually," he said, though the persistent guilt in his stomach—the one like a beast he carried with him at all times—twisted just enough to remind him it was still alive.

Lydia leaned against an old stone well and watched a honeybee digging through the lavender. "How many will be dead before they do?"

She sighed and adjusted her flower crown. Her flowing skirts looked even more delicate when paired with the weapon at her hip. Quinn's mastery was with the bardiche, but she'd shown an aptitude for what swordsmanship he'd been able to teach her.

"I'm sorry. I don't mean to keep bringing it up, it's just... I suppose I feel guilty. Even though the Mapmaker took me against my will, it doesn't mean the Sorrowood isn't partially my doing. Which is why Belimar was able to rally supporters in the first place, wasn't it? And why the Green Country has been so unstable."

She rarely called it the Sorrowood anymore. It was no longer more nightmarish than any other vast wilderness; the contorted trees and shipwrecks giving it a surreal quality. 'The Dreaming Forest,' she'd dubbed it, but the name hadn't caught on among locals who remembered the monsters that used to crawl out of its darkness.

Quinn stood and crossed the garden in a few wide steps. Her face was sun-warmed as he took it between his palms. Though the light between them now only shone when they wanted it to, heat rushed into his veins.

"Don't. Never feel guilty about what happened to you. You were children. You did nothing wrong and even so, you still stopped the wood. Killed Belimar and decimated his army. This country owes you a debt."

She didn't pull away when he kissed her, but the touch of her mouth against his wasn't enough to distract him from his regrets. He hadn't asked to be born the bastard son of a king. Hadn't asked to be anything more than a medic in a small town with more goats than people. Even Rai, in all his zeal, had never managed to convince Quinn he might be the one fey able to rally enough support to overthrow Belimar.

Rai.

Rai had put himself in danger for Quinn—teaching him to fight and keeping his identity from Belimar. And Quinn stole Lydia out from under him, then led his cousin to his death.

Quinn had searched the woods for Rai's body once he was well enough, but there'd been no sign of his weapons or armor among the insect-eaten corpses. Not even a scrap of clothes to bury.

Lydia dropped her head onto Quinn's shoulder. She'd recounted the story of how Rai sacrificed himself to save her and take down the Gyfoal. By the end, both she and Quinn had tears in their eyes.

Quinn owed Rai a debt. A debt he would never have the chance to repay.

"You're changing your mind. I can sense it," Lydia said. Her cheekbones moved against his shoulder as she smiled. There in the sun, with the dragonflies shimmering like sapphires in the garden, he felt his mood lift.

"It's going to be dangerous," he said.

"Don't tell me there are any other prophecies I have to worry about?"

"Not that I know of," he laughed into her hair. "But I meant what I said. Even if the populace backs my appointee, Belimar still has supporters. Cithral wasn't the Hunter King's only devotee. They'll want one of their own on the throne."

Lydia raised her eyebrows. "We'll ask Isst to carry a message to the rebels first. They already know you as Rai's friend. Then we'll arrange a meeting out of the city to tell them we have information on the whereabouts of Llewel's lost son. Hopefully, that will be enough bait for them."

"And if they take the bait?" Quinn asked, feeling the same thrill in his heart as when he'd first seen Lydia dressed in armor, a sword earned in battle at her side.

"We try to figure out what they know and what their plans are. If it seems too dangerous, we can give them a false lead and lie low for a few months. Most fey are still too afraid to come into these woods."

It was the unspoken words that tugged at Quinn like roots trying to pull him into the dirt. What if the rebels wanted his help? What if they were *eager* for him to appoint another High King of Astoria? That would mean returning to the city. Making both Lydia and himself the target of those who would rather see Llewel's line end forever.

"We'll figure out the rest as we go. And I can always slip us into the human world if need be," she said, with the uncanny way she always seemed to know what he was thinking.

"The curse of the Sorrowood has been lifted. There are plenty of scholars in Astoria who'd be able to follow us."

"Then we'll have to be cleverer than they are," she told him.

When she kissed him again, it was with a conviction and warmth that reached his bones. A flicker of light danced between them as Lydia told the magic to flare. A part of him had looked forward to settling into a quiet life out here. He had his practice, and she had every book he could buy her from the traveling libraries that rolled through the Green Country.

But he had to admit she was not the only one who seemed restless.

He sometimes thought back to the time they'd spent on a stolen sailboat and wondered what it would be like to take to the water when there wasn't someone chasing them. To explore the vastness of their realm, including the far-flung regions he'd heard about in rumors and old songs.

Quinn had long ignored the truth about his father's family, but the fey kings were connected to their land by more than a mere title. Just as the Ladies of the Lower World existed in symbioses with the rivers and lakes of the Green Country, the magic of the old fey courts still lingered in its most ancient hills and groves.

"You're thinking again," Lydia said.

"Mm. You should keep up with your swordsmanship. Once a new king is appointed, we could do some traveling. To the east, there's the Desert of Thrones, and south of that, the Hallowed Bog, where the last of the swamp-witches live. It would do you good to know how to defend yourself."

She smiled at him again, and at that moment, Quinn understood the words she had once spoken to him were absolutely true.

I would let this and every other world burn, just for the hope of finding you in the rubble.

"I'll talk to Isst. Once you speak with the new medic, we can reach out to the rebels," Lydia said.

Two weeks later, they raced toward the town of Roldmere at twilight, the sky above them full of violet clouds still pink at the edges.

Perhaps raced was an over-statement. The stag, Landseer, often came to a dead-stop to nibble on dandelion greens sprouting by the roadside. Even worse, his previous owner never had the heart to brand him with the sigils for speed and obedience that covered nearly every other fey mount.

Roldmere was far enough away that the Sorrowood's spread hadn't touched it, but there were signs its residents had prepared to flee. Many windows were boarded up and even though the wide grassy spaces around the square were lively with children, their parents sat huddled together in front of a tavern, speaking in muffled voices as if the fear had not yet left them.

This close to Astoria, it was likely they had felt the political ramifications of Llewel's execution and Belimar's subsequent bloody reign. Quinn sensed eyes on them and was glad Lydia had the forethought to pull her hood over her white hair and round ears.

They rode past the main square, heading for a small barn in an unkempt wheat field. Crickets came awake, along with a number of orange lanterns in the town behind them. Quinn guided Landseer to the other side of the building, where a fairy horse was hitched to a trough filled with sparkling pink wine. Though the silvery mare didn't look like an army mount, she was branded with both the typical runes and others Quinn didn't recognize.

Isst landed on the splintered fence and gave a few clicks. Lydia nodded back. "He saw them go in. Only two rebels, as they promised. No one has come or gone since."

They entered the barn through a creaking door and followed a path of disturbed dust to a root cellar. Quinn's bardiche was invisible beneath a glamour, but he was glad for the weight of it. Lydia caught his eye, an unspoken conversation passing between them. This was the only place the rebels would meet after days of exchanging letters with the aid of a very irritated raven.

It was also the ideal location for a trap. Rai would have been so angry with Quinn for falling for it.

"Let me go down first," he said.

She was back in her armor, sword at her hip, still wearing the flower crown, and with a streak of black kohl above both eyelids. "That wasn't part of the deal, sawbones. We told them there'd be two of us. If you show up alone, they'll get jumpy."

He sighed. Lydia could be stubborn, but it didn't mean she was hot-headed. She analyzed every angle before acting; it was why her sword training was moving along more quickly than he'd expected.

The cellar door opened to the smell of roots and mold.

A lantern flickered at the back of the space. It took a moment for his eyes to adjust enough so he could see the details of the two fey standing before him.

One was small, perhaps a full head shorter than Lydia, with a dark hood pulled low over their face. Quinn could see the straight line of a mouth, but it remained expressionless as he and Lydia arrived on the cellar floor with a puff of dust.

The room's other occupant was of the opposite stature as her companion—she had to crouch to avoid hitting her head on the low ceiling. Heavy armor clanked as she shifted. It was not the typical Astorian design, but then she was not the typical Astorian fey female. Extraordinary height aside, her skin was a rich blue, framing pale golden eyes.

"You're one of the Ettin," Lydia murmured. The small gasp as she said this was enough to disturb the dust again, sending it swirling around them. "I didn't see any of your cousins in Astoria."

It had taken Lydia a few weeks to accept that 'cousin' was also a general term used to address anyone from a sibling to a friendly acquaintance. The Ettin woman ignored this statement and met Quinn's eyes. Something in him bristled, no different from when a fey caught sight of Lydia's ears and asked *him* to ask her if she might convince the squirrels to stop burrowing in their furniture.

"Titania. Puck," the woman said, using the false names Lydia had given in their letters. She straightened as much as she could, resting a hand on the curved sword at her waist.

Quinn knew of the Ettin. Their folk came from the mountains of the far north; a harsh environment which shaped them into excellent hunters, rangers, and survivalists. Belimar had tried to recruit from the bands of Ettin merchants that came through the passes to trade fur and ore in summer, but as far as Quinn knew, none had ever shown an interest in bowing to the Hunter King. Their goal was usually to return to their mountains with as many books of poetry as possible.

"We're all here. Speak your piece and let's get on with it. If all goes well, the villagers will forget the strange folk who rode through their town today," the woman went on. It was impossible not to note the annoyance in her voice.

"We have information on the whereabouts of Llewel's bastard son," Quinn said, using the words he'd rehearsed in his mind.

"Why do *you* care about sharing it with us?" the Ettin woman said. The hooded figure remained so silent and still Quinn briefly forgot there were four people in the room.

He sighed, brushing hair off his forehead with the back of his hand. Quinn had become so used to lying to Belimar that it was easy to slip back into the role of an irritated sawbones treating ungrateful patients. "I served with your old leader in the army. I was a medic, conscripted from a local village, and had no love for the king. Rai confided his plans with me eventually, and…"

The emotion causing Quinn to stumble over his words was not entirely fake.

"He told me he'd tracked down Llewel's bastard, and that if he died, he didn't want the secret to die with him. He was my friend. I promised I'd deliver the information to his rebels when it was safe for me to do so. When Belimar fell, I returned home and heard the rumors of Rai's death from Astorian merchants. So, here I am," he continued with a shrug.

Lydia shifted her weight from one foot to another, staying otherwise silent. They had agreed on the story after days of searching for inconsistencies. If asked, she was to say she was Quinn's wife and a warrior, here to act as a bodyguard.

The Ettin woman chuckled and folded in half so the hooded figure could whisper something in her ear. Quinn's deepest muscles tensed, but did his best to maintain a weary posture.

"Very well," the woman said. "Tell us then, where is the Barrow King?"

He and Lydia had discussed this, too. They'd give a location somewhere in the Sorrowood, where the two of them could observe from a hidden place and attempt to figure out the rebels' intentions.

"Listen, I'm just a sawbones. I don't give a wolf's piss about the politics of the city. However, my creed demands I do no harm unless in defense of myself or someone else. Can I trust you don't intend violence to his man?"

She nodded, golden eyes flashing like those of the sabrecats in the mountains. "I and those I work with were loyal to Llewel. We were his soldiers, his guards, and his spies. We have no desire to harm the king's son. All we wish is to return the rightful ruler of Astoria to the Cloud Palace."

Quinn wished he could pull Lydia aside to hear her thoughts, but they'd rehearsed every word of this. There was no going back now. "There's a lake about seven miles north of here. Llewel's son lives in a cabin nearby and poses as a fisherman. From what Rai told me, he has no interest in returning to the city."

"Funny," the Ettin woman said, flashing a smile that revealed sharp canines on both the upper and lower rows of her teeth. "I've heard that about Llewel's son as well. Which makes it all the more surprising he's climbed into this cellar with his father's weapon concealed behind a glamour."

It seemed even the dust motes hung in place as if waiting to see what would happen next. Lydia was still in his peripheral vision, but she had shifted her left foot back by a few inches—a move that would make it easier to drop into a fighting stance.

"Excuse me?" he laughed. "You think I'm the king's son? I'll be sure to remember the next time I'm bitten while pulling a rotten tooth out of a child's mouth."

The woman grinned, and for a moment, Quinn thought perhaps that had been enough to convince her. Until her eyes narrowed and her expression sharpened. "You may resemble your mother, but I served alongside your father for years. The weapon on your back *knows* me —I couldn't tell you how many times I've sparred against it. So, no more lies, sawbones of Brittlerun. Why are you really here?"

He and Lydia exchanged a glance. They had planned for this possibility, but they'd expected to meet other fey. Not an Ettin and not whatever the small person in the shroud was.

"I'm not—" he began.

The woman cut him off.

"Don't bother. The weapon is old enough and bloody enough to have a mind of its own. Either you have it because it *wants* you to have it, or you stole it from Llewel's true heir, in which case I will kill you or it will. So, which is it?"

"It's his. Rightfully," Lydia said, and he shot her a look he hoped conveyed something like 'You better know what you're doing.' It was a strange thing to realize the feeling in his gut was *trust*. Until recently, his closest friend had been Rai. Though his cousin's intentions had usually been admirable, Quinn hadn't always agreed with Rai's methods of achieving them. With Lydia, their thoughts

matched like a flock of birds moving in perfect synchro-
nization.

The Ettin woman's eyes flickered to Lydia. "What's
your name, human?"

"Lydia Reyes."

"Lydia Reyes. I'm Espen Hollybear."

"It's good to meet you, Espen. May the sun stay at your
back and in your enemy's eyes," Lydia said, which caused
Espen to give another fang-filled smile.

"Wherever did a human learn to greet one of the Ettin
in a traditional manner?" Espen said.

"I'm a librarian," Lydia said. "It's my job to know
those sorts of things."

Quinn resisted the urge to step between them. Even if
this situation called for fighting, a weapon like his bardiche
would be dangerous in this cellar. The hooded figure
moved back into a shadowed corner, and its dark robes
nearly disappeared.

"A librarian?" Espen said. She shook her head and
went on, not bothering to hear Lydia's answer. "My
companion and I have shown our hand. Rai may not have
been able to speak of his true parentage, but he was clever.
He knew how to direct our spies. How to reveal information without saying it himself. We knew it was the rightful
king we were coming here to meet, but that was only half
the puzzle. *Why* are you here? If you were interested in
taking the throne, you could have come forward months
ago."

"I have no desire for the throne," he said, deciding the
time for deception was past them. "My one concern is
putting an end to the violence in Astoria. I can achieve that
by appointing a new ruler. It's within my rights, both politi-
cally and magically. We hoped to learn if your forces were
large enough and organized enough to back our decision."

The hooded figure shuffled up to Espen and whispered something else in her ear, but Quinn couldn't pick it up.

He realized Espen had looked at Lydia far more than Espen had looked at him. Perhaps it was Lydia's kelpie-leather armor or her white hair, which seemed to glow in the darkness.

"After years threatened by a curse and a tyrant's rule, what the people of Astoria want now is safety. Stability. The appearance of Llewel's son, bastard though he is, would appeal to them, but—"

That final syllable stretched on long after Espen cut herself off. Quinn knew it was his fey blood that made him detest unfinished things, but even Lydia's breath held as she waited for Espen to continue.

"It wouldn't *inspire* them," Espen said.

"What is that supposed to mean?" Quinn asked.

"If I may speak plainly, life was hardly better under Llewel than under Belimar. I doubt your average citizen would have noticed the coup had the flags over the Cloud Palace not changed color. They feared the Sorrowood before and they continued to fear it after. Those who were hungry stayed hungry and those in rags stayed in rags, and the whole sorry cycle of the city went on. They might accept your appointee, but how long until another usurper gathers enough forces to threaten their rule?" Espen said.

Quinn crossed his arms. "As you said, we've shown our hand. Now, show yours. It seems as if you've come here with a proposal."

Espen's armor shone in the lantern light as she pointed a clawed hand at Lydia. "*That* is the woman who not only stopped the Sorrowood, but also bent it to her will. She slaughtered the king's high general, then the king himself. She lifted the curse that has kept Astoria isolated for decades. Her death was foretold in a song that every fey child knew by heart before they were old enough to lace up their boots, yet here she stands."

"I know where this is going, and you won't—" he began, but Lydia spoke at the same time.

"I—I'm just a changeling. What are you trying to say?"

Espen cracked her knuckles against her thighs. It was loud and sharp, like lightning striking a tree. "I'm saying if we want the people of Astoria to rally behind us *and* whoever you eventually choose for the throne, we'll need to present them with someone who has truly made a difference in their lives."

Quinn turned to Lydia, half-knowing what Espen was going to say next. Lydia's dark eyes reflected the lantern light as if it was a fire.

"You, Lydia Reyes," Espen went on, "You need to accompany us to Astoria. Not as a changeling. Not as a descendant of the Aés-Caill. But as the consort of the king, and a contender for the throne itself. You, Lydia Reyes, should be the next High Queen of this fey court."

Lydia and Quinn's story will continue in The Drowning Kingdom.

Preorder Now!

THANK YOU!

If you enjoyed The Dreaming Forest, please remember to leave a rating or review!

Visit AuthorLBBlack.com for your free copy of The King in the Woods, a fey fantasy romance novella.

Find L.B. on Twitter, Instagram, and TikTok at @authorlbblack!

Also by L.B. Black

Secrets of the Sorrowood

The Dreaming Forest: Book One

The Drowning Kingdom: Book Two

The Owl King Archives

The Owl's Crown: Book One

Blood of the Wicked: Book Two

The Broken Oath: Book Three

As Dark Things are Meant to be Loved: An Owl King Archives
Novella

Standalones

The King in the Woods: A Fae Romance Novella

About the Author

L.B. Black lives in the misty gloom of the Pacific Northwest. She is the author of the paranormal romance series The Owl King Archives, as well as the fey fantasy romance duology, Secrets of the Sorrowood. Whenever she manages to set her books down, she enjoys exploring the forest and attempting to befriend crows.